MEMORY ROAD

SARAH EDGHILL

www.bloodhoundbooks.com

Print ISBN: 978-1-916978-56-0

CHAPTER ONE

IT WAS one of those unnervingly silent waiting rooms. People were sitting on rows of orange plastic chairs, staring down at their feet or up at posters on the wall, trying to avoid eye contact. One woman had her hands plunged into her handbag, fiddling with the contents, another had brought out some knitting. The wall clock ticked into the silence, as the second hand travelled onwards.

When they arrived, Moira had started flicking through the pages of a magazine. After a few minutes she began to sigh loudly, and was now tutting and shaking her head. Lily put a reassuring hand on her mother's arm and glanced at the clock, willing the door at the far end of the room to open.

'The women in this magazine are too thin,' Moira announced. 'They aren't eating enough.'

'They're models,' whispered Lily. 'They're always thin.'

'Well, they should eat more toast.' Moira sniffed and continued to look through the magazine, flicking the pages so vigorously that each one turned with a crack.

Lily stared down at the book in her hands, reading the words in front of her, but not taking them in.

'If they ate some toast, they would have proper boobies!' Moira exclaimed. 'Their chests are as flat as pancakes!'

Someone sniggered on the other side of the waiting room.

'Mum, shh!' Lily knew her cheeks were burning.

'Look at this one here! She's not wearing anything on her feet, but she's standing in the middle of a field. That's just silly. Who would do that?'

Lily buried her head in her book again; there was always a chance that, if she didn't respond, her mother wouldn't continue with the conversation.

'Cheesecake!' Moira jabbed her finger against the magazine. 'That's one of my favourites. You know that, don't you, Lily?'

'Mum, please keep your voice down.'

'Why? I like the ones with the biscuity bottom. We had one on my birthday, do you remember? I think it had raspberries on top. It was by that famous person who makes frozen cheesecakes. Who was it again? Lee somebody. Bruce Lee!'

A man further along the row snorted with laughter. Lily knew her face was scarlet now. 'It's Sara Lee, Mum.'

'Who is?'

'The person who makes the cheesecakes.'

The door at the end of the room opened, and a voice called out, 'Mrs Spencer?'

'That's us!' Lily said, shoving her book into her bag and putting her hand under her mother's arm. 'Come on, up we get.'

'I haven't finished this magazine yet. It has a lot of interesting articles I want to read.'

'Mum, we need to go in. Give it to me, we can bring it with us.' As Lily took the magazine, she saw her mother had been holding it upside down.

The consultant leapt up from behind his desk as they were shown into the room. 'Mrs Spencer, how lovely to see you. Have a seat.'

'We've been waiting out there for a very long time!' Moira said, as she settled herself into the chair. 'My bottom has gone to sleep.'

'We really haven't been waiting long.' Lily shot the man an apologetic look. 'Mum, shall I hold your handbag?'

'Take your bloody hands off!' Moira clutched the bag to her chest. 'You're not having my Polos.' She leant forward and whispered to the consultant, 'She never buys her own. She has been stealing mine for years.'

Lily sat back, shaking her head and smiling at him; thank goodness this was someone who understood. It had been a stressful morning; Moira hadn't been ready when Lily went to pick her up to bring her to the clinic. They'd spent several minutes searching for her glasses – which were in her handbag the whole time – then Moira insisted she didn't want to wear any of the coats that were hanging by the door. 'I want the green one,' she'd said. 'With the fur collar.' Lily didn't remember her ever owning a green coat. They'd eventually found an olive-coloured scarf at the back of Moira's wardrobe and compromised on that, but the process took a while. Lily had tried to stay calm and not let her frustration show, casting furtive glances at her watch. She really didn't want them to be late for this appointment – they'd waited weeks for it. She wasn't necessarily expecting to learn anything new, but it felt good to be getting things moving, and she was reassured by the knowledge that, after numerous phone calls and a couple of visits to the GP, Moira had finally been referred for tests and was in the system. Even if it turned out there wasn't a great deal the system could do for her.

'We have found a slight deterioration in Mrs Spencer's cognitive abilities,' the consultant was saying now. He looked up at Moira. 'The RBANS results showed your immediate memory performance was not in line with what would be expected, based upon your estimated premorbid level of function.'

'What *is* he talking about?' Moira whispered to Lily.

The consultant was looking down again, flicking through a report. 'The list learning score was slightly lower and the story memory score was significantly lower. The overall results of cognitive testing suggest there is a significant impairment in short-term and delayed semantic memory.'

Lily squeezed her mother's hand. She didn't have a clue what he meant, either, but it didn't sound encouraging.

'I'm sure none of this will come as a surprise to either of you,' said the consultant. 'But having done all these tests, we know what we're dealing with. So, the good news is that we should now be able to look at ways in which we can move forward. How are you feeling in yourself, Mrs Spencer?'

'Oh, I'm right as rain,' Moira said. 'Tickety boo. Couldn't be better.'

'Are you finding your memory is getting a little worse?'

'Not at all. There's nothing wrong with my memory, young man.'

'Mum, you know that's not true,' began Lily. 'What about...'

'Ask me anything! Go on, ask me any question you like and I bet I'll know the answer.' She turned to Lily and poked her on the arm. 'But you mustn't give me any clues.'

Lily sat back in her chair, watching the consultant's face as he chatted to Moira. He was nodding patiently, smiling at her long-winded stories, gently prompting her for answers. He must be used to the intense denial displayed by many of those who sat opposite him in these chairs. Despite the fact that he had a waiting room full of patients to see, he was kind and concerned and there was no sense of urgency in his manner.

What Lily was hearing now was depressing, but not at all surprising; it was a relief to have got to this stage. Over the last year or so, she'd felt she was struggling on her own with a situation she didn't understand and couldn't control. Moira was a bright woman who'd had a successful career as a history teacher. As a child, Lily wondered if her mother had some kind of photographic memory, because her head had been full of dates and places, along with endless lists of confrontations, coups and coronations. She had a sharp wit and a quick mind; she always knew more pub quiz answers than anyone else and was impressively widely read.

But then, about a year ago, Lily had begun to notice slight changes. The occasional moment of forgetfulness, which became more frequent and led to periods of confusion. Moira struggled to concentrate and Lily arrived at her flat to find tasks unfinished: a load of wet clothes left in the machine for so long they needed to be rewashed, a skirt abandoned on the dining table with only half the hem ineptly sewn up. Moira was repeating herself, then getting defensive when this was pointed out. She was struggling to recall friends' names and forgetting appointments. Once Lily took her shopping for a new pair of shoes, but when they got back to Moira's flat, they both stood and stared at the open Clarks box on the bedside table, which contained exactly the same pair, clearly bought by Moira herself a few days earlier. 'What are they doing there?' she'd said, flustered. 'Those aren't mine. They can't be.'

Lily had started googling Moira's symptoms and reading about early-onset dementia, trying to convince herself she'd got it all wrong. It was soon clear she hadn't.

'The most important thing, Mrs Spencer,' the consultant was saying now. 'Is to stay active; keep your brain stimulated. Do you enjoy reading? Do you like crosswords? Sudoku?'

'Oh yes.' Moira smiled at him. 'Very much. I'm also writing a book.'

Lily turned to stare at her.

'It's a book about my life, and I'm writing it for Lily, here, and for my granddaughter, Eleanor. It will tell them all about me – where I lived, what I did, the people I knew.'

'Well, that's excellent!' the consultant said.

'In fact,' Moira was tapping her fingers on her knees, 'I'm going to get Lily to take me on a little holiday, so we can visit the places I'm writing about. I've been planning it. We're going to drive to the town where I was born and the house where I grew up, the church where Lily's father and I got married. I thought that going to all those places again would help me when I'm writing the early chapters.'

'What a good idea.' The consultant nodded. 'That is exactly the sort of thing I would encourage you to do. It will help with your cognitive ability and your recall.'

Lily laughed and shook her head. 'Listen, I'm sorry, but this is ridiculous. We can't do that. Mum, you haven't even mentioned it to me! I might not be able to take the time off work, and we can't just drive off around the country – when you and Dad got married, you lived in Wales! This wouldn't be a little local trip.'

'Don't be so grumpy, Lily,' Moira said, turning to the consultant and rolling her eyes. 'Where's your spirit of adventure?'

'And the van is far too uncomfortable!' Lily turned back to the consultant. 'I've got an old VW campervan and the suspension is appalling.'

'I do think this would be beneficial, if you can make it work,' he said. 'At this stage, your mother needs to do everything she can to maintain her current level of cognition, and revisiting places from her past sounds like a constructive way to re-establish some of those memories and embed them further.'

'Not only that, but my book will be very interesting for you and Eleanor to read,' Moira said.

Lily doubted her daughter would be even remotely interested. It had probably been years since Eleanor had read anything other than the legal documents she had to plough through for work.

'Writing down memories is a positive way of helping slow the process of mental deterioration,' the consultant said. He put the lid on his pen and closed the folder on the desk in front of him. 'Good luck with this trip of yours, Mrs Spencer. Let's make an appointment for you to come and see me in six months' time and you can tell me all about it.'

'That's settled then,' Moira said, turning to beam at Lily. 'We're going on a road trip.'

As they made their way back out through the waiting room, an elderly man was being shown into a different consulting room. He let out a loud fart as he walked towards it; all the people sitting nearby looked away and pretended not to hear.

'Oops, pardon you!' Moira said, cheerfully. 'Brussel sprouts do that to me!'

'Mum, be quiet!' Lily pulled her towards the door.

'Or cauliflower, that does terrible things to my insides.' Moira stopped and turned around. 'Broccoli as well!' she yelled at the old man's retreating back. 'Broccoli makes me fart like a bloody trooper!'

'That's enough!' Lily pulled her mother out into the corridor, as laughter rippled through those left in the waiting room. She marched her mother towards the entrance. 'Honestly! There's no need to swear.'

'Oh, Lily. You worry too much about what other people think,' Moira huffed, as they went into the car park. 'That swear word isn't bad anymore, they say it on Channel 4 quite a lot. Anyway, *you* say it too – all the time – and you say the other one, that's even worse.'

'That's not true. Well, maybe it's a bit true. But we're not

7

talking about me, we're talking about you, and you never used to swear like this.'

'Didn't I?'

'No! Not at all.'

'Well, that's the beauty of getting old,' said Moira, as she allowed Lily to help her climb up into the passenger seat of the blue and white campervan. 'You're allowed to do whatever you bloody well want. Can we go to the supermarket? I really fancy one of those cheesecakes with the biscuity bottoms. Who did you say makes them – was it Bruce Forsyth?'

CHAPTER TWO

'THAT IS the most ridiculous thing I have ever heard!'

'I know it sounds a bit odd, but Granny wants...'

'Seriously, Mum, listen to me. You cannot go ahead with this trip!'

Lily sighed; she knew it was a mistake to answer when she saw Eleanor's number come up on her phone. She had got into work late and they were one member of staff down at the garden centre today, so Lily was way behind with the usual morning tasks. Luckily, because it was October, there was no watering to be done, but there were numerous other jobs needing her attention. Everyone working at Beautiful Blooms had to do a stint outdoors; during the summer months, the staff fought for the chance to be outside rather than stuck behind a till or sorting through deliveries in the warehouse. But at this time of year, it was a different story. This morning it was Lily's turn to be out in the grounds; the sky was molten grey, the wind was bitter against her cheeks and it had started to drizzle.

She switched the phone to her other hand and began dragging netting across a row of redcurrant bushes. 'Darling, I'm sorry but I'm at work, so I can't really talk. Can I call you back later?'

'No, we need to discuss this right now,' Eleanor snapped. 'You cannot seriously be intending to take Granny on this stupid holiday? She's not up to it, physically or mentally.'

Lily could hear a tapping in the background as her daughter spoke, and guessed she was on her laptop sending an email. Eleanor never seemed to do just one thing at a time, she took multi-tasking to a whole new level. Even when she dropped in at the house to see Lily – which admittedly didn't happen very often nowadays – she would be talking while simultaneously texting a friend, drinking a cup of coffee (a takeout she'd brought with her – she always said Lily made disgusting coffee), reapplying her eye make-up and sorting through the contents of her enormous Louis Vuitton handbag. Lily knew she ought to be full of admiration for this energetic, capable daughter of hers. But most of the time, she just felt like slapping her.

'Granny isn't as frail as you make out,' Lily said. 'She's got some issues with her memory, and she gets confused, but she's pretty healthy for her age. We walked all the way down to Hove and back the other weekend.'

'But she's going doolally!' Eleanor exclaimed.

'That's an exaggeration...' Lily balanced her mobile under her chin as she tugged at the netting with both hands, cursing under her breath as it snagged on the thorny branches of the redcurrants.

'She is losing the plot! You know that as well as I do, Mum. Taking her off around the country like this would send you up the wall, and she'd probably do something crazy.'

'I think you're being unfair.'

'I'm not. I'm being realistic,' said Eleanor. 'What's this book of hers about, anyway? It's the first I've heard of it. Is it an autobiography? To be brutally honest, I can't imagine why

Granny thinks anyone would want to read about her life, it hasn't been that spectacular.'

'Oh, Eleanor, how unkind!' Lily let go of the netting and stood up straight, grabbing her phone again with one hand and putting the other on her hip, glaring at the slatted fencing in front of her, as if her daughter's face was being projected onto it. 'Granny has had a very interesting life, but you just don't know much about it. She's doing this book for me and you, so we'll have something to remember her by, which is wonderful.'

'So, you knew she was writing it then?'

'Yes, of course I did,' Lily lied. 'She has told me all about it, and I think it's a great idea. The consultant agreed – he was very keen on it. He says the book and the trip will be good for Granny, and it will also help with her cognitive abilities.'

'He's not the one having to take her halfway across the country in a rusty old van,' Eleanor said.

'It's not rusty! Well, not all of it.'

'Anyway, you know I'm right. You cannot take Granny on any kind of holiday or journey of self-discovery or whatever she's calling it...'

'It's a road trip.'

'For God's sake, Mum, you're not Thelma and Louise!'

After they got back from their visit to the clinic, Lily had made Moira a cup of tea, sat her down and tried to persuade her there was no way they could make this trip together. She'd pointed out it would be physically draining and Moira would be uncomfortable sitting for long periods in the passenger seat of the campervan. She'd mentioned they were short-staffed at work, which meant it might be awkward for her to ask Gordon, her boss, for time off. She'd suggested that some of the places on Moira's list might not be the same anymore – she was talking about revisiting areas she hadn't seen for more than forty years, so there were bound to have been some major changes, which she wouldn't necessarily be happy to see. Lily had also hinted, as gently as she could, that Moira might find it a struggle, mentally, that her increasingly frequent incidents of memory loss and confusion needed to be taken seriously and she ought not to be putting herself under too much pressure. It wasn't the easiest subject to broach, and several times Moira had turned away and started talking about something completely different.

If Lily was honest with herself, she wasn't just reluctant to take her mother away because she was increasingly frail and confused. She was also embarrassed about Moira's erratic, unpredictable behaviour and newly acquired swearing habit. She'd read that the use of foul language wasn't unusual in people who were suffering from dementia, but it was hard to come to terms with; her mother never used to swear and everything Lily had read suggested it was a sign the disease was progressing. It wasn't Moira's fault, but nor was it easy being in sole charge of a potty-mouthed seventy-nine-year-old woman. So, when discussing any possible outing – let alone a long journey around the country – Lily felt all these things needed to be taken into consideration.

With that in mind, she had brought them up with Moira as tenderly and sensitively as she could.

'Bollocks to all that, my darling!' Moira had said, cheerfully. 'We're going on a road trip.'

'We'll see,' Lily had sighed. She'd let it drop, for the time being. But she'd had every intention of knocking this whole thing on the head. It was a bad idea and it would be hard work. She didn't need the hassle.

But that was before she'd had this conversation with Eleanor, her bossy, dogmatic daughter, who invariably thought she knew better than everyone else and managed to make Lily feel that, somewhere along the line, she'd failed as a mother. Eleanor had always been more assertive than anyone else Lily had known, and stubborn should have been her middle name. When it came to a battle of wills, from the age of about two, she won every time. In some ways, nothing had changed: at twenty-six, Eleanor still had the ability to make Lily feel she didn't know what she was talking about and was possibly a bit stupid.

'So, you need to tell Granny this trip is *not* happening,' Eleanor was saying. 'Don't be your usual self about this, Mum. Have some backbone, stand up to Granny and let her know who's in charge.'

Eleanor didn't need to say the words weak and pathetic; Lily was aware they were in her head. That did it.

'Actually, Eleanor, I've decided we're definitely going on this little trip. I'm as keen on the idea as Granny is, and I think it will be fantastic – a real adventure. She will write her book and I'll get to spend some quality time with her and have a break from work – which will be no bad thing, because it's been pretty full on recently. We're setting off this weekend. It's all arranged.'

There was a sharp intake of breath on the other end of the phone and Eleanor was temporarily – and most unusually – speechless. Lily could hear the garden centre phone ringing in the office and wondered if anyone else was going to answer it. 'I've got to go, sweetheart. Have a good day.' She pressed the button to end the call, shoved her mobile back into her pocket and began to walk across the yard. The delight she'd felt at getting one over on her daughter was already fading rapidly. God, what had she got herself into?

CHAPTER THREE

'CHEPSTOW,' said Moira. 'That has to be on the list. It was where your father and I lived after we got married – we had a little house on the edge of town.'

'I remember you telling me.' Lily reached for the bottle of wine and topped up their glasses. 'The one with the pond?'

'No, that was the cottage in Yorkshire. We moved there later.'

'Right.' Lily sipped at her wine, knowing she shouldn't. She had the beginnings of a headache, a dull throb at the base of her skull, which wasn't likely to go away until she took a couple of paracetamol and collapsed into bed. Helping her mother finish off this bottle of Merlot in a noisy bar wasn't going to do the trick.

'And we must go to Mull,' Moira was saying. 'That's where we went on honeymoon. It was June and we'd been warned about the midges, but they were a nightmare. It felt as if we were being eaten alive. Your dad and I had so many bites around our ankles, it looked like we were wearing pink socks. Little fuck buggers.'

'Mum, stop swearing!'

'You'd call them little fuck buggers if they'd bitten your feet to pieces.'

'I wouldn't. Anyway, I'm not sure we can go all the way to Scotland.'

'It is a lot of driving,' said Moira. 'But we'll break it up by staying in nice hotels along the way. I'm paying for all of this, it's my treat. I don't want you to worry about a thing.'

'That's sweet of you.' Lily smiled across at her mother, aware that Moira's idea of not worrying about a thing was possibly rather different to her own. So far, she hadn't been able to think of anything about this trip that wasn't fraught with potential anxiety. First, there was the state of her beloved VW campervan; despite the fact that she had it regularly serviced, it was notoriously temperamental. The other week it had stalled while she was waiting at lights on the busy junction in front of the Brighton Pavilion. In her panic to start it again, Lily had flooded the engine and eventually a couple of students had pushed her and the van to the side of the road while drivers on all sides swore and hit their horns. Even when it was running well, the van wasn't particularly comfortable; the suspension was about as forgiving as a metal dustbin lid and, although Lily had bought padded covers for the front seats, they were still awkward to sit on for long periods of time. Another potential source of worry was the fact that she didn't know if she'd be able to take the time off work – she was still plucking up the courage to mention any of this to Gordon, and the longer she left it, the more awkward she felt about asking to go away at such short notice.

But these were minor issues when put beside her mother's state of mind and her physical and mental ability to deal with any kind of journey. Moira really meant it when she said she didn't want Lily to have to worry about a thing, but she was blissfully unaware of quite how stressed her daughter was feeling, and the fact that for the last couple of nights she had woken up in a cold sweat shortly before dawn, panicking about what was being planned.

But Lily knew this was all immaterial. She had promised Moira they could make this trip – and told Eleanor the damn thing was going ahead – so she needed to put all the negatives to the back of her mind.

'Right. If we're really doing this, we'll need an itinerary,' she said. 'We can't set off without any planning.' She took another slug of Merlot and pulled a pad and biro from her bag.

'There's no need.' Moira tapped her forehead with her finger. 'I've got it all up here.'

'That's as maybe, but I want to know where I'm going. I need it all properly mapped out and organised. You mentioned Cirencester, where you and Dad got married. If we start by heading there, it means we'll go around the M25, then west along the M4. From there, I don't think it's too far to drive to Chepstow.'

'See.' Moira smiled. 'Easy-peasy. I knew you'd sort it out. This is all going to be wonderful. I've bought myself a new notebook from WHSmith, with margins in it, and I'm going to use that when we set off, to start writing my book.'

A group of men chatting at the table beside them exploded into raucous laughter and Lily flinched and rubbed her temples.

'We must go to the Norfolk Broads!' exclaimed Moira. 'We had a wonderful holiday there, while I was pregnant with you, although I was so ill, I kept being sick over the side of the boat and your father fell in once, when we were trying to dock.'

'Really? I've never heard that before.'

'It wasn't very deep, he only fell in up to his knees.'

'We're definitely not hiring a boat, I'm not good on water.'

'Then there was that holiday cottage in the Peak District we rented for a month, after you'd gone off to university.'

'Hang on,' said Lily. 'We can't fit in all this, Mum. We can visit the places you used to live, obviously. But if we went everywhere you've been on holiday, we'd be away for months.'

The men at the next table roared with laughter again and Moira tutted and shook her head. 'How antisocial!' She turned in her chair and jabbed the shoulder of the man sitting nearest to her. 'Will you kindly keep the fucking noise down,' she said, smiling sweetly. 'My daughter and I can't hear ourselves think.'

The man's mouth dropped open as he stared at the diminutive, white-haired lady, whose finger was still prodding him.

'Mum, stop that! I'm so sorry.' Lily smiled at him, and reached across to brush Moira's hand away. 'She's... um... she's very sensitive to noise.'

The man's confusion had now turned to irritation, but he was clearly too polite to react.

'This is a public bar, love!' one of his friends called across. 'If you don't like it, go and sit in a library.'

'They don't serve red wine in libraries, you bloody idiot!' Moira yelled back.

'Right, that's it, we're leaving.' Lily shoved her pad and pen into her bag, stood up and went round to the other side of the table, putting her hand under Moira's arm. 'Come on, let's get out of here. I'm sorry again,' she said to the table of men, some of whom were starting to laugh. She hoisted Moira to her feet, pulled her coat from the back of the chair and began to guide her away. The rowdy laughter followed them to the door and she could still hear it when they were standing outside on the pavement.

'Honestly!' huffed Moira. 'What rude people. There was no need for behaviour like that.'

To her surprise, Lily found herself smiling. 'You're right, they were out of order.'

It was strange, she thought, as they walked towards the van parked at the far end of the pub car park, the mother she'd known and loved all her life would never have lost her rag like that in a crowded bar. Moira had always been unerringly polite; if anything, overly aware of social mores. The idea of causing any kind of scene in a public place would have horrified and appalled her, and she would have been mortified if her daughter had ever spoken out of turn in public. But now Lily wasn't sure if her mother had any idea how badly she was behaving, or if she'd just stopped caring. Either way, it was upsetting and hard to deal with.

Over the last year it had felt as if Moira was developing a dual personality. Lily had begun to think of her as Good Mum/Bad Mum, and was never sure which she'd get on a daily basis. Of course, it wasn't nearly that simple: Bad Mum wasn't bad, she was just naughty sometimes – and extremely rude.

As they drove out of the car park, the men who'd been sitting at the next table were pouring out of the pub onto the pavement. One of them recognised Moira sitting in the passenger seat of the van, and he stood by the edge of the road waving at her and grinning.

Moira stuck her middle finger up at him through the window. 'Fucker,' she shouted.

CHAPTER FOUR

'IT WOULD BE FOR A FORTNIGHT, definitely no longer than that,' Lily said. 'I know it's short notice, Gordy, but do you think you can cover things here? It's a slow time of year.'

'Life is never slow at Beautiful Blooms, you know that, Lily!'

'Slower, then. We've nearly sold out of bulbs, the perennials are away for the winter, I've finished the fruit trees and the footfall is way down already. It won't get busy again until we've got all the Christmas stuff out next month.'

'I'm teasing you.' Gordon grinned. 'Of course, you can go!'

Lily stood up and threw her arms around him. 'Thanks. You're a star.'

'Although it doesn't sound like much of a holiday for you. Is she seriously expecting you'll make it as far as Scotland?'

Lily shrugged and sat back down at the small table in the office. 'God knows. I'm intending to try to talk her out of it, but "determined" is her middle name.'

Gordon shook his head slowly. 'You're a very dutiful daughter to do this,' he said. 'It might not be the easiest of trips.'

'I know,' said Lily. 'But it's important to her.'

She had worked alongside Gordon for nearly thirteen years now, and couldn't ask for a better boss, even though they'd got off to a rocky start when she joined Beautiful Blooms. Two weeks after she began work, he had made a half-hearted pass at her one morning while they were outside weeding the planters. Afterwards, they awkwardly tried to avoid each other – which wasn't easy because, although the garden centre covered a three-acre site, it was uncanny how frequently the two of them found themselves walking towards each other down the same section of path, or bumping into each other as they rounded a corner in the warehouse. The office where the nine members of staff took their breaks was only just large enough to swing a potted azalea. Lily was so terrified at the prospect of bumping into Gordon there that the following day she ate her lunchtime sandwich behind the wicker fencing in the potting area. She was devastated; so far, she had loved working at this place and, until this had happened, she and Gordon had been getting on so well. She lay awake that night, wondering if she might have unintentionally led him on. She hadn't meant to; they'd been sharing stories about themselves, making jokes at the expense of some of the ruder customers. But, always the first to doubt herself, Lily worried she'd been a little too friendly, a little too familiar. The following morning, she mentioned it to Suzanne, who ran the garden centre café, and immediately wished she hadn't because Suzanne informed her she was a local union rep and suggested she lodge a complaint. That wasn't Lily's way at all, she always tended towards the path of least resistance. 'By not reporting this, you're giving out all the wrong signals,' Suzanne had tutted. 'This isn't the nineties, things have moved on.'

But, later that afternoon, Gordon had marched up to Lily and launched into a fulsome apology, he couldn't believe what he'd done and was embarrassed and ashamed at his behaviour. He had totally misinterpreted the conversation they were having and had misunderstood the way she'd responded to him. If she wanted to take the matter further, he would step back from his responsibilities at Beautiful Blooms and ask head office to find someone to replace him immediately. She told him she didn't want him to do anything of the sort and to forget all about it.

'Thank you. I'm really sorry,' he'd said. 'Friends?'

'Friends.' She'd grinned back.

Shortly afterwards, Gordon had found happiness with a woman who worked in the local branch of Lloyds; Hilary wore brightly coloured Crocs, sang in three different choirs and used dozens of kirby grips to pin her hair up into an extravagant but rather chaotic bun. Lily couldn't help thinking that, when it came to women, Gordon certainly didn't have a type. But she'd been relieved – and happy for him – and their own relationship gradually worked its way back to normality, and from there into an even better place than before. Now, he was one of her closest friends and they made a great team at Beautiful Blooms. Having worked her way up to assistant manager, Lily didn't do as much hands-on gardening work nowadays – despite the fact that Eleanor frequently told her she had appalling fingernails – and it sometimes felt as if she spent more time organising staff rotas and dealing with emails from head office, than dead-heading and talking to customers about root rot. But she couldn't imagine working alongside anyone else, or being anywhere else. The building was jaded and could do with new signage, but the outdoor space was fantastic; she was surrounded by plants and flowers, the majority of the customers were lovely and going into work every morning never felt like a hardship. And even though she'd been dreading having to ask Gordon for time off to take this trip, she had known he would be understanding and do whatever he could to make it possible for her.

'It will be good to have a change of scene, even if this won't exactly be a relaxing holiday,' she said to him now. 'I'll go and tell Mum after work tonight, she'll be thrilled.'

'How are things going with Dave?' Gordon asked, as she stood up and began to fill the kettle.

She grimaced. 'Awful. He keeps texting, despite the fact that I haven't replied for the last week. You'd have thought he'd have got the message by now?'

'He doesn't want to give up on you,' Gordon said. 'That's not surprising.'

'You're sweet, Gordy.' She smiled and threw a plastic teaspoon across the table at him. It missed by a mile. She really didn't know what to do about Dave. They'd made contact through a dating app, but within five minutes of meeting him, Lily had known it wasn't going to work. Dave was extremely intense and talked a great deal about himself, leaning too close across the table while telling her about his love of astrophysical engineering. He had a beard (she hated beards), he had awful clothes sense (she knew it was shallow, but couldn't help judging him by his lime-green nylon jumper) and his breath smelt like he'd eaten an entire loaf of garlic bread. When they parted at the end of the first evening, Dave had moved in for a kiss and, as she tried to pull away, his wet lips had landed awkwardly on her ear. She had no idea why the dating app had matched them. He liked Procul Harem and Pink Floyd, she liked The Smiths and Elbow; he listed golf and British Military history as his hobbies, she had put on her profile that she liked gardening, watching soppy romcoms and eating cake.

'Shall we meet again?' he'd asked eagerly. 'It's been a wonderful evening, Lily. I've really enjoyed your company.'

No! screamed the voice inside her head. *I'd rather stick needles in my eyeballs!*

'Yes, that would be lovely,' she heard herself saying.

Poor Dave. The second date had been as terrible as the first, but at the end Lily had managed to come out with a mumbled excuse about being incredibly busy and not very good company and perhaps they should leave it a couple of months? He'd looked so sad, she nearly caved and agreed to see him again. Thankfully, she'd managed to hold back. But he was still texting, hoping she'd change her mind.

'I'll finish it properly,' she said to Gordon, now. 'I really will.'

'Well, stone me,' said Gordon, reaching across to take his cup of tea. 'Is that a pig I see flying past the window?'

After work, Lily drove to Moira's flat.

'Right, it's all sorted,' she said, following her mother into the small sitting room. 'We can leave this weekend! Start thinking about what you'll need to pack, and I'll book us a hotel for the first night in Cirencester. Mum, what's that smell?'

Moira frowned. 'I can't smell anything.'

'There's a strange smell coming from somewhere.' Lily went into the kitchen and saw Moira's slow cooker sitting on the worktop. Lifting the lid, she found it had been turned on and was full of sodden tea towels. 'What's going on? Why are these in here?'

'Don't touch them!' said Moira. 'I'm boil washing them. It's the most hygienic thing to do with tea towels. It's how we always used to clean them in the old days.'

'Mum, this is a slow cooker! It won't boil anything. What's wrong with using the washing machine?'

'Oh, Lily,' tutted Moira, shaking her head and walking away. 'Your new-fangled ways aren't always the best.'

Lily unplugged the slow cooker and pulled out the tea towels, cold, rancid water dripping onto her shoes as she lifted them across to the sink. This road trip was beginning to feel like a very bad idea.

CHAPTER FIVE

LILY DRAGGED the van's side door shut and walked round to the driver's side. 'Right, we're off! Buckle up, Mum – do you want me to help with that?'

'I can do it.' Moira was jabbing the metal end of the seat belt into mid-air, several inches away from the buckle. 'Stupid thing won't reach. These belts are too short.'

'Here, let me...'

'No, I've nearly got it.'

Lily sat back and sighed, briefly closing her eyes. It had been a stressful morning. When she arrived at Moira's flat, she had found her mother sitting on a camping chair on the pavement, surrounded by two suitcases, a polka dot shopping trolley, a picnic hamper, a huge cardboard box held together with Sellotape and numerous bulging plastic bags.

'What's going on, Mum? You can't possibly take all this?'

Moira had crossed her arms and tutted, raising her eyes to the sky. 'Lily, why are you so negative about everything? These are just a few essential bits and pieces I can't do without.'

Now, an hour later, with most of the clutter back in Moira's flat and just one large suitcase loaded into the van, they were ready to set off. Lily was already exhausted, and her temples were throbbing, but she smiled brightly as she turned the key in the ignition and the van's engine roared into life.

'Here we go!' she said. 'Isn't this exciting?'

There had been some weak wispy rays of sunshine glancing off the pavements earlier, but now clouds were gathering along the horizon in ominous steely grey puffballs, and spots of rain dotted the windscreen as they drove along Moira's road. The wipers screeched half-heartedly across the glass while Lily turned on the radio and started tapping her fingers on the steering wheel as something vaguely familiar from the 1980s filled the van. This was all going to be fine. Better than fine, it was going to be great. They were on their way; her mother was happy and the trip was going to be fun.

'Goodbye, Brighton!' called Moira, as they went past a row of shops. 'How long will it take to get to Cirencester? I'd quite like a coffee. Can we stop for a coffee soon, Lily?'

'Mum, we've only just started. Let's at least get round the M25.'

They didn't make it that far. Twenty miles up the road, the van limped into the service station at Pease Pottage, with the temperature gauge rising off the scale and a series of bangs and clanks coming from the engine in the rear. Lily pulled into an empty space in the car park and began to scroll through numbers on her phone. 'Damn and blast, bloody thing,' she muttered. 'I should have the RAC on speed dial.'

'Didn't you call them out last week?' Moira asked.

'Yes.'

'And earlier in the month as well? When you broke down on that roundabout?'

'Yup, then too.' Lily got out and walked round the van as she waited for the call to be answered. Moira wound down her window and sighed. 'I'm surprised they still keep coming out when you call. You must be one of their main customers.'

'Stupid thing!' Lily kicked the front tyre, but the toe of her boot slid to the side and caught on the metal wheel arch. 'Ow! Bloody hell.'

'Swearing at it, won't help,' said Moira.

'That's rich, coming from you!'

'I'm just telling you to stop kicking it.'

'Mum, will you shut up for a second?'

They glared at each other through the open passenger window.

'All I'm saying,' Moira continued, 'is that there's nothing we can do. We just have to sit here and wait.'

'Great. Thanks for the advice,' Lily snapped. 'Since when did you get to be so patient and calm?'

When the operator answered, she ran through what had happened with the practised shorthand of someone who knew exactly which details the breakdown service did and didn't need to hear. 'We're two women travelling alone,' she added. 'And my mother is elderly and extremely frail.'

Moira's eyebrows shot up. 'I'm bloody not!'

'Yes, you *are!*' Lily hissed.

The woman on the other end of the phone asked more questions.

'Well, no we're not exactly in an awkward location,' Lily answered, reluctantly. 'No, we're not by the side of the road. No, there isn't much passing traffic. We're actually in a service station off the A23 at Pease Pottage... Well, yes, it probably *is* quite safe, but my mother is still elderly and frail!'

'What's the point,' she said afterwards, as she rubbed her bruised toe, 'in offering priority assistance to vulnerable women when you then downgrade them again because they don't happen to be stuck on a verge beside a motorway? Vulnerable is vulnerable, wherever you are.'

By the time flashing lights heralded the arrival of the RAC, an hour later, Lily had bought them a second coffee from the Costa machine inside the garage, and played four games of solitaire on her phone. Moira had opened her new notebook and was hunched over it, scribbling away intently. 'I'm not sure if I'll use all of this, but it's useful for background,' she muttered when Lily asked what she was writing.

The young lad who jumped out of the RAC van had a chin splattered with acne and was wearing an outsized orange high-vis jacket that skimmed the top of his knees.

'He doesn't look old enough to have passed his driving test,' Moira said.

'I know,' said Lily. 'But he's all we've got.'

'Ladies,' he said, having assessed the problem in minutes. 'You've got dirt in your carburettor. It's quite common with older vehicles like this.'

'But I just had it serviced,' Lily said.

The lad shook his head and sucked in air through his teeth like a man four times his age. 'I'd change your mechanic, if I was you,' he said. 'Older vehicles like this often need specialist care.'

'Young man, what's your name?' Moira asked.

'Alfie.'

'Alfie! What a fine name. You are going to be making an appearance in my book as a knight in shining orange.'

'Right.' The boy took a step back, his face screwed up in confusion. 'Thank you for that.'

'Sorry about this, Mum,' Lily said, as they sat listening to him banging something loudly against the engine at the rear of the van. 'If I'd have known we were going to break down quite so soon – or at all – I'd have thought about hiring a car instead.'

Moira looked at her in surprise. 'Well, that would have been a waste of money!'

'At least it would have got us further than halfway up the A23.'

'It will be fine,' said Moira, who was still writing notes in her book. 'I'm very fond of this little van.'

'That's sweet of you, I love it too. But it isn't comfortable. The suspension is shot, for a start, and when I go over seventy, it rattles so badly it feels like something's going to fall off.'

Lily ran her hand along the inside of the door beside her. She really did love this little van. It was two-tone, white on top with the lower section a pale sky blue, with alloy wheels and a shiny white bumper. On either side of the metallic VW logo, its headlights peered out at the oncoming traffic like a pair of eyes, wide with surprise.

'Don't you think this is a bit silly?' Eleanor had asked, the first time she saw it parked outside Lily's house, three years ago. 'It's so old – look at the rust! What was wrong with your Ford Focus?'

There had been nothing wrong with the Ford Focus, but Lily had fallen in love with the campervan and everything it stood for. She loved the fact that the doors opened with a loud clunk and needed to be slammed hard to shut properly; she loved the fact that, when she turned the key in the ignition, the engine kicked into life with a throbbing rattle; she loved the little wooden cupboards that lined one wall in the back and the curtains that hung at the windows; she really loved how other VW drivers tooted their horns and waved at her as they went by.

'And when,' Eleanor had asked, 'will you be going camping?'

'I'm not sure exactly,' Lily had said. 'But it will come in very useful.'

Of course she had never spent a night in the van. She wasn't the camping type and had no intention of rearranging the seats into an uncomfortable little bed and trying to sleep on it. But she wasn't going to admit that to Eleanor.

'It's a mid-life crisis vehicle,' her daughter had sniffed. 'How tragic.'

'I'm only forty-seven!' Lily had exclaimed.

Eleanor had just shaken her head. 'As I said, mid-life crisis.'

By the time Alfie drove off in his RAC van and they got back on the road, it was raining properly and the windscreen wipers squealed across the glass, leaving bleary streaks in Lily's line of vision. She had hoped to get to Gloucestershire by lunchtime, but it was mid-afternoon before they arrived at the small village north of Cirencester, following signs directing them up a narrow lane. An overgrown graveyard came into view, dotted with stocky yew trees guarding the church like soldiers.

'It's partly Saxon, you know,' said Moira, as they got out of the campervan.

'Stand there, Mum, in front of the gate,' said Lily. 'I'll take a photo of you.'

Moira puffed out her chest, smiled and gestured at the church behind her with one arm. 'Cheese!' she yelled.

At least the rain had stopped and the sun was streaking tentatively through high, feathered clouds. The wooden door of the church squeaked loudly when Lily pushed it open. As her eyes adjusted to the dark interior, she smelt the mustiness of ancient prayer books mixed with the chemical tang of floor polish.

'It's lovely,' she whispered to Moira. She had no idea why she was whispering but not having set foot inside a church for decades, she felt strangely cowed, as if reverence was not just required but expected.

'Smaller than I remember,' said Moira, her voice echoing as she walked up the aisle. 'Isn't that strange? We had more than eighty guests, but it doesn't seem as if there's room for that many people in here.'

There was a crash from the front of the church and they both jumped and turned towards the noise.

'Can I help you?' A deep voice came out of the gloom beside the altar, then a man appeared, with a thatch of grey hair and huge overgrown eyebrows that clung to his forehead like caterpillars.

'Hello,' said Moira. 'The door was open so we let ourselves in.'

He strode towards them. 'The House of Our Lord is open to everyone,' he boomed.

'Marvellous,' said Moira. 'I got married here, nearly fifty years ago. I wanted to come and visit again. To see if it had changed!'

'Why would it have changed?' the man bellowed, running a finger around the inside of his dog collar, as if trying to tame an itch. He was right up close to them now, and specks of spittle flew from his lips as he spoke. Lily took a step backwards.

'Well, it might have done,' said Moira, standing her ground. 'Fifty years is a long time.' She was smiling, but the vicar didn't smile back.

'Madam, that is a mere drop in the ocean of the history of this church,' he said. 'It's Saxon, you know.'

'Yes, I know,' said Moira, mildly. 'With a Norman arch. I googled it.'

His eyebrows knitted together as he glared at her; he had clearly been about to blast them with some well-rehearsed church history.

'This is my daughter,' Moira said. 'We're doing a little trip

31

together, to visit some of the places that have been important to me throughout my life. Obviously, we had to start here.'

He harrumphed, glancing briefly at Lily. 'Well, I can't stand here all day, talking, I've got a sermon to write.' He spun on his heels and walked back down the aisle. 'Shut the gate on your way out,' he called over his shoulder. 'We don't want sheep getting into the graveyard.'

He disappeared through an arch at the far end and a door crashed shut behind him.

'Rude,' muttered Moira. 'That's someone who should never have devoted his life to other people's happiness.'

They spent a few more minutes wandering around the church, but the romance of the moment had been punctured.

'Come on,' Lily said. 'That's the first pit stop ticked off our list. Onwards.'

Ten minutes later, they were approaching Cirencester when Lily's mobile began to ring. It was in its holder on the dashboard and she could see Eleanor's name and photo flashing on the screen.

'Damn,' she said to Moira, pulling the campervan over onto the side of the road. 'I'd better take this.'

'Hi, darling!' she said, putting a finger into the ear that wasn't against the phone. Even when idling, the engine made a lot of noise, and the old van trembled around them. 'Everything all right?'

'Where are you?' demanded Eleanor.

'Well, right at this minute we're parked up on a lane just outside Cirencester!'

'What? I can't believe you've actually left!' Eleanor was breathing heavily. It sounded as if she was walking; she'd probably come out of work to make the call. 'This whole road trip thing is crazy. When I talked to you on Thursday – oh, hang on a minute...'

There was a high-pitched beeping and Lily pictured her daughter striding across a pedestrian crossing back in the centre of Brighton, phone pinned to her ear with one hand, her Louis Vuitton bag clutched to her side with the other.

'When I talked to you before, I thought you'd realised it was a terrible idea?' Eleanor carried on, as the beeping faded into the distance. 'I can't believe you're going ahead with this. You should know better.'

'We've had this conversation so many times...' began Lily.

'Well, let's have it again. We'll keep having it until you see sense. This trip isn't just foolish, it's downright dangerous. Put me on to Granny, let me talk to her.'

Lily silently handed the mobile across to Moira, grimacing.

'Hello?' said Moira. 'How are...'

Although the phone wasn't on speakerphone, Lily could still hear Eleanor's voice, tinny and shrill, on the other end of the line. It wasn't quite loud enough for her to make out every word, but she got the gist.

'Eleanor, calm down,' Moira was saying. 'You're going to give yourself a heart attack if you carry on like this. We know how you feel about our trip, but you've made your point and your mother and I have set off now – we have hit the road, Jack, as they say, and we're having a marvellous time – aren't we?' She looked at Lily and winked.

The squawking continued and Lily stared through the windscreen, thinking how strange it was that at times – like right now – her mother seemed totally in control and compos mentis. As she listened to her speaking calmly and rationally to Eleanor, it was hard to believe this was the same woman who had, only last week, been forcibly evicted from Poundland after opening several boxes of cereal and pouring the contents onto the floor. Later, when Lily asked her why she'd done it, Moira had stared at her in confusion. 'Why do you always say I've done something? I just went in to buy toothpaste, but I had no end of trouble finding it. I think they'd hidden all the Colgate away somewhere.'

Lily wiped at a smudge on the side window of the van, wondering where they'd eat tonight. It might be easiest to book a table in the hotel restaurant. The menu looked interesting: there was sea bass – she hadn't eaten sea bass in years.

Now Moira was handing back the mobile. 'She wants to speak to you again.'

'You're being bloody irresponsible,' snapped Eleanor.

'Sweetheart,' said Lily. 'The consultant was all in favour of this, he said our trip was a good idea and–'

'I don't care what he said,' interrupted Eleanor. 'He's a man for a start, so I bet he wasn't really listening to what you were telling him. Also, he didn't know what you had planned. He probably drives a Tesla, so for him a road trip would be the height of luxury. He had no idea you were intending to drive hundreds of miles across the country in a bloody campervan.'

'He works for the NHS, Eleanor, I doubt he drives a Tesla.'

'Whatever. I bet you didn't tell him what you were planning.'

Lily sighed and rubbed her eye with the heel of her hand. Eleanor knew they'd told the consultant exactly what they were planning, but there was no point arguing with her, she wasn't the sort to back down. When she was growing up, Eleanor had been what Lily's friends kindly referred to as 'a handful'. As a small child, she had thrown tantrums of epic proportions, while Lily looked on in bewilderment, often not sure what had caused the frenzy, let alone how long it would last. She tried to reason with her daughter, she tried bribery, she tried to plead with her. As strangers stared, Lily would feel her cheeks flaring and impotent fury building up inside her as she dragged the screaming child away from the pursed lips and heads which were being shaken in disapproval. By the time she started at secondary school, Eleanor's insistence on always being right made her unpopular in the playground and alienated teachers and sports coaches, as well as adults who paid her to babysit their children, deliver newspapers or wash up in pub kitchens. Eleanor stormed through school and college, then forced her way out into the world with a self-confidence which Lily found astounding. When she chose the law as a career, it had seemed appropriate, but God help anyone who dared challenge Eleanor's world view. Lily herself rarely did so. Many years ago, she had learnt that, when her daughter fired a shot across her bows, it was safer to stand well back and duck.

'Stop making excuses.' Eleanor hadn't paused for breath. 'You need to turn around now and come home.'

'We don't want to come home,' said Lily. 'Granny is happy and she has planned everything down to the last detail. This is what she wants.'

'She doesn't know what she wants!' screeched Eleanor. 'She's losing her marbles.'

'I heard that!' said Moira. She reached for the phone, took it out of Lily's hand and put it back to her own ear. 'I am perfectly in control of all my marbles. Each and every single one. We have to go now, I'm afraid. I would say it was nice to speak to you, but it really wasn't. Goodbye.'

She held the phone away from her face, screwing up her eyes as she looked for the end call button before stabbing at it with her forefinger. 'Right,' she turned to Lily and smiled, 'on we go.'

CHAPTER SIX

THE HOTEL in Cirencester was luxurious. Delicately woven Indian rugs were scattered across the polished wooden floors, velvet drapes fell on either side of the large windows and a wide staircase swept upwards from the reception desk, where the staff greeted them like royalty. Lily's immediate reaction was dread; this place and its staff were far too grand to react well to an elderly lady who wasn't always on her best behaviour. As they waited to be checked in, she watched her mother anxiously for telltale signs that she might start singing at the top of her voice or begin to rip off her clothes and run half-naked around the entrance hall.

But Moira was surprisingly calm. 'This is all very beautiful,' she said to the young man who showed them up to their capacious twin room. 'How lucky you are to work here!'

Lily wondered if it was something to do with the atmosphere. The hotel was peaceful, there were no slamming doors or ringing phones, no raised voices or even a clattering from the direction of the kitchens, and the tranquillity of the place seemed to have a calming effect on Moira. They had a gin and tonic in the bar, followed by a delicious, leisurely meal in the dining room – the sea bass was every bit as good as Lily had anticipated. Both weary after their long day, they were in bed in their twin room by 10pm and, just minutes after turning off the bedside light, Lily heard her mother's breathing settle into a soft, regular snore. She smiled to herself in the darkness, feeling the tension in her own body start to ebb away. Maybe the two of them would be all right on this journey, after all? She just needed to keep her mother calm and ensure they avoided any potentially stressful situations.

Breakfast was an equally sumptuous affair. They filled up on home-made muesli and freshly squeezed orange juice, then struggled to finish piles of soft, bright yellow scrambled eggs. Toast appeared on the table, along with another huge pot of tea.

'This is the life,' said Lily, sitting back in her chair and clutching at her stomach. 'Thanks, Mum, what a fantastic place to stay. I've really enjoyed it.'

'Nice to start off our trip with a little luxury,' said Moira. 'I can't promise everywhere will be this good though.'

'I'm pleased to hear it, you'd bankrupt yourself. Have you booked a hotel for tonight?'

Moira waved her hand in the air. 'Oh, yes. It's somewhere in the north.'

'I thought you said we were going to Worcester?'

'Yes, that will be it.'

'Have you booked ahead?'

'It's all sorted,' Moira said. 'Don't worry.'

'Well, it might be a good idea if I ring and...'

'Did I tell you that your father and I stayed here on our honeymoon?' Moira said, suddenly. 'Right here, in this hotel?'

'No! You didn't tell me that.'

'We had our reception here, after we'd got married in that little church with the awful vicar. Not that he married us, thank goodness. What a disaster that would have been. Just having that miserable bugger standing up in front of you, spitting in your face, would ruin a wedding.'

For once, Lily thought Moira's language was entirely appropriate. 'Did you have a sit-down meal here?' she asked.

'Oh yes. Four courses, and then we had a beautiful cake, which we cut just over there in the corner. They stood it on a carved wooden table; it was ever so pretty.'

'Mum, that's lovely! Why didn't you tell me? No wonder you wanted to stay here – I'm so glad we managed it. Has the hotel changed much?'

Moira sat back and looked around at the dining room. 'Not a great deal. Those curtains weren't here though. I remember the ones in this room were burgundy with a lovely trim on them. The tables all had white linen tablecloths and there were spring flowers everywhere – it was April when we got married, all the daffodils, hyacinths and tulips were in full bloom.'

'That's wonderful,' said Lily. Part of her wasn't surprised Moira had such a clear recollection about an event that happened so many decades ago. From what she'd read, it was the recent memories that disappeared first when dementia began to take hold. Those recollections from many years ago, which were stacked towards the bottom of the pile somewhere inside her mind, would be the last to go. Even when she was struggling to remember her own name, Moira would still probably be able to recite exactly what she and her guests had eaten at their wedding breakfast. Lily's stomach lurched as she imagined herself sitting opposite a mother who didn't know who she was. Over the last few months, she had learnt enough about this cruel condition to realise it was highly likely – possibly inevitable – that Moira would one day fail to recognise her own daughter and granddaughter. She would eventually forget where she'd lived and who her friends had been; all the knowledge, wisdom and happy memories inside her head would be obliterated by a rolling fog that would wipe away everything she'd achieved in her life.

Stop this, Lily told herself. *It's pointless.* She took a deep breath and smiled across the table as Moira chatted about the speeches at her wedding reception. Even if this was the scenario that was waiting for them, there was nothing either of them could do about it. But it underlined the value of what they were doing: they were revisiting places that had been important to her mother while she was still fit and healthy enough to not just remember them, but also enjoy those memories.

'I hope you're writing all these things down in your book,' Lily said.

'Of course I am,' said Moira, tapping her fingers on top of the notebook, which was lying beside her plate. 'Everything is going in here, don't you worry. Your father and I had the honeymoon suite upstairs. It was very fancy indeed. It was quite a raunchy night, what with one thing and another.'

'Mum, please! I do not want to hear about that!'

Less than an hour later, they were packed and ready to get back on the road. Lily took the bags out to the van, while Moira stopped at the reception desk and asked for the bill. A few minutes later, having got her mother settled in the front seat, Lily popped back into the hotel again.

'Sorry, this might sound odd,' she said to the man behind the desk. 'But I just wanted to check that my mother *has* sorted out the bill with you? She's getting a bit forgetful nowadays.'

'Absolutely.' He beamed. 'And she left a generous tip. I'm glad you both enjoyed your stay.'

'Oh good.' Lily's relief was tinged with regret that she'd doubted Moira. She had been listening to too much of Eleanor's nagging, picking up on her negativity and expecting her mother to get everything wrong and muddled. How unfair.

'We've had a great time,' she said. 'It has been lovely for my mother to be back. She had her wedding reception here, did she tell you?'

He looked surprised. 'No, she didn't mention that.'

'Yes! She and my dad got married in Daglingworth Church, fifty years ago, and they came here afterwards for their reception, then stayed for the first night of their honeymoon.'

'Ah.' The man's brow was furrowed in confusion. 'I see.'

'They had your honeymoon suite, upstairs.'

'We don't actually have a honeymoon suite,' he said.

'Oh. Well maybe you did back then. I mean it was a long time ago! The hotel must have changed hugely over the years.'

He was looking embarrassed now, staring down at the register in front of him and tapping his biro on the desk. 'It wasn't actually here then.'

'Sorry? What wasn't?'

'The hotel. It wasn't here fifty years ago. Well, that is, the building was here, naturally. But it wasn't a hotel.'

Lily was confused. 'I don't understand?'

'This building was a private house until ten years ago,' the receptionist said. 'Then the owner sold it to Maddisons and they converted it into one of their flagship hotels in the south west.'

'So, you're saying my mother didn't stay here when she got married?'

The man was still fiddling with the register, not meeting her eye. 'I couldn't possibly comment on that, madam. But I'm wondering if she might be getting a little confused?'

'Do you know, it must be my mistake,' Lily blustered. 'I obviously wasn't paying attention when she was talking to me, just now.'

As she walked back out to the van, there was a heaviness in

the pit of her stomach. Maybe she should say something to Moira? But what was the point – there was no way she'd got the wrong end of the stick during the conversation they'd had at breakfast. Her mother had definitely been talking about this hotel. She opened the door and climbed into the driver's seat of the van, reaching for her seat belt. Moira was already strapped in, scribbling in her notebook and humming to herself.

'Off we go then!' she said, looking across at Lily and beaming. 'To Wales!'

'Yes,' said Lily, turning the key in the ignition. 'To Wales.'

CHAPTER SEVEN

IT WAS a long time since Lily had driven Moira further than the doctor's surgery or the local supermarket, and during those ten-minute journeys she had never thought much about her mother's credentials as a travelling companion. But now that the two of them were buckled in, side by side, feeling every bump in the road and having to yell to make themselves heard above the roaring engine and the rattling interior of the campervan, going on a journey with Moira had taken on a whole new meaning.

Lily considered herself a patient human being; tolerance was something she possessed in spades. But by the time they'd crossed the Severn Bridge, she was at the point where she would scream if her mother made one more comment about the idiocy of the radio DJ, the lunacy of other motorists, or the way Lily herself was driving.

'Look at that one! He's going far too fast. He's going to get stopped by the police... Did you see that grey lorry? He shouldn't be in the outside lane. Who is this stupid bloody man on the radio? Why doesn't he stop talking and let us listen to the music? Not that it's very good music. Although I like this one by Abba. You know this one, don't you, Lily? I remember the two girls were wearing those flared pantsuits when they sang it. Whatever happened to pantsuits? Lily, I think you're too near to that car in front – you won't be able to stop if it brakes suddenly!'

When they came off the motorway, Lily breathed a sigh of relief as the engine noise decreased; at least her mother could bend her ear at a normal volume now. She wound down her window and took several deep breaths in and out, relaxing her shoulders and trying to connect with her inner calm as she changed the radio station and found something soothing and classical.

'I've never been to Chepstow,' she said. 'Can we have a look around first, before we go and find the house where you and Dad lived?'

'Well, it's not a very interesting town.' Moira sniffed.

'You've always said it was lovely?'

'I don't think I did, Lily. I would definitely remember if I'd liked Chepstow. It looks like a bit of a dump to me.'

They parked and had a walk around the castle, then sat outside a café, sharing a piece of cake and gazing up at the imposing stone ramparts towering above the river, the air filled with the cackling of rooks floating high up on the thermals.

'When were you last here?' asked Lily, spooning the chocolate sprinkles off the top of her cappuccino.

'We left in the mid-seventies,' said Moira. 'When your dad got a new job. While we lived here, he was working for Cadw, as a groundsman at the castle. There wasn't a lot happening socially though. Every Thursday night we used to drive up to Gloucester, to go dancing.'

'I never knew that?'

'He was a lovely dancer, your father. Very light on his feet. We went to the Ritz Dance Hall and we'd spend the whole evening whirling around.' Moira raised her cup and circled it around in the air.

'Mum, you're spilling coffee on me!'

'We did the quickstep and the fox trot – and the rhumba! Oh, my word, how your father could gyrate his hips to the rhumba. He was a very sexy man, you know.'

'Please, stop.' Lily dropped her head into her hands.

'Anyway.' Moira put her cup back down on its saucer. 'Let's go and find 14 Mount View. I'm looking forward to this. I wonder if the people who live there now will let us inside to have a look round? It was our first home, you know, did I tell you that?'

'Many times.'

'I ran up some curtains for the kitchen window – they were the only things I'd ever made and the material had big red flowers on. They didn't quite meet in the middle, and one was shorter than the other, but I was very proud of them.'

As they got up from the table, Lily pulled out her phone. 'Let's have a quick picture of you, Mum, with the castle in the background.'

'Good idea,' said Moira, pulling her coat tightly across her body with one hand and throwing out her other arm to indicate the towering ramparts behind her. 'Stilton!' she yelled, as Lily took the photo.

When they got back to the van, Lily's phone pinged with a text from Gordon:

> Hope you're having a good time? Is Moira behaving herself?

She tapped out a quick reply:

> We're doing fine! She hasn't trashed any shops or insulted too many people yet x

They got into the campervan and drove through the town. Moira was leaning forward in her seat, directing. 'Down here to the end, then take the next right.'

'I'm impressed you still remember the way after all these years!'

'Oh, that little shop is still there! It used to be run by such a lovely man. Alan, I think his name was. Or Aled? This is it, this road just here. The house is about halfway along on the left: number 14.'

Lily pulled up outside a small semi-detached house and they both sat and stared at it.

'Oh dear,' said Moira.

The grass on the front lawn was knee-high and littered with brightly coloured children's toys. What had once been a flowerbed was now so overgrown that the shrubs in it lurched towards the sky, untamed green tendrils shooting out at angles, like water spouting from a fountain. A section of guttering was hanging below the roof, and a pane in one of the upstairs windows was broken, with a piece of cardboard flapping across it. They could hear music coming from inside the house, a pounding bass as regular as a heartbeat.

'Shall we knock?' asked Lily. 'We can ask to go in and take a look round?'

Moira shook her head violently. 'Absolutely not.'

'It might be better inside, maybe they're the kind of people who don't like gardening.'

'No, let's go,' said Moira, reaching for her seat belt.

'Sure?'

Her mother nodded, keeping her head down, fiddling with the belt.

Lily started the engine and pulled away from the kerb, accelerating as soon as she had left the small estate and was back on the main road. For a few minutes, neither of them spoke.

'There were all those toys in the garden, so they obviously had young children,' Lily said, eventually. 'It can be hard work, keeping everything together when you've got a family.'

Moira didn't answer; she was staring the other way, through the side window. Lily glanced at her, suspecting she might be crying, but unable to see her face.

They drove on in silence for a few more minutes.

'The state of that border!' Moira said, suddenly. 'I remember planting some roses in that flowerbed, when we moved in. They were beautiful. We pruned them every winter and the scent was wonderful. Such a waste. And there was ivy all over the side wall – did you see that? It's going to get into the brickwork if they're not careful.'

'I know,' said Lily. 'It's a real shame.'

Moira reached into her bag and pulled out her notebook and pencil, bending her head over the pages as she wrote. 'Bloody idiots,' she muttered. 'Bloody selfish idiots.'

Lily was furious with herself – why hadn't she done more research before they set out? She could have looked on that street view website, then she would have realised the house was in a mess. She might not have been able to persuade Moira not to visit, but at the very least she could have prepared her for the shock.

'Where are we off to now?' Lily asked, brightly. 'We're going towards Gloucester but do I need to get onto the motorway?'

'Maybe,' muttered Moira, her head still over her notebook.

'Mum! You said we were staying in Worcester – is that right?'

'We are going to stay with Oliver,' Moira announced.

'Oliver? Who the hell is that?'

'He's an old friend.'

'What kind of old friend?'

'How many different kinds of old friends are there?

Honestly, Lily, you can be very stupid sometimes.' Moira sighed and shook her head.

'Charming, thank you. When did you last see him?'

'Oh, I don't know. Years ago. Years and years. When you were a little girl. I think he came to see us once when we lived in Yorkshire.'

'So, the two of you haven't actually seen each other for more than forty years? Wow, this is going to be interesting. Why have I never heard you talk about him?'

'You don't know everything about my life, Lily! There are many things I've never spoken to you about.'

Lily sighed. 'No, I realise that, but I do need to know where Oliver lives. Have you got his address?'

Moira tutted and raised her eyes. 'Of course I have. Sometimes you treat me like a five-year-old.' She reached down into her bag again and pulled out a scrap of paper. 'Here you are.'

Lily pinned the note to the steering wheel with one hand and glanced down at it. 'Wolverhampton? Mum, you said Worcester!'

'No,' Moira said. 'I most definitely said Wolverhampton.'

'Fine, whatever. Does this Oliver person actually know we're coming to stay?'

'Of course. It's all arranged, I wrote him a letter.'

'But did you hear back from him?'

Lily's phone pinged as a text came in and she glanced at the dashboard. Although only part of the message was showing, she could see it was from Eleanor. She reached up and swiped to clear the screen. She certainly wasn't going to respond to that for a while; she was still angry about yesterday's phone call, the way her daughter had shrieked at them both and tried to bully them into abandoning the trip.

'You shouldn't let her boss you around, you know.' Moira

had guessed who the text was from. 'She doesn't treat you very nicely.'

'I know,' Lily said. 'But I don't think she's ever going to change. My daughter is a force of nature.'

'For years you let Nick get the better of you. Now Eleanor does the same.'

'I know, Mum,' Lily said. 'You don't need to tell me that.'

'Well, you should do something about it then.'

Lily changed gear more forcefully than was necessary, and the van stuttered and nearly stalled. She knew Moira was right, but she wasn't in the mood to hear it. Eleanor had always been so much more like her father than like Lily. She could hear her daughter's voice in her ear, during their phone conversation a couple of days ago, telling her to have some backbone and stand up to Moira. The irony of it all wasn't lost on her. Thirteen years after the divorce, Nick's voice still rang in her ear, coming out with the sort of belittling things he'd said to her dozens of times during their marriage: *'You're such a pushover, Lily. You should learn to stand up for yourself.'*

It still stung, even after all this time. The memory of how he had constantly put her down was like an open wound that never quite healed. Over the years it would stop itching for a while and she would almost forget about it, then something would fire it up again; usually Eleanor would make some throwaway comment about how amazing her dad was or what a good time the two of them had recently had together – and Lily would be right back where she'd started: vulnerable, insecure and desperate to scratch at an old itch that had never really gone away.

CHAPTER EIGHT

'STOP!' Moira yelled, banging her palms on the dashboard.

'Jesus, Mum!' Lily slammed her foot onto the brake pedal and the campervan shuddered as it slowed down. 'What's the matter?'

'We've got to go back!' Moira was turning around in the passenger seat, staring through the rear window at the stretch of road they'd just driven along.

'Why?' Lily's heart was thundering almost as loudly as the cars that were flying past them as they sat on the side of the dual carriageway. A horn blared out as a lorry rumbled by, the flow of air rocking the van.

'I just saw the road where the Ritz was!'

'What the hell is the Ritz?'

'The dance hall, Lily! The one where your father used to take me. Quickly, turn round, we need to go back, it's down there on the other side.'

More horns blasted as Lily moved back into the traffic. 'There's a roundabout up ahead, I'll turn there. Honestly, Mum, you nearly gave me a heart attack.'

'Never mind that, go back. That's it. Down here. Keep going. Now, do you see that turning up ahead? That's the one.'

Lily pulled off the main road. Moira was leaning forward in her seat, pointing. 'Up there. Then take a right. Now pull into that car park.'

Lily cut the engine and they sat in silence for a few seconds. 'Mum,' she said, gently. 'This can't be it.'

'I'm sure it is.'

'But this is an Asda superstore?'

Moira was shaking her head and tutting. 'This is the Ritz Dance Hall, I remember it as if it was yesterday. We used to park over there, by those trees. Thursday was always a popular night. You could hear the music playing as soon as you got out of the car.'

Lily reached across and put her hand on her mother's arm. 'I think you may have got this wrong. Or maybe it's just not here anymore? It was probably knocked down to make way for the supermarket.'

'I have not got anything wrong,' snapped Moira, pulling her arm away. Before Lily had a chance to react, her mother had unclipped her seat belt, opened the passenger door of the van, stepped down onto the tarmac and was making her way across the car park, the edges of her coat flapping behind her.

'Shit!' Lily muttered. 'Mum, come back here!' She got out and began to follow, running back to the van when she realised she'd forgotten to lock it. By the time she was halfway across the car park, Moira was disappearing through the supermarket's huge sliding entrance doors.

It was now Sunday afternoon and it seemed as if the entire population of Gloucestershire had picked this particular time to do a weekly shop. Lily pushed her way past people who were coming out through the doors, apologising as she bumped against their over-stacked trolleys, her eyes darting backwards and forwards as she looked for Moira's dark red coat.

'Hey, watch it!' said a man with a small child balanced on one hip and a bag of shopping in the other hand.

'I'm sorry!' Lily said. 'I've lost my mother.'

She ran through the fruit and vegetable section, then along the back of the store, aware of the pungent smell of freshly baked bread as she stopped at the top of the dairy aisle, peering through the crowds of shoppers. She could feel panic rising in her chest and her breath was coming in jags. There were so many people, she was never going to find her like this. She ran down the aisle, banging her hip against one trolley and sending it spinning into another. 'Sorry!' she called over her shoulder. 'Really sorry!'

At the far end, by the tills, she looked up and down again. No sign. Turning the corner, she ran up the length of the next aisle. Then the one after that. She went past pasta and packets of soup, then past home baking and tinned fruit. Ahead of her was the bakery section and, as she got near, she noticed some sort of commotion going on and a woman was shouting. Heads were turning and at the top of the aisle shoppers were moving to get a closer look at whatever was happening just around the corner. Lily squeezed past a family with young children and spotted a flash of burgundy up ahead, just as she realised the woman's voice was terrifyingly familiar.

'Get your bloody hands off me!'

'Madam, you can't do that.'

'Don't you tell me what I can or can't do, young man. How old are you? You look about fifteen, shouldn't you be in school?'

Moira was standing beside a security guard; she was clutching a half-eaten doughnut, while vigorously trying to shake off the guard's hand which was curled tightly around her upper arm.

'Let go of me, you fucker! Get off my arm!'

'Calm down, lady,' the guard said. 'There's no need for language like that.'

'Fucking fuckwit!' yelled Moira. 'You're hurting me!'

The children beside Lily were sniggering, and a young couple were laughing out loud while the man pulled a phone from his pocket.

'Please, let go of her!' Lily said, walking forward. 'This is my mother. I'm sure she hasn't done anything wrong. Mum, what are you doing? What have you got there?'

Standing to one side was a woman wearing a hairnet and a plastic apron over an Asda T-shirt. 'She stole that doughnut!' she said, pointing at Moira. 'Picked it up off the counter and took a big bite out of it. When I told her she had to pay for food before she ate it, she stuck up two fingers and walked away, bold as brass.'

'I stuck up one finger, you idiot!' Moira shouted.

'Oh God, I'm so sorry.' Lily grabbed the doughnut Moira was waving in the air and passed it back to the woman. 'She's not well and doesn't always know what she's doing.'

'I'm fine!' yelled Moira. 'Give that back to me!'

'She's taken a bite out of that, you need to pay for it!' the woman said, holding up her palms in front of her as if to ward off the offending doughnut.

'It's custard! I like ones with custard in the middle.'

Lily pulled her purse from her coat pocket and pulled out a five-pound note. 'Here, this should cover it. I'm really sorry.'

'I can't take that. You need to pay at the till!' snorted the woman. 'What are you trying to do, get me sacked?'

'No! Of course not. Look, we'll pay on the way out. I'm really sorry again, for causing all this trouble.' The security guard – who actually did only look about fifteen – had dropped Moira's arm and stepped back; Lily threw him a grateful look and put her arm around her mother's shoulders. 'Come on, let's get back to the van.'

'What about my custard doughnut?'

'You can have it when we get outside. I need to pay for it first.'

'I don't want it outside, I want it now!'

Lily pulled her mother through the crowd of gawping onlookers, knowing her own face was scarlet. The young man with the phone was now taking photos and she glared at him, imagining herself reaching out and knocking the mobile from his hand so it shattered into hundreds of pieces on the polished tile floor.

People were laughing out loud behind them, and she could hear the woman from the bakery counter talking indignantly to the security guard. Suddenly Moira stopped and shrugged off Lily's arm. 'It's here somewhere, I know it. Maybe on the other side.' She started walking back the way they'd come and Lily followed her. 'It's definitely here.'

'Mum, please! Where are you going?'

Moira turned into the next aisle, which was lined with washing powder and conditioner.

'There was a band at one end, up on a stage with a bar along the far wall,' she called back over her shoulder. 'Your father bought me Campari and soda, that was my favourite drink. I always had a Campari and soda before the dancing started, then I'd have another one in the break. I was sometimes a little tipsy by the time we finished. All that spinning around, with your father doing that sexy thing with his hips.'

She suddenly stopped in the middle of the aisle, and a woman glared at her as she was forced to move her trolley to one side. Lily caught up and took Moira by the arm again. Her expression had changed. She no longer looked animated; now her brow was furrowed and she was staring around her in confusion. 'I don't know what's happened, Lily. Why are we here?'

'Come on,' Lily said. 'Let's get back to the van.'

'Why did I come into this place?'

'I'm not entirely sure, Mum, to be honest. But let's leave now.'

She dragged Moira towards the self-service tills, where she handed the five-pound note to a bemused looking shop assistant. 'It's for this doughnut,' she said. 'Keep the change.'

'I can't do that!' the assistant called after them. 'You have to scan it through the till.'

'Can you do it, please?' Lily called over her shoulder, pulling Moira towards the entrance doors.

By the time they got back to the van, Moira was walking so slowly that Lily felt she was half carrying her. She helped her up into the passenger seat and gently pushed a strand of white hair back from her mother's forehead. 'Are you okay?' she asked, reaching for the seat belt and pulling it gently across her body.

Moira looked at her and smiled. 'Oh yes. I'm right as rain.'

'Good,' Lily said. 'Then let's get away from here.'

Even though they were out of that place, she was still trembling and her heart was racing. She couldn't stop thinking about the expressions on the faces of all those shoppers as they'd gathered around Moira like spectators at a circus. The disbelief, the amusement and – in some cases – the contempt. There had probably also been a few sympathetic faces: people who understood what they were going through. But if so, Lily hadn't noticed them. The whole thing had been horrible. As she put the keys into the ignition and the van engine roared into life, she made herself take several deep breaths. It was over now; everything was going to be all right. That scene had been upsetting and worrying, but none of it was Moira's fault.

Putting the van into gear, Lily remembered the text she'd sent to Gordon this morning:

> We're doing fine! She hasn't trashed any shops or insulted too many people yet x

Maybe that had been a little premature after all.

CHAPTER NINE

EXHAUSTED AFTER DANCING in the aisles at Asda, Moira fell asleep before they joined the motorway. Lily glanced over, watching her mother's head resting on her chest, hoping the van's poor suspension wouldn't jolt her awake again too soon. She kept thinking back to the laughter all around them in the supermarket, the scorn on the faces of most of the other shoppers. Didn't those people have elderly relatives who weren't quite as lucid as they had once been? Did none of them know how painful it was to watch somebody you loved beginning a slow decline into a world that was foggy and unfamiliar? Surely many other people would have been through something similar, and would have understood the horror of the situation. But they weren't the ones standing around, watching, laughing and taking photos on their mobiles. The people who knew what Lily and Moira were going through would have turned and walked away, anxious not to aggravate an already distressing situation.

Earlier, when Moira handed her the scrap of paper on which she'd written down Oliver's address, Lily had put the postcode into the Google Maps app on her phone; now it was telling her they were an hour away from their destination.

Who on earth was this man? She kept racking her brains and trying to remember whether either of her parents had ever spoken about him, but she came up with nothing. Maybe he had been a work colleague of her dad's? If so, it was possible he and Moira had kept in touch after Ken died, nearly twenty years ago now, even if it was just through the occasional Christmas card. In that case, part of the reason Moira was telling her so little about him was because she didn't know much herself. She may have only met Oliver a few times, many years previously. If so, why had she decided to include him on this road trip? It was useful, Lily acknowledged that much, because it meant they weren't having to pay for another hotel this evening. She just hoped that, whoever Oliver was, he had actually been told they were on their way – and that he'd have some food ready for them; she hadn't eaten since they'd shared that slice of lemon drizzle in Chepstow and, even above the noise of the VW engine, she could hear her stomach rumbling.

Moira woke just as Lily was reversing the van into a space outside a row of terraced brick cottages.

'Where are we?'

'I think we're at Oliver's, but I can't see a house number. How are you feeling, Mum? A bit better after that sleep?'

'I'm feeling fine, why wouldn't I?'

'I just meant, after what happened in Asda.'

Moira turned and stared at her. 'Lily, what are you talking about? What happened in Asda? You do say the strangest things sometimes.'

Lily sighed, it wasn't worth pursuing. She edged the van forward a few feet and they both peered over the top of the wooden gate. 'What does that sign say, beside the door?'

'*Beware of the dog*,' read Moira. 'I hope he hasn't got something big and jumpy, like a Great Dane.'

'Look, there's a number 12 on the house next door, so this one must be 11,' said Lily. 'We're definitely in the right place.'

They sat staring at the little cottage, neither of them making a move.

'Do you know,' said Moira. 'I'm a bit nervous?'

'I'm not surprised. You haven't seen him in such a long time.'

'What if he's disappointed?' asked Moira. 'What if he looks at me and sees a wizened old bat, who's nothing like the woman he remembers?'

'Well, don't take this the wrong way,' said Lily. 'But you are seventy-nine. I'm not for one minute suggesting you're a wizened old bat, but you're no spring chicken. On the other hand, unless he's had extensive plastic surgery, he won't be much of a catch either.'

Moira took a deep breath in. 'You're right. Come on then, in we go.'

They got out and walked up the path to the front door. There was no reply at first, and Moira had to ring the bell again. Then, from inside came the sound of footsteps, followed by a clattering as bolts were drawn back. Then a crash that made them both jump.

'Fuck!' bellowed a voice.

The door was flung open. The man standing in front of them had one hand on the door, the other grasped around a bunch of half-dead carnations, water dripping down his arm from the stems.

'Mind the glass,' he said, indicating the shattered pieces on the floor at his feet. 'Stupid place to put a vase of flowers.' He turned and walked away from them down the passageway. Lily looked at her mother, whose mouth was hanging open.

'Oliver?' Moira called after the man. 'Oliver, is that you?'

'Of course it's bloody me,' he yelled over his shoulder.

The kitchen at the back of the house was large, with a dining table at one end and an old wooden dresser running along most of one wall. Every surface was taken up: pots, pans, piles of dirty plates, half empty glasses, crumpled newspapers, boxes of cereal, opened tins of food. Even the chairs around the table were covered with discarded jumpers and books. There were also empty bottles. Lots of empty bottles. On the dining table alone, there were green, brown and clear bottles that had once held wine, beer, gin, vodka and whisky.

'Sit, sit!' ordered Oliver, waving his hand towards the table. Then, realising there was nowhere to sit, he dumped the flowers in the sink and began to sweep debris from chairs.

'Sorry, wasn't expecting you today,' he said.

'But I did say Sunday?' said Moira, lowering herself into a chair and running her palm across the table in front of her, brushing bits of decayed food onto the floor.

'Yes, but that's tomorrow,' said the man, putting his hand to his forehead and frowning. He was hugely overweight, the distended belly sticking over the belt of his trousers looked solid enough to belong to a woman on the point of going into labour. His face was fleshy and blotchy, and his white hair, which he was now sweeping back across his forehead in jerky, awkward movements, was badly in need of a trim.

'It's Sunday today,' said Moira, quietly. Lily noticed her mother's hands, as she laid them on the table, were trembling.

'Oh, really? That's strange, must have lost a day. Hah! Oh dear. Anyway, tea? Coffee? Or how about something stronger? I've got gin or whisky. Or maybe you ladies would like some sparkling wine?'

'Tea would be lovely,' said Lily. 'Just normal tea.' It wasn't even four o'clock, so she couldn't face the idea of a drink just yet.

She sat down beside Moira, who was sitting ramrod-straight in her chair. She put her fingers on top of her mother's hands, squeezing them gently. 'Can I help at all, Oliver? I'm Lily, by the way, Moira's daughter.'

'Jolly good,' he muttered, holding open a cupboard door and peering into it. 'I've got Darjeeling, whatever the bloody hell that is.'

Moira turned to look at Lily, her lips pinched together. She raised her eyebrows.

'So how long is it since the two of you saw each other,' said Lily. She could hear the enforced jollity in her own voice, but Oliver wouldn't know the difference and her mother was too shaken to care. 'It must have been back in the eighties, is that right, Mum?'

Moira nodded.

'This is a lovely house, Oliver,' Lily persevered. 'When did you move here? I bet it's got a beautiful garden.'

He was throwing teabags into a giant brown teapot and boiling a filthy grey kettle that looked as if it might once have been silver.

'Something like that,' he said. 'Milk. Not got any fucking milk. Won't be long.'

He turned and marched out of the kitchen, his tread heavy as he went down the passageway; after the front door slammed behind him, the silence rang in their ears.

'Bloody hell,' said Moira. 'I can't quite believe this.'

She looked as if she was going to cry, and Lily put out her arm and hugged her, aware of the sharp ridges of her shoulder bones.

'I'm guessing,' she said. 'That he's changed a bit in the last forty-odd years?'

The two women looked at each other and Moira shook her

head in disbelief. 'He's got so fat! And I can't believe how rude he is. He hasn't even properly said hello to me, yet.'

There was a row of framed photographs on the dresser and Lily got up and went over to look at them. They were all faded, the glass covered in dust, and most had been taken many decades ago. The same young man featured in several of them, and she presumed that was Oliver in his prime. He was tall and skinny, with cheekbones that jutted from his face with artistic perfection; his blond hair went below his ears and looked bouffant enough to have been expensively blow-dried in a London salon. He wasn't Lily's type, but she could see he had been handsome – in an old-fashioned sort of way.

'Is this him?' she asked, passing one of the photos to Moira.

'Oh yes.' She peered at it closely. 'That's definitely him. That's the Oliver I remember. He was such a good-looking man.'

'He hasn't aged well,' said Lily.

'I was a little in love with him,' Moira said suddenly, still staring at the photo. 'He was such a wild boy, so free. Nothing like your dad – although that was a good thing, of course. Oliver wasn't the sort of man you would have married.'

'But you were already married to Dad, when you met him?' Lily asked.

'Yes, of course. I didn't mean that. Just that he was so dynamic and such fun to be with.'

'Did he have a wife?'

'No, although there were regular girlfriends, none of whom ever seemed good enough for him, in my opinion. They were all beautiful young things, but they didn't have many brain cells between them.'

Lily looked at her mother, still studying the photo. 'Mum, you sound jealous,' she teased.

'Don't be ridiculous,' Moira snapped. 'Anyway, your father

saw much more of him than I did, the men all drank in the pub together.' She put the photo frame onto the table in front of her. 'At least I don't have to worry about him thinking I'm a wizened old bat. That man has really let himself go.'

'He has,' said Lily. 'In spectacular fashion.'

By the time Oliver got back, Lily had scrubbed the kettle, stacked all the dirty plates and bowls at the far end of the worktop, near the sink, and had discovered some bin liners, into which she had thrown as many of the empty bottles as possible. She had also found another vase and put the wilting carnations back onto the hall table. Now she was unsuccessfully trying to sweep the floor with a broom whose bristles were full of fluff and dead insects, while Moira ran a cloth across the surfaces.

'Ah,' he said, standing in the doorway. 'Domesticity. Marvellous. Should have asked you over years ago.'

When the tea was made, they sat down at the table and sipped from their mugs.

'So, Oliver,' said Moira. 'How have you been?'

He shrugged and put his head on one side, as if pondering the answer to a much more complicated question. 'Pretty good,' he said, eventually. 'Can't complain.'

'Are you working?' asked Moira.

Another shrug, and this time he leant back in his chair and tilted his face towards the ceiling before answering. 'You could say that.'

'Oliver was an artist,' Moira told Lily. 'He did the most fantastic portraits. All black and white, charcoal, weren't they?'

He nodded.

'He could really capture someone's personality,' Moira continued.

'Did one of you, once,' said Oliver, staring at the ceiling.

Lily looked at her mother and saw shock register on her face. For a moment no one spoke.

'Really?' asked Moira at last. A flush was spreading up her neck and across her cheeks. She looked embarrassed, but gratified at the same time. 'A portrait of me?'

Oliver nodded again and took a noisy slurp of his tea.

'Have you still got it?' asked Lily. 'I'd love to see that.'

He put out his bottom lip and shook his head. 'Gave it to Ken, just before you moved away,' he said. 'Thought your old man might want to get it framed or something, give it to you as a present.'

Moira's brow was furrowed and Lily could see she was trying to work all of this out. 'But he never said anything? I didn't know he had it. I wonder why he didn't tell me?'

Oliver finally turned towards her and shrugged again. 'Don't ask me,' he said. 'He was a funny fish, your Ken. Bit protective.' He turned to Lily. 'Husbands didn't always like me,' he said. The comment could have sounded seedy – even arrogant – but it just struck Lily as sad.

'Food!' he announced suddenly, getting up so fast that the wooden chair tipped over behind him and crashed onto the floor. 'Let's have something to eat.'

It turned out there wasn't much in the house and, on his fifteen-minute round trip to the local shop, Oliver hadn't thought to buy anything other than milk. He stood helplessly in the middle of the kitchen, running his hands through his hair and looking confused, until Lily stepped in.

'I'll sort something out,' she said. 'Why don't you both go and take a look at the garden while it's still light and have a chat.' They made their way out through the back door, and Lily heard Oliver swear loudly as he carried a couple of faded deckchairs around from the side of the house and tried to set them up.

'They're no better than fucking hammocks!' he yelled, as there was a crash and the first chair collapsed.

'Bloody idiot,' said Moira. 'You're not doing it properly.'

Lily rummaged in sticky shelved cupboards and found unopened tins of tuna, sweetcorn and button mushrooms. There were eggs in the fridge and a lump of cheese that looked surprisingly fresh. It would have to do.

As she whisked the eggs, she stared out of the kitchen window at the elderly couple. It was getting dark, and certainly wasn't warm outside, but they were both lying back in the deckchairs, facing the house rather than looking at the garden. Moira was talking to Oliver, gesticulating with her hands, explaining something that was making him frown with confusion. Although, whatever it was didn't need to be particularly complicated. Lily noticed that, while her mother was still sipping from her mug of Darjeeling, Oliver had somehow smuggled a bottle of wine outside, and was working his way through it, splashing red liquid into his empty mug and knocking it back in deep gulps.

What the hell had gone on between these two? The passing of time hadn't been kind to either of them, but four decades ago they had obviously been an attractive couple. Although they *hadn't* been a couple – as Moira had been quick to point out.

There was nothing remotely attractive about Oliver now, but in his day he had been a catch – a good-looking rogue. Her own father, Ken, had been entirely different: shorter, dapper, unfailingly polite, a mild-mannered man and a lover of cricket, who drank in moderation. Had Ken known all there was to know about handsome Oliver? Not that it mattered now, her father had been dead for such a long time. But there was something about this man that made Lily uneasy. She brushed the thought aside. She was overthinking it all; he was just a blast from the past, and there was nothing wrong with that. It was what this entire trip should be about.

They ate omelettes at the kitchen table, and by early

evening Lily could see Moira was flagging. She had kept up a show for the last couple of hours, chatting brightly, telling Oliver stories about Brighton and their lives there, asking him questions that elicited increasingly slurred, senseless answers. But it had clearly been a huge effort.

'Come on,' Lily said. 'I think we're all in need of some sleep.'

Oliver insisted they went to bed and left him to clear up so, after fetching the suitcases from the van, Lily carried them upstairs and helped her mother settle into one of the spare bedrooms.

Later, curled up on a lumpy single mattress, from which she'd had to remove further piles of clothing and books before she could lie down, Lily listened to Moira singing softly to herself through the thin dividing wall. She was finally drifting off, dreamlike thoughts about castles and motorways chasing her towards sleep, when there was an almighty crash from downstairs.

'Fuck!' yelled Oliver. 'Stupid place to put a vase of flowers.'

CHAPTER TEN

BREAKFAST WAS INSUBSTANTIAL – there was only enough dry bread in Oliver's dusty bread bin for them to have one piece of toast each. Lily ate quickly, desperate to get away from this dirty, oppressive cottage. She had slept badly and was in a foul mood.

Moira, in contrast, was irritatingly chirpy. 'Oliver,' she said as she scraped margarine across her toast. 'Do you remember when we all went to the theatre, that time? There was me and Ken, and we went with the Johnsons – do you remember them?'

'Nope.' Oliver shook his head.

'You were with that Danish girl, the one with rather large bosoms. What was her name?'

Oliver squinted across the table at her. 'Bosoms?'

'Yes! She wore very low-cut blouses and had a gold pendant thing that hung down into her cleavage.'

Oliver was shaking his head. 'Can't say she rings any bells.'

'Karina?' Moira said. 'Or maybe Katrina?'

'How big were they?'

'Bloody huge!' said Moira. 'If she turned sideways, she could

hardly get through doorways. And that gold pendant was big too
– the size of a hard-boiled egg.'

'In that case, I would have thought I'd remember her,'
mused Oliver, sitting back in his chair and staring at the ceiling.
His breath was rank this morning and his teeth were purple.
Lily hoped he hadn't already been on the wine, but it was a
distinct possibility.

'Keira?' Moira asked. 'Karolina?'

'Kara!' Oliver yelled. 'Kara with the massive bosoms!'

'Yes.' Moira nodded, excitedly. 'That's the one.'

Lily pushed her chair away from the table; she couldn't take
much more of this. 'Right, we must get back on the road, Mum.
Is your case packed? I'll go and put it in the van.'

As she carried the suitcases downstairs, a few minutes later,
she heard chortling from the kitchen.

'After that,' Oliver was saying. 'She only went and put that
sodding gold pendant down his trousers!'

Moira screeched with laughter, as Lily went towards the
front door. 'I'll take these out,' she called. Ironic that the two of
them were finally getting on like a house on fire. It didn't sound
as if they shared the same memories of the time they'd spent
together, but it clearly didn't matter in the slightest. It must be
so strange to meet up with someone from your past who had
once been important to you, but who had changed so
dramatically. She wondered if this would be her and Gordy in
thirty years' time, then immediately dismissed the thought. For
one thing, she was going to make sure they didn't lose touch.
Even if she stopped working at Beautiful Blooms or Gordy and
Hilary ended up moving away, she was sure their friendship
was strong enough to endure. Anyway, times had changed and
modern technology made it so much easier to keep tabs on
people. If you didn't have the time for a proper phone
conversation, it only took a few seconds to send a text to check

up on a friend, whereas forty years ago, you had to make more of an effort if you wanted to stay in touch. When Moira and Ken left Chepstow and moved to Yorkshire, they would have written letters and sent postcards and used landlines to have proper conversations with the friends and neighbours they'd left behind. There were mobiles around in those days, but Lily knew her parents hadn't owned one. Moira had reluctantly allowed Lily to sign her up for a phone contract after her father died, but she'd never really got the hang of how to use it and for several years kept the old-fashioned Nokia handset shut away in a drawer in her desk, only turning it on when she wanted to make a call.

There was another shriek of laughter from the kitchen.

'We thought she was going to get arrested!' Oliver was saying.

'Oh, dear me!' Moira yelped. 'What a sight that must have been!'

Lily opened the front door and carried the cases down the path. Just because she was tired and grumpy this morning, it was unfair to drag Moira away too quickly; she ought to let the pair of them have some time together. So, once she'd loaded the cases into the campervan, she cleared out the empty food and drink wrappers from the day before. Then she wiped down the dashboard and swept bits of mud out of the footwells with her hand. At one point, her phone pinged and she groaned when she saw it was a text from Dave with the blubbery lips:

> Hi Lily, fancy a drink? It's been a while 😊

She deleted it, then immediately felt guilty. Her brief involvement with Dave had taught her he didn't take gentle hints and clearly wasn't aware he was being ghosted, so unless she said she didn't want to see him again, he would carry on texting.

When she finally went back into the cottage, the two elderly people were still sitting at the kitchen table, silent now, but grinning at each other.

'Thank you for having us, Oliver,' said Lily. 'It has been nice to meet you.'

'Yes.' Moira nodded. 'Good to catch up after so long, you fat old toad.'

They went down the passageway and Lily helped Moira into her coat, while Oliver jingled coins in his trouser pocket, humming something unintelligible.

'I'll come back another time,' said Moira, going up to him and rising onto her tiptoes to give him a kiss on the cheek. 'Take care of that big belly of yours.' She put both her hands on his enormous stomach and tapped out a rhythm on it, as if she was playing a set of snare drums.

'Mum!' Lily was shocked, but Oliver didn't seem bothered.

'Marvellous,' he said, beaming down at her. 'Take care of yourself, you old witch.'

He stood by the side of the road, waving, as Lily started the van and pulled away.

'Well, that was fun,' said Moira, waving back through the rear window until Oliver was just a speck at the end of the road. 'What a jolly time we had. Right, onwards Lily, next stop the Lake District.'

They headed through the outskirts of Wolverhampton, following signs towards the M5. Back in the uncomfortable driving seat again, Lily realised she was still tired from the hours she'd spent sat in it yesterday. Her arms ached as they found themselves back in the familiar positions on the steering wheel.

Beside her, Moira had her notebook on her lap and was

staring through the windscreen, tapping absently on the front cover with her pencil.

'You'll have a lot to write about now,' said Lily. 'I'm so pleased you enjoyed seeing him.'

'Me too,' Moira said. 'He definitely needs to go into my book. Not just what we did at his house now, but the things he did all those years ago. The way he was.'

'What sort of things?'

'He was very important, Lily,' she said. 'That man played a big part in my life.'

'I can tell that. It all felt a bit awkward yesterday, when we arrived, but once you both relaxed and started to feel comfortable with each other again, it was obvious you'd been close.'

'Very close indeed,' Moira said.

Lily glanced sideways; her mother was nodding and looking thoughtful. 'I'm so happy the two of you have met, Lily. It means a great deal to me, to have introduced you to Oliver.'

'Good,' Lily said. 'I'm glad too.'

Moira opened the notebook and flicked through the first few pages. 'Right, I now need some peace and quiet while I get all of this written down. I can't decide whether to include the bit about that Danish girl, but I suppose I can always cross it out again.'

'Yes, better to have too much there than too little,' said Lily.

'True.' Moira nodded. 'That's what the men always used to say about her bosoms.'

CHAPTER ELEVEN

'WELCOME, LADIES, TO OUR HUMBLE *RESIDENCE*.'
The man held out one hand, indicating the large Victorian
house behind him. 'Please would you be so good as to reposition
your vehicle within one of the parking bays, as marked?'

Lily stared down at the tarmac. Now it had been pointed
out, she could see that the area in front of the guest house had
been divided into uneven rectangles by a series of wobbly white
lines. They looked as if they'd been painted in a hurry by
someone with a pastry brush and a tin of white emulsion.

'Er, are these the bays?'

'Why, naturally!' The man's clipped Edinburgh brogue
boomed across the car park. 'I see no other bays?'

'Of course,' she said. 'So sorry.'

As she restarted the engine and tried to manoeuvre into a
space – which was too narrow for anything except a Smart car –
the man took Moira's elbow, while a skinny woman beside him
grabbed her other arm. Lily watched as the pair propelled her
mother towards the front door. She followed a minute later,
feeling like the hired help as she heaved their cases up the steps.
There was a shabby sign above the portico: *Glenmorrow Guest*

House. When her mother had given her the address, as they left Wolverhampton, Lily had wondered why a small hotel in the Lake District would have a Scottish name. Now they had met the owners, it made perfect sense.

'And this is our dining room!' The man's voice was booming out from the right. 'It is where you'll experience our world-famous breakfast. Joan here does the continental stuff, but full English is my department. If you want anything hot in the morning, I'm your man.'

Lily caught Moira's eye as her mother was hurried back out into the hallway; she was trying hard not to laugh.

'Aha, there you are at last!' said the man, as if Lily had deliberately been kicking her heels in the car park. 'You are missing the tour. I am Archie Campbell and this is my wife, Joan. We're now moving on, to the residents' lounge. Keep up.'

Lily dumped the cases in the middle of the hall and followed them into a room on the other side.

'Sofas,' Archie Campbell said, waving his free hand across the room.

'Bookshelves!' added his skinny wife, Joan, from the sideline.

'A television!' Archie threw his arm dramatically in the direction of the small set in the corner, as if he had just invented the thing himself.

'Heavens!' Moira said, trying to extract her arm from Archie's grip. 'You've got all mod cons, haven't you?'

'When did you say you were last in Keswick?' asked Joan.

'Years ago,' Moira replied. 'My parents brought me here on holiday one summer – it must have been in the early fifties. We stayed for two weeks and I remember going out on the lake.'

'And you stayed here, at our little guest house?' Archie beamed. 'How marvellous. Of course, it would have been a little different then. My grandparents ran the Glenmorrow in those days – they opened just after the war and then Joan and I took over in the nineties – but I know they would also have given the sort of all-round personal service provided by my good lady wife and myself.'

Moira finally managed to pull her arm out of his grasp and she frantically brushed the sleeve of her coat as if getting rid of specks of dirt he might have left on there. 'I can't remember what the people were like,' she said. 'But the place seems exactly the same to me. It doesn't look as if it's had a coat of paint since then.'

Archie Campbell's eyebrows shot so far up his forehead that they almost disappeared into his thatch of thick grey hair.

'Right, Mum!' Lily said, quickly. 'Let's get you upstairs to your room, so you can have a rest. Shall I grab those cases, Mr Campbell?'

Moira's room was spacious and the double bay window had a view down the hill, with glimpses of Derwentwater sparkling in the distance. 'This is nice,' she said, collapsing onto the bed and starting to cough.

'Have a lie down while I unpack for you,' said Lily. She had just poked her head into her own room but wasn't inclined to stay for long; it was half the size of this and at the back of the building, with a view over the industrial wheelie bins and the flat roof of the kitchen.

She opened Moira's case and began to take out some of her clothes. 'You didn't pack this very well,' she muttered, as she pulled out crumpled blouses, skirts and underwear.

'Oh, leave it all in there, I can do it another time,' said Moira, coughing again.

'You don't sound well?'

'A bit of a tickle, that's all. A sore throat as well. But I'm probably just tired.'

'I think you could do with an early night,' Lily said, taking

Moira's toiletry bag into the en suite and putting the toothbrush and toothpaste into the plastic beaker by the basin. Her mother had a point, this place didn't look as if it had undergone any sort of makeover for decades. The walls above the avocado bathroom suite were covered in tiles which had presumably once been white, but now looked slightly grey, and the shower curtain hanging from a rusty rail was covered in spots of mildew.

'I'm sure we can find somewhere nicer to stay?' she said, coming back out of the bathroom. 'It's a bit basic.'

As they'd driven down the hill into Keswick, they had passed several other hotels, most of them in a better state of repair than this. Lily had never been to the Lake District before, but had been looking forward to this leg of their trip. She wasn't a snob and didn't have particularly high expectations about their accommodation, but surely they could find somewhere slightly better? It was October, the area wouldn't exactly be overrun by tourists.

'Do you want me to see if I can book us into somewhere else tomorrow?' Lily said. 'I'm happy to contribute to the cost, I don't want you to feel you have to pay all the bills.'

'No, it's being here that matters,' said Moira. 'When we stayed in this guest house it was the first family holiday I can remember going on, and I need to write about it. It's not very grand, but being here will help my creative juices.'

Lily snorted with laughter. 'Get you!' she said. 'Creative juices indeed.'

There was a rap on the door, which opened before either of them had a chance to say anything. Archie Campbell's ruddy face appeared around the edge, followed by one outstretched arm.

'Joan has forgotten your bath sheets!' He tutted, placing a pile of worn brown towels on the chest of drawers. 'I sometimes think that wee woman would forget her own head if it wasn't right there on top of her shoulders when she woke up every morning.'

'These people are priceless,' said Moira, when he'd slammed the door shut and they'd listened to his heavy tread descending the stairs. 'The bed is comfortable though.' She began to cough again, her shoulders heaving with the effort. 'Leave me be!' she spluttered, waving Lily away with one hand. 'I'm fine. I just need to rest. Why don't you go out and have a wander round? Get yourself a glass of wine and some supper. You've done a lot of driving today, you must be tired too. Anyway, you deserve some time away from me. Ask them to bring me up a sandwich in a bit, and I'll see you in the morning.'

Joan was behind the reception desk as Lily went out, but when she asked for a sandwich to be sent up to her mother's room, the skinny woman looked aghast, as if she'd requested that a five-course banquet be delivered to the first-floor bedroom by a handsome Eastern European waiter dressed in nothing but a mankini.

Collecting herself, Joan sighed heavily then picked up Post-it notes and a pen. 'Ham or cheese?' she asked. 'Oh no, wait a moment. I don't think we have any ham.'

'I guess it will be cheese then,' Lily had said, smiling. 'I suppose it would be asking too much for you to stretch to some pickle?' She'd meant it as a joke, but Joan didn't smile back.

CHAPTER TWELVE

HER PHONE PINGED when she got down to the lake. She stopped and clicked on the message.

> Where are you? Why haven't you answered my text?

Lily had long ago stopped feeling offended that Eleanor never signed off with x, let alone xx. She wondered if, away from public view, her daughter was more loving with her boyfriend, Paul. They'd been together for three years and Lily had no doubt who had the upper hand in the relationship. They'd just bought their first flat together in Hove and it sounded as if Eleanor had chosen everything from the location and the number of bedrooms, through to the art they'd hang on the walls. Paul was a nice lad though and he clearly adored Eleanor, so it seemed as if being bossed around was a price he was willing to pay. Anyway, when it came to standing up to her daughter, Lily was in no position to criticise.

> We're in Keswick. Arrived this afternoon having stayed last night in Wolverhampton xx

She didn't mention Oliver, that would really set the cat among the pigeons. As she carried on walking down the hill, her phone pinged again almost immediately.

> Why?? That's miles away??

Lily could hear the exasperation in her daughter's words as clearly as if she was standing beside her saying them.

> It's lovely here.

> We're near Derwentwater and the sun is shining xx

The blue text icon started flashing: *Eleanor is typing* her phone helpfully informed her. Lily stood watching it; this message was a longer one. Why didn't she have the strength to carry on walking and ignore her daughter?

> Has Granny done any weird stuff? I just spoke to Dad about all this and he thinks you're crazy and you're being irresponsible. He agrees with me that you should come home.

'Oh, does he indeed!' Lily said out loud, glaring down at the screen. 'Well, he can just sod off!'

A woman walking past, stared at her, but Lily was too angry to care. This was typical of Eleanor, talking to Nick about what was going on; and it was typical of Nick to wade in with an opinion. Of course he was going to agree with his daughter that Lily wasn't being sensible; in the twenty-eight years they'd known each other, he had rarely given her credit for anything. But this was none of his bloody business! Come to that, it wasn't any of Eleanor's business either.

She swiped to delete the message notification and turned off the phone, shoving it into her pocket and marching on around the lake, blood pumping through her temples. She should be used to her ex-husband and daughter ganging up on her – she *was* used to it. But it still hurt. She couldn't remember a time when the two of them hadn't seemed pitted against her in every sense of the word and, while the father/daughter alliance had been hard enough to bear while she and Nick were still married, it was even more galling now. He hadn't been part of her life for years, so he had no right to offer an opinion on how she lived it.

The trouble was, Eleanor didn't see it that way. She had been the ultimate daddy's girl when she was growing up – from the moment she'd started talking and taking her first steps, Eleanor was Nick's little princess. Lily adored her daughter, but she could also see the need for creating boundaries and setting rules. Nick, on the other hand, behaved like some throwback hippie parent from the sixties, insisting rules were wrong for children and too much dull routine would rot Eleanor's young brain. Lily found it infuriating, and was convinced he only said those things to wind her up. Which it did. But their clashing parenting styles quickly drove a wedge more deeply into what was already a rift in their relationship. By the time Eleanor was toddling around on her little chubby legs, poking sticky fingers into electric sockets and upending bowls of cereal on top of her own head, her parents were at loggerheads most of the time.

Nick told Lily she was too hard, too controlling; he indulged while Lily tried to discipline, he praised everything Eleanor did, while whatever Lily said was taken as criticism. Petulant, spoilt behaviour from their daughter was always Lily's fault, because Nick insisted she was handling the situation badly. She hated being cast as the bad cop, but it invariably ended up that way. She'd always wanted more than one child and, as Eleanor got older, that desire intensified. She didn't care whether it was a boy or a girl, she just longed for another baby who would even things up a little. Their next child would be calmer than Eleanor, more rational, less needy. She was determined that, second time around, she would do a better job and make sure she and Nick treated this next baby differently, not over-indulging to the point where their lives were ruled by their child, instead of vice versa.

But she never got pregnant again. Many years later, she looked back on that period in their lives and wondered if it was the stress and unhappiness which had been messing her up physically, as well as mentally. But realistically, she didn't get pregnant because she and Nick were rarely sleeping together. To all intents and purposes, the marriage was over long before Eleanor was old enough to start school, and Nick's affairs were numerous and invariably blatant by that time – even though Lily tried not to let herself acknowledge them.

The late afternoon sun on the water was beautiful and, despite her anger, she was cheered by the sight of it. Some sailing boats were moored at the edge of the lake, and gulls shrieked as they swooped down to gather up crumbs left by picnickers along the shore. She lifted her face as she walked, catching the last rays of sunshine and enjoying how the warmth stroked her skin and made it tingle.

Although Eleanor still consulted her father about everything, and shared her disapproval of most of what her mother did or said, Lily knew Nick didn't care. He had moved on and whatever had gone wrong in their marriage, or with their joint parenting, was ancient history. But, of course, he still felt entitled to give his opinion and make sure Lily knew about it.

She often wished she could be as relaxed about it all, but her exclusion from their family unit and her ongoing unhappiness had underpinned everything the three of them did together. It was only when she looked back on Eleanor's childhood, years later, that she was able to understand the damage it had done to her own relationship with her daughter. After Nick left, she and Eleanor – then in her early years at secondary school – struggled to get along, but by that time the pattern of their dysfunctional relationship was already too established and raging teenage hormones and resentment on all sides did nothing to make life any easier. Lily loved Eleanor and longed to find a way to improve the frostiness between them, but her daughter's lack of respect for her, coupled with her adoration of the father who'd walked out on them, made her feel she'd failed as a mother.

The sun was now setting on the other side of the lake, throwing beams of orange and burnt umber across the darkening water. The wind had dropped but it was chilly and Lily pulled her coat more tightly around her. Up ahead was a hotel called The Hamilton, with beautifully tended window boxes and a pretty little garden to one side. It looked smart but by no means exclusive. She stood and stared through the windows, which were lit by the soft glow of table lamps, and before she knew it, she was walking up to the front door. She would have one quick drink, as a reward for her long day of driving and all the accompanying angst of dealing with Moira's unpredictable behaviour.

When she pushed open the door she was hit by a gust of warm air and a subtle combination of wood smoke and furniture polish. The place was quiet, with just a few tables in the bar occupied.

'Gin and tonic, please,' she said to the barman.

'Double?' He smiled back.

'Why not.'

She had brought her bag with her, but her book was in the suitcase, still sitting unpacked on the bed in the rear bedroom at the guest house. Not wanting to sit and drink with nothing to do, she grabbed a newspaper from a pile at the end of the bar, and took it to a free table. A group of women were further along on one side, their heads bent forward in animated discussion over glasses of wine. A man was sitting alone at a table on the other side. He glanced up as Lily sat down and she smiled at him, mellowed by the clink of the ice in her glass and the prospect of a quiet hour to herself. She tended to catch up with the news through her phone and the television, and rarely read a newspaper. It made a nice change to flick slowly through the pages, reading about other people's lives and crises that were far removed from her own worries about Moira and Eleanor. There were graphic photographs of a riot in a South American capital city and looking at them made her feel small, reminding her how minor her domestic dramas were, when compared to the hell going on in other people's lives.

After half an hour, she reached for her glass and realised it was empty. Damn it, she was going to have another gin. It didn't seem entirely responsible, sitting here while Moira was on her own back at the guest house; she felt like a schoolgirl who'd bunked off double chemistry. But her mother had suggested she go out and have a couple of hours to herself. Anyway, Moira was probably already asleep, and there was definitely no point Lily hanging around at the Glenmorrow on her own. The only place to go was the residents' lounge and, if she popped in there to test out the sofas and tiny television, she risked getting dragged into the dining room by Archie and Joan to sample some of their spectacularly mediocre home cooking.

The thought of food made her realise her stomach was rumbling.

'Can I eat here?' she asked the barman, as she paid for her gin.

'Of course, go on through to the dining room,' he said,

pointing towards an archway. 'Monday evenings are always quiet, no need to book.'

As a waitress showed her to a small table in the corner, Lily realised the man who'd been drinking in the bar had moved in here as well. He was at the next table, tucking into a plate piled high with meat, potatoes and vegetables and he grinned as he looked up and caught her eye.

'I can recommend the pork casserole,' he said. 'This place has the best menu in Keswick.'

'Thanks, I might go for that,' she said.

She had worked her way through the newspaper, so folded it over and studied the crossword while she waited. The clues were ridiculously complicated – or maybe she was just tired – but by the time her food arrived, she'd only managed two answers.

'Would you like some wine with your meal?' asked the waitress, as she set down the plate.

'A glass of Pinot Grigio would be lovely,' said Lily.

She began to eat, thinking again about Eleanor's text. There was no point dwelling on it, but she couldn't get the hurtful words out of her mind. If Moira had been here, she would have told her about it, needing to share the hurt and seek reassurance that she wasn't being oversensitive. Over the years her mother had always been Lily's champion, constantly offering support and bolstering her against Nick's criticism and disparagement. After he dropped his bombshell, packed his bags and left Lily for the first of several younger models, Moira had hardly been able to contain her rage. 'He was never good enough for you,' she said. 'I could murder him for treating you so badly.' But, of course, they both had to swallow their anger, because while Nick was moving into a pretty little mews house with a woman half his age, Lily and Moira were left to pick up the pieces and their main priority had to be the disturbed, wounded – yet still ferocious – twelve-year-old child whose father had left her. So, they put their own feelings to one side and tried to adjust to the new normal, which – with hindsight – ensured that Eleanor's self-centred, egotistical view of the world, was never challenged.

'Excuse me?'

Lily jumped at the voice right next to her.

'This is really cheeky and I promise I don't normally do this sort of thing. But I saw you sitting here on your own, digesting your pork casserole, and I'm sitting over there on my own, doing the same. I wondered if you'd mind if I joined you, while we finish our drinks, and we can do some digesting together?'

Lily stared up at the man who'd been at the next table. She was so taken aback, she couldn't think of anything to say.

'God, that was naff, sorry.' He looked so appalled at himself, that she started to laugh.

'It was fine until you got to the bit about digesting.'

'I know.' He shook his head. 'Mutual digesting. Jesus, I'm so embarrassed.'

'Sit down. Please.' Lily pointed to the free chair on the other side of the table.

He pulled it out and sat, setting down his glass of red wine in front of him. 'I'm Jake,' he said, reaching out his hand.

'Lily.' She smiled, taking it. 'Nice to meet you.'

'Apologies. I honestly don't think I've ever come out with something that cheesy in my life.'

She laughed again. 'I'm flattered you thought I was worth the effort. How long did it take you to come up with all that digesting stuff?'

'Hours,' he said. 'I've been planning it since I saw you walk into the bar.'

He had the most amazing brown eyes. Lily found herself staring at them for slightly too long, and lowered her own eyes to the table again, feeling a flush spread across her cheeks.

'Are you staying here?' he asked.

She shook her head. 'I wish! I'm staying at a guest house, further up the hill. I was out walking and saw this place and thought I deserved a drink. Then it somehow turned into dinner.'

'The pork was good though, wasn't it?'

'It was very good, thanks for the recommendation.'

As he grinned back at her, she noticed the laughter lines spreading out from the edges of his eyes, his skin still lightly tanned from the summer. He had dark hair, with a few flecks of grey, but it was hard to tell how old he was – possibly mid to late-forties, like her?

'So, what are you doing in Keswick, Lily?' he was asking. 'Here for work? On holiday?'

'Just passing through,' she said, as she lifted her glass to her lips and stared at him over the top of it. 'I've never been here before, it's beautiful.'

For some reason, she was strangely reluctant to tell this handsome stranger about the road trip or the fact that she had an elderly mother tucked up in bed, half a mile away. It was exciting to be having a conversation with a man who knew nothing about her, but who had liked the look of her enough to risk being knocked back when he asked to sit at her table in a restaurant. Nothing like this had ever happened to her before.

'You're lucky with the weather,' he was saying. 'It's not always so sunny at this time of year.'

'It was beautiful, looking out over the lake this evening,' she said, twisting the stem of her wine glass between her thumb and forefinger. She was rubbish at small talk, and he clearly wasn't much better. Her heart was beating slightly faster than usual and she felt light-headed – mostly because of the alcohol, but also because of the way this good-looking man was leaning towards her across the table, his brown eyes seeming to bore right into her soul.

'Fancy another one?' he asked, glancing down at her empty glass.

She smiled across at him. 'Why not?'

CHAPTER THIRTEEN

FOR A FEW MOMENTS she had no idea where she was. Sunlight was seeping through a gap in the curtains and panning across the pale carpet. A dark shape next to the wall looked like a dog about to pounce but, as her eyes adjusted to the light, she saw it was just her coat, thrown carelessly over a chair. In the distance there was the sound of a door slamming and footsteps coming close before receding again. A couple of seconds later she heard a low mechanical clunking and subconsciously recognised it as the sound of a lift making its way to meet a pressed call button.

For some reason, the room was spinning. Lily closed her eyes, then opened them again, but it didn't help. Lying on her side she stretched her legs out behind her and her foot hit something. As she started to roll over, she suddenly realised it was someone else's foot. By the time she had turned fully the other way, Jake's face was just inches from her own. His eyes, those lovely rich brown eyes, were looking at her.

'Good morning,' he said. His voice was slightly husky.

'Oh God!'

'Nice to see you too.'

'Oh God. No, I mean... Shit!' Lily flung back the covers, then – realising she was naked – dragged them back over herself, rolling onto her side, reaching down to the floor and feeling around frantically with her fingers, soon coming across the clothes that lay strewn where she must have left them the previous night. Her head was pounding so hard it was as if someone was tapping on the front of her skull with a frying pan.

She found her shirt and pushed her arms through the sleeves, hearing one of the buttons pop off and fly across the carpet. There was no sign of her knickers, but her jeans were right beside the bed, so she grabbed them and wriggled into them, only then finally leaving the safety of the covers and standing up. Her entire body lurched with the effort and a wave of nausea flooded over her. She caught sight of herself in the mirror above the dressing table and dragged her hand through her wild hair to try and flatten it.

She finally turned round to look at Jake. He was on his side, his arm across the space beside him in the bed where she'd been lying.

'Are you okay?' he asked, squinting up at her.

'No. I think I might die,' she whispered. 'How much did we have to drink last night?'

'No idea,' he muttered. 'More than we should have done.' He closed his eyes and a smile spread across his face. 'It was worth it though. Come back here.'

She groaned and looked down as the room span. One trainer was on the floor in front of her and she slowly knelt down and ran her hand under the bed, where she came across the other one, as well as her knickers. She scrunched them into a ball in her fist and sat back against the edge of the bed, breathing deeply to steady herself as she pushed her feet into the shoes.

'What's the time?' she asked. She usually kept her phone nearby at night but there was nothing on the bedside table, where the hell was it? As she looked around, she remembered switching it off and putting it in her coat pocket yesterday evening as she walked by the lake.

Jake's weight shifted in the bed as he turned to look at his watch. 'It's 9 o'clock,' he said. 'Christ, I need to get up, I'm late for work!'

Lily suddenly went cold. Nine o'clock? It couldn't be. She'd been out all night, leaving her mother on her own at Glenmorrow. How could she have done that? What had she been thinking? She had somehow come to this hotel room with a man she hardly knew – although she couldn't actually remember coming here – and done goodness knows what with him, while her elderly mother had been left alone in a strange guest house. Worst of all, she hadn't been feeling well – she'd had that cough. This was awful, truly awful.

Lily pushed herself up from the floor, but had to put out both hands to steady herself as she stood. This was not good. She was so hungover and her brain so foggy, she could only remember snippets about last night. They'd stayed in the dining room for some time, she knew that, and they'd ordered another bottle of wine. She remembered shrieking with laughter at something Jake was saying. After the bottle of white wine, hadn't they moved onto red? Then there was the lift. They'd fallen through the opening doors and he'd pushed her up against the wall and started kissing her. She remembered his hand resting on her stomach, then pushing downwards, moving the material of her jeans away from her skin.

'Bloody hell,' she groaned. 'This is terrible.'

Glancing sideways into the mirror again, she saw her hair wasn't the only overnight casualty. Her mascara had smudged below her eyelashes and there was a red mark on her neck that looked like a bruise. She must have bumped into something the previous evening? Then, when she leant closer to the mirror, she realised what it was.

'Shit!' At the age of forty-seven, she had a bright red love bite on her neck.

'I've got to go.' Rubbing at the black marks under her eyes, she walked across to the chair and picked up her coat, fumbling to pull the phone from the pocket and swearing under her breath as her trembling finger stabbed at the button to turn it on. What if Moira had tried to phone her? What if she'd felt really ill in the night and hadn't been able to call for help?

'Can I see you later?' Jake was now sitting up on the other side of the bed and, even hungover and highly anxious, Lily's heart did a little flip at the sight of his bare back, the muscles rippling across his shoulders and down the top of his arms.

'This is appalling,' she said, struggling into her coat. 'I can't believe what we've done.'

'It wasn't that bad!' he said, turning towards her with a smile on his face. 'I've not...'

'You don't understand!' she said. 'This should never have happened, I shouldn't be here.'

He looked confused, then hurt.

'I've got to go,' she said.

She turned and went towards the door, pulling it open with one hand, the other still clutching the mobile out in front of her, willing the screen to flicker into life. As she stepped out into the corridor, the wall lights blinked on. She had no idea where the lift was, but headed for a pair of doors at the far end of the corridor. The room door slammed shut behind her, sending reverberations thundering through her aching head. Through the double doors was a stairwell and she began to go down, clutching on to the black handrail for support. As she got to the bottom and came out into the hotel reception, the screen on her phone finally lit up and she stopped and scrolled through the notifications, her heart thumping so hard against the wall of her chest that she was sure anyone standing nearby would be able to hear it.

There were several texts from Eleanor, of course. She flicked past them. Then something from Gordon, which she deleted accidentally. Didn't matter, she could call him back later. But to her relief, there was nothing from Moira. Thank God. Her mother rarely used her mobile phone, but she had Lily's number on speed dial and she knew how to use it in an emergency. There weren't any missed calls from a local landline either, so Archie Campbell hadn't been trying to contact her – this must mean all was well. It was even possible Moira was still asleep? She'd been fighting off a cold last night and they'd had a busy couple of days, so her body would have needed the extra rest.

Coming out of the hotel entrance and walking back beside the lake, Lily felt some of the tension ebb away. It was all going to be fine; she would be back at the Campbells in less than ten minutes, and no one would have missed her. Moira would never need to know she'd spent the night elsewhere.

But, bloody hell, what a night it had been. That man! She hugged her arms around herself as she walked, unable to get Jake's face out of her mind. Or the rest of his body, come to that. This was all so crazy. She'd never had a one-night stand in her entire life – let alone fallen into bed with someone like him. Dave's face briefly popped into her head. Dave with his scratchy beard and wet lips and total lack of respect for personal space. A fortnight ago she'd been unable to refuse Dave's desperate plea for a second date, and just yesterday morning she hadn't been able to pluck up the courage to dump him properly. Now, she was walking away from a hotel room in Keswick where she'd just spent an extremely enjoyable night – what she could remember of it – in the company of a complete stranger. What had she been thinking? This was so *not* like her.

Turning away from the lake, Lily walked up the hill as fast as her wobbly legs would carry her. She was still feeling sick and took deep breaths to try and quell the waves of nausea curdling up in her stomach. It had been years since she'd had so much to drink – she couldn't remember the last time she'd felt this hungover. What an idiot. She tried to put her phone back in her coat pocket but there was something in the way. She plunged in her hand and pulled out her knickers, realising she must have shoved them in there a few minutes earlier. Her face flared again as she remembered Jake's hands on her body, his lips meeting hers, the feel of his naked chest pushing against her as she fell backwards onto his hotel bed. She stared down at the scrunched material in her hand, smiling despite herself.

Lily Bennett, she thought to herself. *You total hussy.*

CHAPTER FOURTEEN

THERE WAS a young lad behind the reception desk at the guest house. Lily had never seen him before, but he looked too much like his father to be anyone other than Archie Campbell Junior.

'Can I help you?' he called as Lily rushed in.

'No, I'm fine thanks!' she said, short of breath after the walk up the hill. 'I'm a guest, I'm staying here.'

She took the stairs two at a time, relieved to have made it back so quickly. It was still only 9.15am and there was a swell of conversation coming from the dining room. The smell of bacon wafting upwards after her, did nothing to quell the nausea that was still rolling around in her stomach. She stopped to get her breath back at the top of the stairs and ran her hands through her hair again. Moira would be the first to notice the state she was in, although she obviously wouldn't guess why. Lily decided she would say she'd been out for an early walk and had rushed back after getting lost or forgetting the time.

'Mum?' She rapped on the bedroom door, before pushing it open. The room was in darkness and smelt slightly stale. 'Good morning!' She walked across to the window and dragged the heavy curtains back on either side. 'It's beautiful out there today. Did you sleep well? How are you feeling...?'

She turned around to see the bed was empty, the duvet rumpled and pushed back.

'Mum?' Lily went over to the en suite, but the door was open, the room in darkness. Maybe Moira had already gone down to have breakfast? Her dark-red coat was still hanging on the back of the door, where Lily had put it yesterday afternoon, and the mobile phone that she hardly ever used was sitting on top of the chest of drawers. She obviously hadn't gone far, so she must be downstairs in the dining room?

Lily went back out and down the stairs, holding on to the banister. The walk had helped clear her head and the world wasn't spinning quite so badly, but she still wasn't feeling at all well. She didn't think she would ever be able to face alcohol again – just the thought of a glass of wine made bile rise in her throat.

Young Campbell watched her as she came down the stairs and Lily smiled at him as she went into the dining room, brushing her hands through her hair again. She must look a real sight. She scanned the room, but there were only a handful of tables occupied and Moira definitely wasn't there.

'Excuse me,' she said to one of the waitresses. 'Have you seen my mother this morning? I'm not sure what she'd be wearing. Her name's Mrs Spencer and she's in room 6?'

The waitress looked at her blankly. 'Don't think so.'

Panic was rising up in Lily's throat. Where else could she be? She crossed the hallway and put her head around the door to the residents' lounge, which was empty.

'Is she quite short, with white hair?' asked a voice behind her. It was Young Campbell.

'Yes!' Lily spun round, relief pulsing through her. 'That sounds like her. Thank God! Have you seen her? Where is she?'

'Oh, I have no idea,' the boy said. 'She went out for a walk a while ago.'

'A walk?'

'Yes, you know – that thing you do with your legs?'

Lily glared at him; like father, like son. 'How long ago? Where did she go?'

He shrugged. 'Not sure, maybe an hour ago? I was answering the phone. I just saw her walk through.'

'How could you have let her go out on her own?'

The boy stared at her in surprise, then his expression changed as he took in her messy hair and the traces of make-up still clinging to her cheeks. Lily glared back, aware it must be obvious she'd spent the night elsewhere. The other thing that this young man didn't need to say, but which was obvious to both of them, was that her elderly mother was *her* responsibility, and it wasn't up to him to keep an eye on the guests. She turned and ran out of the front door and down through the badly marked-out parking area. She had just come from the direction of the lake, so Moira couldn't have been walking that way. She stood on the pavement, staring at the houses further up the road, but there was no one in sight. Where the hell would she have gone? Lily felt really sick now. This was serious; she'd messed up badly. She began to run up the road, before stopping and turning back again. This was crazy – she didn't know where to start. Maybe she should get in the van and drive around? Moira couldn't have got very far. Although, of course, that depended on how long she'd been gone, and if the lad was right, and she'd left the guest house an hour ago, she could be a couple of miles away by now. But she could still cover more ground in the van.

Her phone began to ring and she reached into her pocket, hoping it might be an unknown mobile number; someone who had met a confused little old lady who shouldn't be out walking on her own in a strange town. Although, as she pulled the phone out, she realised that wasn't likely. Moira didn't have her own phone with her, and even if she wasn't confused and hundreds of miles from home, Moira would have struggled to remember Lily's mobile number off the top of her head. If she wasn't feeling well and was panicking at finding herself lost in a strange town, there was no way she'd be able give anyone the information they needed to call for help.

It was Gordon; she couldn't speak to him now. She rejected the call and ran back towards the front door of the guest house. Thinking about it, she ought not to get behind the wheel of the van – she'd had so much to drink last night, she was probably still over the limit.

'We need to get the police!' she said to Young Campbell, who had now come out from behind the reception desk. 'My mother has got early-onset dementia and she shouldn't be out on her own, she gets confused and she'll have no idea how to get back to this place again. We have to find her. Please help me!'

As she pressed 999 and waited for the call to connect, Lily closed her eyes. Her head was thumping and her mouth was so dry, it hurt to breathe. She listened to the phone ringing at the other end, willing someone to pick up quickly. Nausea was flooding over her in waves again and she could hardly think straight, but it was the guilt that felt overwhelming. What kind of a selfish daughter was she? How the hell could she have let this happen?

CHAPTER FIFTEEN

'SO, you don't know what she was wearing?'

'No! I told you, her coat is still in her room, but I think she may be in a blue skirt because she wore that yesterday. But I'm not sure which cardigan she's got on.'

'And you don't know of anywhere she might have gone?'

'No. She hasn't been to Keswick for years.'

'Nor do you have any idea precisely what time she left?'

Lily shook her head, miserably. She really ought to know the answers to these questions. She should have been here this morning to see her mother and notice what clothes she was wearing. But of course, if she had been here this morning, she would have guided Moira into the dining room for breakfast and there would be no need to work out where she was heading or what time she'd left the building. Because she would still be in it.

'We're just wasting time!' she said. 'We need to be out looking for her. She's in the early stages of dementia and she doesn't always think clearly. If you don't know her, you'd think she was fine, but she does get confused and I'm sure she won't be able to remember how to get back to Glenmorrow. Can't you send out a search party or something?'

'This isn't television,' snorted the police constable, who looked barely old enough to have done his GCSEs. 'We don't have search parties just hanging around at the station, waiting to go looking for missing people.'

'Well, can't you send out a message or something?' Lily said. 'You must have ways of letting everyone know she's missing! I can give you a photograph.'

'That would be helpful,' said the policeman. 'And, if you would let me do my job, I *am* just about to issue an alert to be sent out to all our units in the area. But I can't do that without some basic information from you first.'

Joan Campbell came into the residents' lounge holding a mug of tea. 'Have this and sit yourself down,' she said to Lily. 'Toby has gone out to have a scout around for your mother. Don't fret, she can't have gone far.'

'Who's Toby?'

'Our boy! Archie would have gone, but to be honest his knees aren't up to it.'

Lily wrapped her hands around the mug and sipped at it gratefully. Joan had added sugar, clearly thinking she needed it for the shock, and there was so much milk the liquid was nearly white. Usually, Lily would have found it undrinkable, but right now it was just what her empty stomach and hungover body needed.

'Have you tried calling her mobile?' asked the police constable, writing notes.

'It's upstairs in her room, she didn't take it with her,' Lily said.

'Hmm, interesting. Does that strike you as suspicious? Do you think she intended to leave it behind so that she couldn't be found?'

'No, don't be ridiculous!'

'There's no need to be rude, ma'am.'

'Sorry, I just mean, she hardly uses it. She's seventy-nine years old and doesn't know how to work it properly. She never remembers to take it with her when she goes out, unless I remind her. She probably didn't even think to charge it last night.'

The young man looked bemused. The concept of not being able to use a mobile was clearly alien to him, as was the idea of letting the battery run down overnight. 'That's extremely interesting,' he said. 'My gran is seventy-seven and she's on Facebook. We even taught her how to tweet last year – she's got 300 followers. Does your mother not do any social media?'

'No! But why's it such a big deal? Even I don't do much social media.'

He shook his head and tutted as he wrote something in his notebook. Obviously, Lily and her strange mother were beyond the pale.

'So, to be clear. You don't think Mrs Spencer left the premises with the intention of not being found?'

Lily glared at him. 'Are you going to report this?' she snapped. 'All these questions are bloody ridiculous. I'd stand more chance of finding her if I was out there looking for her myself, rather than sitting here wasting precious time talking to you.'

'There's no need to be offensive. We are all doing the best we can. In a situation like this, we need to make sure the person who is being reported as missing, hasn't just gone somewhere and forgotten to mention it. Might your mother have popped to the SPAR to get herself something to eat?'

'No!' Lily snapped, putting the mug down on a side table. 'She doesn't know where the SPAR is! I don't know where the bloody SPAR is – we only got here yesterday.'

The young police officer sighed and flicked over a page in his notebook. 'It's a cause for concern that you're not being more helpful, in the circumstances,' he said.

Lily suddenly heard a familiar voice coming from the entrance hall. 'A bit of bacon might be nice. Have you got any fried bread?'

'Mum?' She got up from the sofa and ran towards the open door.

Moira was standing just inside the front door beside Toby Campbell, who had his hand protectively under her elbow. 'Fried bread it is,' he was saying. 'I think we can even stretch to a couple of poached eggs.'

'Oh, I do like a poached egg,' said Moira. 'It has to be runny in the middle, mind. None of that hard-boiled crap for me.'

'Mum!' Lily ran across the hallway and threw her arms around her. 'Oh my God, I'm so glad to see you! Where have you been? I was really worried. Why did you leave without telling anyone?'

Moira stepped back and stared at her in confusion. 'What are you going on about, Lily? I just went for a little walk.'

'I found her in the park up the road,' said Young Campbell. 'She was sitting on the roundabout, singing.'

Lily put her hand on his arm. 'Thank you so much! I can't tell you how grateful I am. That's so kind of you to have gone out looking. Mum, I've been beside myself with worry!'

The police constable cleared his throat behind them. 'If your mother is fit and well, I'm happy to consider this incident closed,' he said.

'Why are the police here?' asked Moira. 'Have I missed something exciting?'

'No, they were here because we were looking for you!'

'For me?'

'Yes, we didn't know where you'd gone.'

'How ridiculous. I was on a little walk.' Moira started to cough, her body trembling with the effort.

Lily turned back to the young officer. 'I'm sorry we wasted your time,' she said.

He was sliding his notebook back into his pocket and shaking his head. 'As I said, ma'am, in these situations there is often a rational explanation.'

'How about some breakfast?' asked Joan. 'We've officially stopped serving, but if you want to take your mother through, Archie will rustle you up something special.'

As Lily started leading Moira towards the dining room, she noticed she had bare feet. 'Where are your shoes? Did you leave them somewhere?'

Moira stopped and looked down at herself, surprised. 'I don't think I had any on.'

'But you must be freezing! I'll go and get a towel and your slippers. Why did you go outside without any shoes on? That cough is sounding really bad.'

'But you weren't here, Lily.' Moira's expression had changed. She suddenly looked exhausted and fragile, and her voice started to wobble. 'I couldn't find you.'

'Oh, Mum.'

'I looked for you, but I couldn't find you anywhere. Where did you go, Lily? Why weren't you here?'

Lily had been intending to lie. In her head, earlier, she'd been practising a long-winded story about how she'd decided to go for an early walk herself, and walked so far around the lake that she forgot the time. But as she stood there, staring at Moira's pale, confused face, she couldn't find the words.

'I'm sorry,' she said again. 'I should have been here. This is all my fault.'

Her mother was still coughing. Lily put her arm around her shoulders and hugged her, before starting to guide her towards the dining room again, where Joan was standing to attention, looking as if she was about to drop into a deep curtsey and welcome a member of the royal family. As they got to the door, Moira turned towards Lily again.

'What have you been up to?' she asked. 'You've got eye make-up all over your face and your hair's a mess.'

Lily nodded. 'I know. I can't really explain.'

'It's not like you to let yourself go,' said Moira, shaking her head. 'You usually look so smart!'

'Come and have a seat, right here,' called Joan. 'Archie is doing something rather magnificent with eggs and bacon.'

'Don't forget to tell him I want my egg to have a runny middle,' Moira said, collapsing into a chair at a table by the window. 'None of that hard-boiled crap.'

CHAPTER SIXTEEN

'I'VE DECIDED we're going home. You're not well, so I think you should rest up today, then tomorrow we'll head back to Brighton.'

'We are absolutely not doing that.'

'Mum, don't be silly. You've got a bad cough and it didn't help that you went out walking in your bare feet.'

Moira was sitting up in bed, clutching a hot water bottle provided by Joan, and glaring at Lily, her eyebrows beetled together. 'My feet are fine and this is just a little cough. We are not leaving Keswick until I've got more material for my book. I've nearly written the first three chapters now, and so much is coming back to me.'

Lily perched on the side of the bed. 'I know how important your book is to you, but can you understand why I'm worried?'

'There is no need for you to worry about anything,' said Moira, before succumbing to another coughing fit. When it was over and she could speak again, she looked back at Lily, her eyes watery. 'All these memories are wonderful. Just being here is making me think about what we did on that holiday when I was a child, the places my parents took me. It's bringing it all back! I need to get on and write it all down while we're here.'

'But it's not...'

'Lily, please!'

Looking at her mother, she felt her resolve trickling away, as usual. It did seem cruel to bring the trip to such a sudden end. She remembered the consultant's enthusiasm for their plans, the way he thought this holiday would help Moira. It probably wouldn't do any harm to stay for a few more days, if nothing else it would give her a chance to shake off this nasty cough and regain her strength.

'Okay, you win. We won't go home tomorrow. But I'm not making any promises about the rest of the trip. Let's see how you feel in a couple of days. It may be best to head back before the weekend.'

Lily was so tired, she could hardly think straight, and she didn't have the energy to argue with her mother. She couldn't face the thought of the long drive home right now, but everything would look better once she'd recharged her batteries. The only downside about her mother being confined to bed was that they wouldn't be able to find a nicer hotel in Keswick. The Campbells had been very kind, but the facilities in this place weren't up to much.

'It would be silly not to go to Durham, while we're here,' Moira said, reaching across to the bedside table for her notebook and pencil. 'It's almost on the way home. We had a weekend there, just after we got married.'

'Durham is not on the way home, it's on the other side of the country!'

'Yes, but the country isn't very wide up here.'

'We are not going to Durham.'

'Suit yourself,' said Moira, beginning to cough again. Lily

grabbed a blanket from the end of the bed and wrapped it around her mother's shaking shoulders.

'We'll talk about it when you're better,' she said. 'And I'm only saying we can stay here for a few more days on the condition that you promise me you won't go anywhere on your own again. You mustn't leave this room without me. Understand?'

Moira shrugged. 'You weren't here before,' she muttered.

Lily sighed; she had no right to order her mother around. If she'd been where she should have been and had spent the night in the cramped back bedroom of the guest house, none of this would have happened.

Suddenly, her head was full of Jake again. She saw him sitting on the edge of the bed earlier this morning, the definition of the muscles running across his lightly tanned back. Then he was lying beside her in the hotel bed, his brown eyes inches away from her, his hand running slowly across her stomach and down the side of her thigh.

She shut her eyes and willed herself to focus on something else. Anything else. There was no point thinking about this man, because she was never going to see him again. In the panic of the last couple of hours, it hadn't occurred to her that she had rushed out of Jake's hotel room without giving him her number. Or asking for his. Now the realisation hit her and the disappointment and regret were so intense, they were almost a physical ache in the pit of her stomach.

Was it worth going back to the hotel to try and find him? She didn't even know his room number; she'd been in such a state when she left that she had no idea how many flights of stairs she'd raced down while she desperately waited for her phone to turn on and start loading texts. It occurred to her, for the first time, that he might also be feeling more than a little confused about the whole situation. She had rushed away within two minutes of waking up, and had barely spoken to him, let alone acknowledged that something rather amazing had taken place between them the night before. He might think she was regretting what had happened, or – even worse – that she hadn't wanted it to happen at all. No, surely not? There was no way that man could think she hadn't been up for it, or that she hadn't had a damn good time.

But she couldn't go back and try to find him, it would be too embarrassing. Anyway, he might not want to see her; for him it probably hadn't been such a big deal. If he stayed in hotels regularly, she was unlikely to have been the first woman he picked up and lured back to his bedroom. Not that she'd needed much luring. More, slightly wobbly, memories of the previous night were starting to flood back now that her hangover was easing, and she felt herself blushing as she remembered the way she'd behaved. Not to mention some of the things she'd done to – and with – that gorgeous brown-eyed stranger.

'Are you all right?' asked Moira. 'You've gone a bit pink.'

'I'm fine!' she said, over-brightly, as she stood up from the bed.

It was probably just as well she had no way of contacting Jake, because the memory of their night together – which had, without question, been one of the best nights she'd had in an awfully long time – would always be tainted by her guilt at how irresponsibly she'd behaved.

'I'm going to find a chemist, to get you some cough medicine and paracetamol,' she said. 'I'll be back in about twenty minutes. I don't want you to move from this bed, do you hear me? Why don't you close your eyes and try to get some sleep?'

Moira smiled up at her. 'I will do. I promise. You're such a good girl to me, Lily. Such a good daughter.'

No, she thought. *I'm really not.*

When she went downstairs, Archie Campbell was standing behind the reception desk.

'Thank you for all your help, with my mother. I really appreciated everything you and your son did for us. You've been so kind.'

'All part of the service.' He beamed at her.

'I'm just going to find a chemist. Can you make sure... I mean, if my mother gets up and comes downstairs, would you mind sending her back to bed again? Or at least stopping her from going outside?'

'Naturally. I will barricade the door, if necessary.' He smiled but, as Lily turned and walked towards the front door, she noted the sarcasm in his voice. He had a point; it wasn't his job to look out for Moira, it was hers.

CHAPTER SEVENTEEN

THERE WAS a branch of Boots on Main Street and she stood in a queue waiting to ask the pharmacist what she should get for Moira's cough, listening to the conversations buzzing around her. She still had a slight headache, but was surprised that she actually felt pretty good. Better than good. She felt bloody marvellous. That was what a bit of unexpected sex did for you, when you thought you were only going out for an afternoon stroll.

It had been a while since she'd been told she was attractive, let alone slept with anyone. Things had never got that far with Dave, he'd been too intense, too obsessed with talking about himself and astrophysical engineering. She grimaced at the memory of his squashy lips planting themselves against hers; she really must stop thinking about Dave.

People in the queue in Boots were shuffling their feet and sighing. The woman at the front appeared to be buying enough painkillers to knock out an elephant. Lily tapped her fingers against her purse. The only downside about last night, was that she couldn't remember every single second of it in detail. Why had she got so drunk? Not that she'd intended it to happen, but it was a shame she could only remember fleeting glimpses of gorgeous Jake and the things they'd done to each other. God, it felt good to have sex again.

Although she hadn't had much of a love life since she and Nick divorced, thirteen years ago, the same couldn't be said for him. Nick had deserted Lily and Eleanor to set up home with someone called Josie, whom he'd chatted up in a supermarket. She was barely out of her teens, and Lily – still raw from the rejection and shattered at how easily he'd been able to walk away from his home, his marriage and his child – was relieved when the relationship broke down within months. Shortly afterwards, when she was on the point of suggesting to Nick that for Eleanor's sake they probably ought to try again, her daughter coldly informed Lily that her father was seeing someone called Sophie, who was twenty-four and a ballerina. Lily met her the following weekend when they came to pick up Eleanor. However unhappy her marriage to Nick had been, seeing another slim, pretty young woman draping herself across her former husband, did nothing to help Lily's feelings of low self-esteem.

By the time the decree absolute came through, Nick and Sophie were engaged. His second wedding was a grand affair; Lily attended – against her better judgement – but at the time she'd felt she needed to be there to support Eleanor. Her daughter was a prima donna of a fifteen-year-old bridesmaid, but Lily was sure that, deep down, she was struggling with the whole thing and would need support. As it turned out, Eleanor seemed to enjoy every second of the day, while Lily spent most of it feeling out of place, humiliated and on the point of tears, from the moment the bride and groom arrived at the church, to the elaborate first dance. Eleanor took great pleasure in telling her that Nick – who'd always insisted he loathed dancing – had been taking lessons and he certainly swirled his young bride around like a contestant on *Strictly*.

But despite the extravagance of the ceremony and the fact that Nick had boasted to Lily that he and his second wife were at it like rabbits, his marriage to Sophie lasted for less than a year. The resulting divorce was messy. Lily never spoke to Nick about it, but heard some of the details indirectly from Eleanor. She had to bite her tongue when Sophie's lawyer managed to get such an over-generous financial settlement that Nick couldn't afford to contribute to Eleanor's Year 12 geography field trip.

Nick seemed cowed for a year or so but, by the time Eleanor left school, he had moved in with someone called Rachel. After that, when things went tits-up with Rachel, hadn't there been an Adriana? Over the years – and well over Nick – Lily had lost track of his dalliances; the girlfriends were invariably half his age, always blonde and pretty, and she couldn't for the life of her work out what they saw in him.

Just a few weeks ago, a glossy invitation had landed on the doormat. It was for Nick's wedding number three, which was taking place at the end of October in a large country house near Worthing. Lily knew nothing about the next victim, Helen, and had no idea why the happy couple had even invited her. The whole thing felt a bit weird and she had no intention of attending.

The woman in Boots finally left, armed with a bulging paper bag full of drugs. The queue started moving forward more swiftly and, when Lily reached the front, the pharmacist sold her a bottle of cough linctus but suggested that, in view of her mother's age, a call to the GP might be in order. 'Just to make sure there's nothing more unpleasant going on,' he said.

As she went back out onto the pavement, her mobile rang. Her heart sank as she saw Eleanor's number come up and she rejected the call. She didn't have the energy for a grilling. As she walked up the hill towards the guest house, Eleanor called again, and when the phone rang for the third time, as Lily was walking into the badly painted car parking area, she gave in.

'Hello, darling,' she said, sitting down on a low wall behind the campervan.

'What are you doing? Why haven't you been taking my calls?' Her daughter sounded out of breath, as well as angry. 'Honestly, Mum, this is ridiculous. You can't just ignore me. What's happening with Granny? Have you persuaded her to come home?'

'We've had a couple of conversations about it, but...'

'That clearly means no. Why are you being so weak? You should be the one in charge of this situation. She's an old woman who's not in full command of her senses and you can't let her bully you.'

Lily almost laughed out loud, Eleanor was still completely oblivious to the irony of what she was saying. 'We're going to stay in Keswick for a few more days, and then we will probably head home. Granny isn't well, she's got a cough. So, I'm making her stay in bed.'

'Ha! So, she's now ill? I knew this ridiculous trip was a mistake. What have you been letting her get up to?'

'I'm sure she'll be fine,' said Lily. 'I've just been to get her some cough medicine and she needs to take it easy. Anyway, it was nothing to do with what she's been getting up to. She had the cough before she went out this morning.'

'What happened this morning?'

Oh shit. Lily frantically wondered how she could backtrack. 'She just went out for a walk. But it was quite cold and the grass was wet in the park.'

'What do you mean the grass was wet?' Eleanor's voice was terrifyingly calm.

'It was dewy, that was all. Her feet got a bit wet.'

'Her feet?'

'She forgot to put her shoes on.' As the words came out of her mouth, Lily wanted to swallow them back in again. Why did Eleanor have the ability to make her say exactly what she wanted to keep to herself?

'So, you're telling me that you let Granny, who has dementia and isn't capable of behaving sensibly, go out for a walk with no shoes?'

'I didn't let her do it, Eleanor! She went off without me knowing. When I got back I...'

'When you got back? Bloody hell, Mother, where were you? I don't believe this. I knew it was a mistake to let the two of you go off together – you're as bad as each other. You need to stop this nonsense and bring her home right now.'

'I agree!' said Lily. 'But Mum won't leave, she wants to finish the trip. She's not well, so we'll stay here for a couple of days, then I'll persuade her to go home. I do understand how important it is to her that we're here, she's writing so many notes in her book about all the places we've visited.'

'She's an old woman; you just need to tell her what's going to happen, don't give her a choice!'

'Eleanor that's an awful thing to say.' Lily stood up and started pacing across the car park. 'She's a human being, I can't just impose my will on her.'

'Yes, you can, she's demented and doesn't know what's going on.'

'That's ridiculous and cruel. She's fully of aware of everything that's going on. Well, most of the time.'

'I'm coming up to sort this out, you clearly can't deal with it on your own.'

'You really don't need to do that...'

Eleanor was calling out to someone else, away from the

phone. 'Find out how I can get up to the Lakes tomorrow! I don't want to drive, I'll need to do some work en route.'

'Darling,' said Lily. 'There is no need for this. I can cope.'

'There is every need, Mum. You clearly can't.' She yelled away from the phone again. 'Can I fly to Manchester and hire a car? Or else look up train times from London?' Lily didn't know whether she was yelling at her brow-beaten boyfriend, Paul, or at her poor secretary. Either way, someone down in Brighton was jumping to attention.

'Eleanor, stop! I've got things under control.'

'You clearly have nothing under control, Mum, which is why I need to get up there and sort everything out.'

CHAPTER EIGHTEEN

MOIRA SHRIEKED and spat out some of the cough mixture. 'That is fucking disgusting!' she yelled at Lily. 'I'm not drinking that muck!'

'The chemist said it would help, so you need to take it. Stop making a fuss.'

'I wouldn't be making a fuss if you weren't trying to poison me!'

'Mum, please don't shout at me. I've got a headache and we're both tired and stressed, so let's just try to be civil to each other. Look, you've got medicine all down the front of your nightie now.'

'I would be fucking civil if you weren't trying to kill me!' Moira took the spoon and hurled it across the bedroom. It clattered against the wall, then dropped down and landed on a side table, on a tray that held the kettle, cup and saucer and a neatly arranged selection of tea and coffee sachets. 'Would you look at that?' Moira turned to Lily, beaming. 'A perfect shot!'

Lily smiled and nodded. Today she was being treated to an extraordinarily unpredictable array of Good Mum/Bad Mum. In the dining room earlier, Moira had wolfed down an enormous fried breakfast and asked for more toast, before telling Joan she'd never eaten such an awful meal.

'Sorry!' Lily had whispered to Joan, raising her eyes to the ceiling. 'We're a bit grumpy this morning.'

Moira was now propped up in bed with her notebook open on her lap.

'Are you going to show me any of what you're writing?' asked Lily.

'No.'

'I'd love to see how it's going?'

'No. Bog off. You'll have to wait until it's finished. There's a long way to go yet – I haven't even got to the bit about you.'

'But I was born when you were living in Chepstow. I thought you said you'd written about that?'

'Oh no, not that.' Moira waved her hand dismissively in Lily's direction. 'The rest of the bit about you.'

'What rest?'

'Oh, Lily.' Moira sighed. 'You're so impatient. You will find out all about it, in good time. I'm getting along pretty well but you can't hurry genius.'

'Right,' said Lily. She was sitting in the armchair by the window, with the book she was reading open on her lap. It was hard to concentrate and she would have given anything to be able to go outside and wander back down to the lake. In the distance, she could see the sun sparkling on the water, and resented being cooped up inside. But there was no way she was leaving this bedroom again. Joan had said she'd bring up a couple of trays at lunchtime and, in the meantime, Lily had to resign herself to a quiet morning, keeping an eye on her mother.

She picked up her phone and stared at the screen. No one had called, of course they hadn't. Anyway, the only person she wanted to hear from couldn't call because he didn't have her number and had no idea where she was staying. Lily clicked onto the internet and searched for the Hamilton Hotel. A website appeared with photographs of the hotel's garden and the views across Derwentwater. There was a link to *Accommodation* and when she clicked on that, a picture came up of one of the hotel bedrooms. It could well have been the one in which she'd spent the previous night – the curtains looked identical, the carpet was the same colour. She'd been pretty close to that carpet a few hours ago, when she'd been on her hands and knees in a panic, scrabbling around under the bed and coming across her knickers, which were still scrunched up in the pocket of her coat. Mortification flooded over her again. How was she ever going to forget about this, or forgive herself? Although, if truth be told, it was only the forgiving bit that mattered. She didn't want to forget about any of it, not one wonderful, thrilling, pulsating second.

Where would Jake be now? She was sure she must have asked him what he did for a living, but by that time she was already pretty drunk and she had no idea what he'd said. Did he have an office job or was he outside doing something more physical with those strong arms and gentle hands? Despite the hangover and the tiredness, she felt a tickle of something stirring in her loins. *Stop it*, she told herself. *This is doing no good at all.*

Moira was muttering to herself. 'I need to make sure he's happy about all this, I need to go over it all with him.'

'Who?'

'Oliver, of course.'

'Are you writing about our visit to him?'

Moira shook her head with irritation. 'No, that wasn't very interesting. I'm writing about the old him. The him I used to know.'

'I'm sure he won't mind that.'

'It was good he finally met you,' Moira was saying. 'That was important. I don't think he knew.'

'Knew what?'

'Knew any of it.'

'Mum, you are making no sense whatsoever. Why did Oliver need to meet me? And what didn't he know about?'

'You don't understand,' Moira said, shaking her head and breaking into another bout of coughing. 'You have no idea.'

'Tell me, then?'

'No, you'll have to wait to read my book.'

Lily sighed, this damned book was taking on a life of its own. She picked up her own paperback again and flicked back through the previous few pages, trying to remember where she'd got to. She'd been enjoying it back in Brighton, but hadn't managed to read for a couple of days.

What did Moira mean about Oliver? She wanted to probe further but knew her mother wasn't in the right mood. She had been particularly bolshy since Toby Campbell had found her singing to herself on a roundabout in the park. Lily glanced up and watched for a few seconds as Moira scribbled energetically in her notebook. Irritatingly, her mother was right, she would just have to be patient and wait until this cough was better and Moira had forgotten about her barefoot bid for freedom.

CHAPTER NINETEEN

'AH, here you are. How the hell did you find this place? It's like Fawlty Towers.'

Eleanor swept into Moira's bedroom like royalty. She was wearing a smart red suit with a pencil skirt and high-heeled red shoes. Her hair was bundled up on top of her head into what could pass for a casual bun but, looking at the wisps of hair trailing delicately down on either side of her face, Lily reckoned the hairdo had probably taken ages to get just right.

'What is *she* doing here?' asked Moira.

'Lovely to see you too, Granny,' said Eleanor, swooping down towards the bed to air kiss her cheek.

'Eleanor thought she'd come and join us for a couple of days,' said Lily. 'Isn't that nice?' It wasn't, and none of them would have claimed otherwise, but she couldn't think of anything else to say.

'Didn't you tell her I was coming?' Eleanor asked, turning to Lily and delivering a second – even more distant – air kiss in her direction. 'Honestly, Mum. I sometimes wonder if you're losing the plot too.'

Lily deliberately hadn't mentioned Eleanor's impending arrival to Moira. It was partly because she didn't know how to explain the visit, and also because she was half hoping something else would crop up and her daughter would be summoned to a work meeting of such crucial world-changing importance that she would need to cancel her travel plans. Sadly, that obviously hadn't happened.

'Hello, darling, how are you?' Lily said. She knew her smile wasn't reaching her eyes. She was still furious about their phone call the previous morning, as well as the fact that Eleanor was here at all. But as usual her daughter had outmanoeuvred her. 'You look very smart. How did you get up here in the end?'

'Caught an early morning flight to Manchester from Gatwick, then a train into the city, then another one to Penrith, then a bus to Keswick. Bloody long journey.' Eleanor had wheeled a large hard-shell suitcase through the door with her, and now threw her handbag and laptop case onto the end of Moira's bed. 'This is a godforsaken place. How did you end up here? I need a coffee – haven't you got anything other than those horrid little plastic sachets?'

'No, that's all there is,' snapped Lily, slamming shut her paperback. 'Apologies if this isn't up to your usual standards, Eleanor. But no one asked you to come.'

'I certainly didn't,' Moira said.

'You clearly couldn't cope up here on your own,' continued Eleanor, ignoring her grandmother. 'So, I decided it was the only option. Believe me, I could have done without all this travelling and being away from the office.'

Moira was glaring at Lily. 'Why didn't you tell me she was coming? We don't need her here, she'll interfere with my writing.'

'I won't interfere with anything,' said Eleanor. 'I'm just here to make sure you both stay out of trouble. I hear you went wandering off on your own yesterday, Granny? What on earth were you thinking? You know you shouldn't do that sort of thing. Don't you remember how worried everyone was back in the summer, when you went to the swimming pool and didn't tell anyone what you were doing?'

'I can go wherever I want!' Moira sniffed and crossed her arms in front of her chest. 'I don't know why you keep on about the swimming pool – it was a hot day! I only wanted to have a little dip.'

'Granny, you were stripping off in the men's changing rooms!' Eleanor said. 'Then you jumped into the shallow end wearing just your underwear! I don't understand how you can possibly think something like that is normal, let alone acceptable.'

'I was trying to cool down,' muttered Moira.

'Even if Mum was careless enough to lose you yesterday, I'd have thought that after all the trouble we've had recently, you would realise that you can't do that sort of thing.'

'I didn't lose her!' Lily said.

'There were only a couple of men in the changing rooms,' said Moira.

'Well, I sort of lost her, but you're making it all sound much worse than it really was,' added Lily. As she said the words, she could feel her face colouring, it was every bit as bad as Eleanor was making it out to be. Thank God her daughter only thought she had taken her eye off Moira briefly. If she knew that Lily had spent the entire night elsewhere in the arms of a strange man, she would be – rightly – appalled.

'I spoke to Dad when I was on the train, and he wasn't surprised by any of this,' Eleanor said. 'He reminded me about that time when you left me on a bus when I was a baby, Mum.

Do you remember that? I mean, what kind of mother forgets her own child on public transport!'

'That's typical of your father to bring that up,' said Lily. 'Anyway, I didn't actually leave you on the bus, I remembered you were there when I'd got to the bottom of the stairs and I went straight back up to get you. Lots of women do things like that when they've just had babies – it's the hormones. There was no harm done – why do you always exaggerate?'

'I remember that.' Moira cackled. 'It was so funny! We teased you about it for months afterwards.' Her laugh turned into a coughing fit.

Eleanor raised her eyebrows at Lily. 'That doesn't sound good.'

'I'm fine,' Moira wheezed.

'And I do wish you wouldn't talk about all this with Nick,' Lily continued. 'It is none of his business.' She didn't know why she was bothering to make a fuss. Eleanor had always taken his side and always would. When she was younger, Lily had sometimes wondered if she was a bit scared of her overbearing father? But that wasn't it, they were just too alike. Eleanor was a pea right out of Nick's arrogant, critical, self-obsessed pod.

'Young lady, you are very bossy!' Moira said. 'I'm perfectly capable of making my own decisions.'

'But you aren't, are you, Granny?'

The two women glared at each other across the bed. Eleanor gave in first.

'I'm going to freshen up. Is this the bathroom, through this door? God, this place is grim. I don't think I can bear to stay here. The taxi passed a nice five-star hotel on the way from the station. I may book in there.' She went into the bathroom and slammed the door behind her.

Lily looked at Moira and saw her mother's mouth twitching. The two of them burst into snorts of laughter before Lily put her finger to her lips. 'Shh! She'll get even more cross if she hears. She hates it when she thinks people are laughing at her.'

'That child of yours,' said Moira, shaking her head. 'She's like a mini hurricane in a posh frock. If she didn't look so much like you, I'd think you were sent home from hospital with the wrong baby.'

CHAPTER TWENTY

LILY FINALLY REMEMBERED to call Gordon. She sat in the residents' lounge, listening to his phone ring, hundreds of miles away in Brighton.

'Gordy, I'm so sorry not to have got back to you. I know you've called and texted a couple of times. Things have been a bit chaotic over the last few days.'

'No problem. How's it going?'

'It *was* going fine, but we're now in the Lake District and Mum did a bit of a runner yesterday morning and went missing. I had to call the police, but luckily some kind boy from the guest house found her before things got out of hand. She went walking without any shoes on though, and she already had a bad cough, so that has only made it worse.'

'Oh, Lily, I'm sorry.'

'It's all fine, really. But I'm not sure she entirely understood why she'd gone off on her own, and definitely not why it was such a big deal. Her memory is getting worse and now I'm spending more time with her, I'm realising how confused she is about a lot of things. Anyway, that's just the way it's going to be from now on. The big downer is that Eleanor has decided to come up and sort us out. She thinks I'm not coping so she arrived a couple of hours ago and is busy steam-rollering her way through both of us, while making enemies of the couple who own the guest house.'

'Oh dear, that's not good.'

'It's not good at all. The only saving grace is that she won't be with us all the time, because she hated this place so much, she has booked herself in to stay at a hotel down the road, somewhere much more grand. To be honest, I never realised my daughter was such a snob, but I can't say I'm surprised. But the best news is that she says she won't be able to spend much time with us during the day because the wifi is so bad she can't even conduct her very important business meetings here. So, she'll have to do that in her own hotel bedroom and will be out of earshot, which will be a blessed relief for all of us!'

'Hmm, lovely.'

'Gordy, you're sounding very distracted! What's going on?'

'Nothing.'

'Are you sure? Did I call at a bad time?'

There was a silence on the other end of the phone, then a sigh.

'Gordy, what's happened?'

'It's Hilary. She left me.'

'Oh my God!' Lily clapped her hand to her mouth. 'That's awful! I'm so sorry. Why didn't you say? You've let me witter on about Mum and Eleanor and our trip. What happened?'

'Not sure really. I think she just got bored with me. She says there isn't anyone else, but she may be saying that to ease the blow.' His voice was wobbly and it sounded as if he was trying not to cry.

Lily stood and began pacing up and down the lounge. 'When did it happen? Did you have a row?'

'No, nothing like that. She just came out with it, a couple of days ago. Said she wasn't feeling anything for me anymore. She has moved out and taken all her stuff. It has been so sudden, I don't know what to do with myself. The house feels very strange without her.'

'Oh, sweetheart, I'm sorry. This is dreadful. Are you okay? Stupid question, obviously not.'

'Not really.' Gordon sighed again. 'I feel so empty inside. We've been together for such a long time, nearly twelve years. I can't quite work out how I'm going to carry on without her.'

'You will, Gordy, you really will. But obviously it doesn't seem like that, at the moment. Have you told anyone else about this? Any of the others at work.'

'No. It didn't seem fair to bother them.'

'You need some support though. How about telling Hannah? Or Richard?'

'Maybe.'

'I wish I was there with you,' Lily said. 'What awful timing. Why did she have to do this right now, when I'm so far away?'

'When are you coming back?' Gordon's voice was definitely quavering now. 'It would be good to see you, Lily. To be able to chat about all this.'

'I can't come home yet, I'm really sorry. Mum isn't well, so I need to give her time to recover. But maybe by the weekend?'

After Lily had ended the call, she walked across to the window and stared out at the pale blue and white campervan, squeezed into the miniscule parking space outside the bay window. She felt so useless. One of her closest friends was having a bad time and needed her. But she couldn't be there because her priority had to be her own mother, who was in the bedroom directly above her head, struggling to fight off a cough that didn't seem to be getting any better. Lily hated feeling so inadequate, but she was being pulled in too many directions.

Two of her favourite people needed her, but right now she wasn't being a decent support to either of them.

As she walked up the main stairs, she could hear Moira coughing inside her bedroom. She plumped the cushions behind her mother's back and topped up her water glass, perching beside her on the bed.

'You're not sounding good. I wonder if we ought to get a doctor out to see you?'

She had expected Moira to bat her away and insist she was fine, but her mother nodded. She looked exhausted; there was a sheen of sweat across her forehead and her eyes were rheumy. 'Maybe that's a good idea,' she said, her breath coming in scratchy wheezes.

When Lily rang down to the reception desk, Joan was delighted to be asked to help. 'Doctor's appointments are like hens' teeth round here, but leave it to me,' she said. 'My friend Sandra is the receptionist at the local surgery, I'll see if she can get you onto the list for home visits this afternoon.'

Eleanor walked into the bedroom, just as Lily was finishing the call. 'Well, that's good.' She sniffed. 'Although to be honest it's something you should have done days ago.'

'You're probably right. But I've done it now, so let's hope they can send someone.'

'If it had been up to me,' Eleanor was saying. 'I would have handled this very differently.'

Moira opened her eyes and smiled at them. 'There you both are,' she said. 'I was wondering why nobody was here. Is Oliver coming to visit later?'

'Who's Oliver?' Eleanor asked.

'No, Mum. It's just us,' said Lily.

'He said he'd come,' muttered Moira. 'That's rude if he doesn't turn up.'

'What's she talking about?' Eleanor picked up a magazine

125

and flung herself into the armchair, knocking Lily's paperback onto the floor.

'Nothing,' Lily said, going into the bathroom to get a damp flannel to hold across Moira's forehead. There was no reason to tell her daughter about Oliver. In any case, she wasn't sure exactly what there was to tell.

She'd been thinking a great deal about yesterday's conversation with Moira. Oliver had clearly been a good friend, but it sounded as if there had been more to their relationship than that. Had the two of them been having an affair? The idea didn't particularly shock her. It was no surprise to learn her mother had led a more eventful life than she'd been aware of. Moira had always been feisty, full of energy and enthusiasm. She had also been very attractive when she was younger. Nowadays, all Lily could see were the wrinkles and paper-thin skin, the liver spots across her mother's arms and hands and the white hair that had grown so fine on the top of her head that you could see her scalp through it. But there were plenty of photos of a much younger Moira, taken when Lily was a girl, and she had been gorgeous. A couple of days ago she had said she'd been a little bit in love with Oliver, and it would be understandable if Oliver had been a little in love with her too.

Lily held the damp flannel against her mother's forehead, listening as her breaths rattled in her chest. Maybe Moira was hinting at something that had happened between herself and Oliver in the past, as a way of preparing Lily for revelations along those lines when she finally shared the memories she was documenting in her book?

Watching her mother drop off to sleep and listening as Eleanor flicked noisily through the pages in the magazine, Lily ran her fingers softly across the top of her mother's hand. Moira was right, this book she was working away at would be something for her and Eleanor to treasure.

CHAPTER TWENTY-ONE

JUST BEFORE 4PM, there was a knock on the door. When Lily opened it, her heart went into freefall inside her stomach. She stood gaping, one hand on the doorknob. She tried to speak, but nothing came out of her mouth. The blood was pumping around her chest, forcing itself up her neck and thundering through her skull and her legs were suddenly weak, as if they might give way beneath her.

'Who is it?' Eleanor called, from inside the bedroom behind her.

'Just... just someone,' she said, her voice sounding squeaky in her own ears. She went out into the corridor and pulled the door shut behind her, leaning back on it to steady herself against a wave of giddiness. Her cheeks were burning, as if a hairdryer on its full heat setting was being pointed straight at her face.

'What are you doing here?' she whispered.

'I was going to ask you the same thing!' Jake looked as shocked as she felt.

'God, it's good to see you.' The words were out of her mouth before she could stop herself. But it really was so good. Over the last day and a half, she had thought about this man almost constantly; she'd pictured his rich brown eyes and his neatly trimmed hair, speckled with grey, the fringe flopping across his forehead. She'd thought about his mouth, laughing as they talked, moving towards her to kiss her. When she closed her eyes, she found it hard to think about anything other than the strength of his arms as he held her and the way her stomach contracted as he ran his hand along it.

'It's good to see you too,' he said.

She realised she was holding her breath as she stared at his face, inches from her own. She wanted to launch herself at him; throw her arms around his neck and hold him as tightly as she had done two nights ago. She wanted to run her hands through his hair and smell his skin, feel his cheek soft against her own.

But at the same time as her body was rebelling with desire for this other human being, her head was telling her this was all wrong. What was he doing here? How on earth had he tracked her down to this guest house? To this very door?

She was suddenly aware that she could hear movement in the room behind her. 'Why are you here?' she whispered. 'How did you find me?'

'I didn't! I mean, I didn't know you were here.'

She shook her head in confusion. Part of her didn't care how or why he'd tracked her down, she was just ecstatic he had. She'd thought she would never see this man again. She'd been riddled with regret about running out of his room the previous morning, when she'd been in such a panic about Moira that she hadn't even said goodbye. But ever since she'd left him behind, she'd been telling herself it was just one of those things. She'd had a one-night stand; the man in question was bloody gorgeous. But circumstances meant they would never see each other again, so that was the end of it.

Now, here he was, standing inches away from her in the

corridor of the Campbell's guest house, with the smell of Archie's home cooking wafting up the stairs around them.

There was another noise on the other side of the bedroom door and the handle began to turn. Lily had her hands behind her back, holding on to it for dear life, pulling the door towards her, straining against Eleanor, who was trying to open it on the other side.

'You have to leave!' she hissed at Jake. 'My mother's in this room – and my daughter's here too, my bloody daughter! Oh shit. She can't find out what happened. She can't see you out here or even meet you.'

He was looking bewildered and opened his mouth to say something.

'Please, just go!' Lily whispered. 'We're waiting for the doctor to come and see my mother because she's not well. So, you'll have to leave. How did you find me again? Oh, Jake. I'm sorry, this is all so horrible. I really don't want you to leave, but you must!'

'Lily,' he said. 'I can't go.'

'I know! I know! I feel the same. But they can't come out and find you here.' She was getting wafts of his aftershave; it wasn't one she was familiar with, but breathing it in now took her straight back to the hotel room down by the lake.

The door was rattling behind her.

'Mum?' Eleanor called. 'What's going on?'

'Lily!' he said urgently. 'Stop!'

Her heart was beating so hard now that it sounded as if an incoming tide was roaring in her ears. He put out his hand and rested it on her arm. His fingers were warm and soft and the feel of them against her skin was almost too much to bear. She wanted to let go of the door handle and launch herself at him, but her arms were now being pulled backwards as Eleanor tried to open the door.

'Lily,' he said again. 'You don't understand.'

She frowned, shaking her head at him. 'Just leave, Jake!' she begged.

'I can't!' He still had one hand on her arm, and he raised the other hand so she could see what he was carrying: a large black leather bag. 'I can't leave; I'm the doctor.'

CHAPTER TWENTY-TWO

'SHE SHOULD NEVER HAVE BEEN out on her own anyway, especially when she wasn't wearing any shoes, but there's not much we can do about that now,' Eleanor said, turning to glare pointedly at Lily. 'The main thing is that we deal with this cough and make sure there are no other underlying symptoms.'

'I've not got underlying anything,' said Moira. 'I just have a very bossy granddaughter.'

Jake was sitting on the edge of the bed. He had opened up his black bag and taken out a stethoscope and a thermometer and was gently monitoring Moira's pulse and breathing.

'What's your name, doctor?' she asked.

'I'm Dr Jordan, I work at the local surgery.'

'Well, it's nice to meet you,' Moira simpered, putting her head on one side. 'Extremely nice. Do you want me to take my nightie off?'

'No!' said Eleanor and Lily, at the same time.

'That's fine, Mrs Spencer. I can listen to your chest like this.'

'The thing is, she has got *dementia*,' whispered Eleanor. 'It's not particularly far advanced yet, but it means we need to be extra vigilant about what she does and where she goes. To be honest, doctor, there are times when she really can't be left alone.'

'Oh, shut up about my dementia,' Moira said. 'I can hear every word you're saying, Eleanor, you fuckwit.'

'See what I mean?' Eleanor said, sotto voce, to Jake. 'Completely unpredictable.'

'It's because you're discussing her like this!' Lily couldn't resist putting in. 'She is right here in front of us, Eleanor. Show some sensitivity!' She had been standing at the side of the room, not saying a word. As soon as Eleanor managed to pull open the bedroom door and she and Jake stumbled through it, her daughter had taken over; it was actually just as well, because Lily wasn't sure if she would have been able to act normally and hold a conversation with Jake while he examined her mother.

'This whole trip was a ridiculous idea,' Eleanor was now saying. 'I tried to point out that it would only end in tears, but of course my *mother* thought she knew best.'

'The consultant agreed it was a good idea,' Lily said, through gritted teeth. She didn't want to have a showdown with her daughter in front of Jake, but nor could she bear to just stand there while she got slagged off – yet again. She would have been angry with Eleanor anyway, but it was even more galling that Jake was hearing all this. She *knew* she'd been a rubbish daughter; she *knew* she should have taken better care of Moira. But she could do without this man hearing all the sordid details.

'You've obviously got a nasty cough, Mrs Spencer,' he was saying now. 'There is a slight rattle on your chest and you have a moderately raised temperature. But there are no other signs of an infection, and I don't think it's viral, so I'm going to prescribe you a short course of antibiotics, just to make sure we knock this on the head. The good news is that we've caught it early, so I'm confident you'll be fine.'

'Well, that's a relief,' said Eleanor. 'No thanks to some people though.' She glared at Lily again, and this time Jake saw it.

'I don't think your barefoot walk yesterday made things any worse,' he said, turning back to Moira. 'Some people might suggest that dancing on damp grass is very good for the circulation.' He smiled and Moira beamed back at him.

'Oh, you are a lovely boy!' she said. 'I wasn't dancing when I went out on my walk, but I'm quite good at it. Ken used to take me to the Ritz Dance Hall, near Gloucester. Do you know it? I don't really like taking pills, but if you think it's a good idea, I'll give them a go.'

'Marvellous,' he said, pulling out a prescription pad from his bag. 'I'll write this out now and maybe your granddaughter could take it straight down to the chemist?'

'What, me?' Eleanor looked taken aback.

'Here you are,' said Jake, ripping off the form and handing it to her. 'If you go now, you'll catch Boots before they shut. That would be a great help because she really needs to start taking these tonight.'

'Right,' Eleanor said. 'I see. Well, okay then.'

As the door closed behind her, Moira lay back on her pillows. 'She can be a right witch!' she whispered to Jake.

'Mum! That's an awful thing to say.'

'Fucking true though.'

Jake laughed. 'Nice to meet you, Mrs Spencer. Take it easy for a couple of days and then you should be well enough to head home.'

'Oh, I'm not going home,' said Moira. 'We're going to Durham next.'

'I'll show you out,' Lily said, more loudly than she needed.

Once they were both outside in the corridor, she pulled the bedroom door shut behind her.

'Why didn't you tell me you were a GP?' she whispered.

'I did!' he whispered back. 'I told you all about it.'

Lily crossed her arms in front of her chest. She had no recollection of any of that. 'So, if you live in Keswick, why were you staying in the hotel?' she asked.

Jake grinned. 'Blimey, you really were drunk. Don't you remember?'

'No! I don't. I don't think we discussed any of that. We were too busy... too busy doing other things.' She looked up and smiled back at him.

'That's true, we were quite busy. But I did tell you all about myself,' Jake said. 'My house has just been sold, I'm moving into a rented flat at the other end of the town, next week. In the meantime, I'm staying at the Hamilton.'

Lily grimaced. 'Really? I don't remember.'

'And my wife is divorcing me.'

'Shit, I should have remembered that.'

'You should, but we did drink quite a lot,' he said, and put his hand up to her cheek.

'Lily!' Moira's voice sounded quavery from inside the bedroom, then she started coughing.

Lily put her hand on top of his and leant forward. Her eyes closed as their lips met and she breathed in the smell of his skin, the underlying scent of that aftershave. Something lurched in the pit of her stomach.

'Lily!' Moira was still coughing. 'Where have you gone?'

'I ought to go,' he said. 'I have a long list of home visits to make this afternoon.'

'Lily! I need some water!'

'I'm coming!' she called, then turned back to him. 'It's so good to see you again. I'm sorry about running out yesterday

134

morning. I had such a shocking hangover and I was in a panic about Mum, I wasn't thinking straight.'

'I thought you weren't that interested in me,' he said.

'No! That really wasn't the case – the opposite. I mean, I just wasn't thinking...'

There was a crash from the bedroom and the sound of glass breaking.

'Fucking fuckers!' yelled Moira.

Jake stepped away from her and raised his hand awkwardly. 'You need to go,' he said.

She nodded. 'Bye then.' She stood and watched him walk away down the stairs, and her heart – which had just been dancing with delight at having him so close by – felt as if it was plummeting down into the soles of her feet again.

CHAPTER TWENTY-THREE

JOAN HAD OFFERED to find Lily and Eleanor a table in the dining room for supper but, without even consulting her daughter, Lily knew the suggestion wouldn't go down well. When she got back with Moira's prescription, Eleanor threw the packet onto the bed and marched across to push open the bedroom window. 'The smell of that man's cooking is appalling!' she said. 'It hits you when you walk in through the front door and the whole building stinks of school dinners. I can't believe people choose to eat here.'

'We don't actually have any choice,' said Lily. 'Granny has been told to stay in bed, so we'll be eating up here and personally, I'll be grateful for whatever the Campbells decide to give us.'

'I won't,' said Moira. 'Eleanor's right. The food here is a bit shit.'

'Too bad,' said Lily. 'We'll have to put up with it for a couple of days.'

'Well, I won't be joining you.' Eleanor sniffed. 'The menu at the Roxborough sounds wonderful – I looked at the Specials board earlier and there's fresh rainbow trout with ginger and scallops on the menu tonight. I'll definitely be eating there.'

'Good,' said Moira.

Although she didn't particularly want to spend the evening listening to her daughter criticise her actions and list her faults, Lily wouldn't have minded a decent meal this evening. Despite being well and truly over yesterday's colossal hangover, she'd been more hungry than usual all day. It was a long time since she'd drunk so much, but she vaguely remembered that this was what happened after you'd pumped your system full of alcohol. This afternoon she'd eaten all of the packets of biscuits on the tea trays in both bedrooms, and had also worked her way through a jumbo bag of Haribo she'd found in the glove compartment of the campervan. The bag was already open and had been in there for a while, but beggars couldn't be choosers. She was still hungry now, but couldn't leave Moira alone, so for her it would have to be supper in the room again. But, as she said goodbye to Eleanor, she couldn't help hoping the rainbow trout wouldn't be quite as delicious as it sounded.

'It's shepherd's pie this evening,' Archie announced later, as he carried in the two trays. 'With green beans, petits pois and carrot batons.'

'These are just sticks of carrot!' said Moira, prodding the vegetables with her fork.

'That's what a baton is,' Lily said.

'So, why don't you call it a carrot stick?' Moira asked Archie.

'It's a culinary term, dear lady. Used by chefs who are used to catering for the most discerning palates.'

'That's not you, then. How ridiculous. If I was you, I wouldn't bother using fancy names for bog-standard vegetables.'

Lily grimaced at Archie apologetically as he backed out of the room, but he just smiled, clearly not offended. The Campbells were certainly getting the measure of her mother.

Either that, or they were so thick-skinned they had absolutely no idea when they were being insulted.

While Moira was still picking over the remains of her meal, Lily texted Gordon.

> How are you? Hope it's all feeling less raw? Xx

His reply pinged in almost immediately.

> Just so sad. Don't know how to fill my time. The house is empty without her x

She tapped out:

> It will get easier xx

It didn't sound as if he'd taken her advice and confided in anyone else about what had happened with Hilary, which was a shame because she was sure it would help him to talk. Another reply pinged in straight away.

> I'll never meet anyone else now. Not at this age. For me and you, the best parts of our lives are now behind us x

'Huh, charming!' Lily muttered to herself. Gordon was a good ten years older than she was, and she wasn't impressed that he was being so negative about her own chances of happiness. She felt like texting back and hinting at her unexpected night of passion with a stranger, but that would be cruel – there was no way she could tell him about Jake when he was at such a low ebb.

She got up and went to draw the curtains across the bedroom window, staring out across the car park at the spotlights cast onto the pavement by the streetlights. Poor

Gordy; it must be awful to find yourself alone again so suddenly. Oliver came into her mind, with his huge stomach and red wine-stained lips. Seeing him alone and out of his depth in his messy, filthy house had been depressing, but it must have been much harder for Moira to process. There was a man who had let himself go, who didn't seem to have anyone who cared enough to help him get his life back on track. Did her mother feel guilty about the fact that her former friend was now in such a bad way? Even all those years ago, when they'd apparently been so close, he hadn't been her problem. But deep down she might feel as if she'd let him down.

There was no way Lily was going to let that happen to Gordy. As soon as they were back in Brighton, she would go round to check he was taking proper care of himself, then drag him out of his empty house to drink cocktails and do a bit of dancing and generally remind him that his life was far from over, and he had the right to throw caution to the wind and behave like a man half his age.

CHAPTER TWENTY-FOUR

'THERE'S a letter here for you, Mrs Bennett!' Archie was waving a white envelope at her.

Lily walked over to the reception desk and held out her hand. The envelope was flimsy and had her name scrawled across the front.

'Handwritten,' said Archie.

'Yes.' Lily turned it over but there was nothing on the back of the envelope; she had no idea what this was.

'I didn't see who delivered it. Someone must have dropped it off earlier, while I was in the kitchen.'

'I guess so.'

'Do you know people in Keswick?'

'No,' said Lily. 'Not a soul.' There was a tiny rip on the back of the envelope, at the edge of the glued-down flap. She guessed Archie had been trying to have a sneaky peak at the contents, just before she came down the stairs. She was surprised at his lack of initiative; she would have thought a man with such a lengthy history in hospitality would have learnt how to quickly and efficiently steam open an envelope. She tucked it into her pocket as she turned towards the door.

'Are you not going to find out who it's from?' He sounded disappointed.

'See you later!' she called out. She was desperate to rip open the envelope, but wasn't going to give him the satisfaction of doing it right here. She'd been on her way out to the campervan, to see if she had a spare phone charger in the glove compartment – hers had taken to working intermittently or not at all. Having slid open the side door, she hopped up and sat at the little table, fishing the envelope out of her pocket.

It was from Jake.

Her eyes had flown straight to the bottom of the single sheet of paper, and when she saw his name in neat, forward slanting writing, she gasped with delight, initially skimming through what he'd written, before reading it properly a second time, then a third and a fourth. He was asking her to meet him this evening, down by the lake. And he'd scribbled his phone number at the top of the sheet of paper. She caught her breath and her heart started to flutter a little faster as she brought the note up to her face, hoping to catch a waft of his aftershave. It smelt of absolutely nothing.

'Idiot,' she muttered to herself. She must stop behaving like a lovestruck teenager.

***

'I don't get it,' said Eleanor. 'Why would you want to do that?'

'I just need a couple of hours to myself,' said Lily. 'I'm going to make some calls, have something to eat. I need some "me" time, Eleanor. You must be able to understand that?'

'I suppose so. It's not hugely convenient though. What time will you be back?'

'No idea,' Lily said, cheerfully. 'I'll see you when I see you.

You and Mum can watch some TV together and the Campbells will bring up supper trays, as usual.'

The expression on Eleanor's face was priceless.

'I don't want to be stuck in here with you, either!' Moira called from the bed. She started coughing again. 'In fact, I'm the one who deserves some "me" time.'

'Sorry, Mum, but you aren't going anywhere,' Lily said. 'You need to take it easy and give those antibiotics time to work. Don't forget to take your pill this evening, I've left the packet on the table, to remind Eleanor.'

When she went out of Moira's bedroom, she almost skipped down the stairs. She felt like a schoolgirl who'd managed to get out of lessons by telling a massive lie – and got away with it. She couldn't remember the last time she'd persuaded Eleanor to give up what she was planning and step in to take some responsibility for Moira. Mind you, that was because she, Lily, never asked for anything from her corporate powerhouse of a daughter. She just went ahead and did everything in life without expecting any offers of help or support – which was a self-fulfilling prophecy, because it meant she never got any. She giggled to herself as she remembered the shock on Eleanor's face and the annoyance on Moira's; the two of them were going to irritate the hell out of each other over the next couple of hours. Good.

Leaving the guest house, she walked briskly down the hill towards the lake. The light was already fading and she wrapped her coat more tightly around her to keep out the October chill. In the note, Jake had suggested meeting a little way along from the theatre. He wrote that he'd be on a bench beneath a large oak tree, at 6pm. As she walked along, she suddenly realised she hadn't told him she was coming. How stupid! Maybe he wouldn't be there? She was a few minutes late, so he might have given up and gone home. She pulled her phone out of her pocket, thinking she should text him, but then put it away again – by the time she did that, she'd be nearly there. She increased her pace, her footsteps ringing out on the path. She almost wanted to laugh out loud with relief when she saw a figure up ahead, sitting back on a bench, legs stretched out in front, one foot carelessly slung over the other.

He stood up as he saw her and she stopped a few feet away. He was smiling, tiny pale crow's feet rippling out from the sides of his eyes.

'Hi!' he said, running his hand nervously through his hair, pushing his fringe back from his face. 'I wasn't sure if you'd come.'

She suddenly felt ridiculously awkward and tongue-tied. She opened her mouth to speak, but couldn't think of anything to say.

'But thanks anyway,' he said. 'For coming, I mean.'

'Thanks for inviting me.' Argh! What a stupid thing to say! Why was she being so formal? Plus, her voice sounded strangely squeaky, and higher than usual. She wished they could start over again.

He moved forward until he was inches away from her. Now she breathed in the scent of that aftershave and then his lips were on hers. She closed her eyes and kissed him back, reaching up to put her arms around his neck as she felt his hands go around her waist. His lips were soft and the kiss was firing up every nerve in her body. She leant against his chest, feeling as if her legs might give way beneath her.

When they pulled apart, a few seconds later, he was smiling.

'Hello, Lily Bennett,' he said.

'Hello, Dr Jake Jordan.'

'This is all highly unethical. Doctors aren't meant to arrange furtive encounters with patients' relatives.'

'Don't worry. I'm not going to tell anyone.'

They sat on the bench and Jake pulled a rucksack onto his lap. 'I've got hot chocolate or wine,' he said. 'I didn't know which you'd prefer, so I thought I'd cover both bases.'

She laughed. 'It's bloody freezing, so I ought to have hot chocolate, but I think I'd rather start with wine.'

'Good,' he said as he produced a bottle and two glasses. 'Just don't neck it quite as quickly as you did the other night. I want you to remember some of our conversation this time.'

'Oh God, I'm sorry,' she said, watching him pour the wine. 'I'm so embarrassed about how I behaved. I haven't been that drunk in years, honestly. And I want you to know that I don't make a habit of falling into bed with men I hardly know.'

'Glad to hear it,' he said, as their glasses clinked. 'I don't make a habit of falling into bed with women I hardly know, either.'

As darkness fell across the lake, lights flickered on around them. She turned sideways, watching his face as he talked, their shoulders touching. It was so cold, they could see their breath creating tiny puffs of cloud in the air.

'At the risk of making you repeat every word you said to me the other night, tell me about you,' she said. 'How long have you lived here?'

'Eleven years. My wife's family live up here – ex-wife, should I say. She was working in Penrith so I relocated when we got married.'

'What's her name?'

'Claire.'

'Has it been amicable?'

'Mostly. We drifted apart over the years. We tried to have children but it didn't work out, and after a while we found there was nothing tying us together any longer.'

'I'm sorry,' said Lily.

'No need to be. I still love her, but I haven't been in love with her for a long time, and she feels the same about me. I'm ready to move on. It hasn't been much fun dividing up our lives and selling our home, but at least we've managed to stay civil with each other. It could have been much worse. It sounds like things were pretty awful for you?'

Lily grimaced. 'Did I bore you with all that the other night? Sorry.'

'You didn't say much, but it sounds like your husband was a shit.' Jake picked up the wine bottle and topped up their glasses.

'He really was.' Lily sipped at her wine. 'He still is. Eleanor is very like him and they've always got on so well. I felt like a spare wheel for most of her childhood. She blamed me after the divorce – although it was Nick who'd had an affair – but we don't ever seem to have got past any of that. When she was a teenager, I hoped our relationship would improve once she grew up and left home, but she's twenty-six and there are no signs of that happening yet.'

'She's certainly forceful, your daughter.'

'Yup, and convinced she knows the best way to do everything. I really didn't want her to come up here, but she just rages through life, doing whatever she wants.'

'How does your mum get on with her?'

'She loves her, obviously. Eleanor is her only grandchild. But she has always been frustrated by her behaviour, and it used to make her angry when I was upset by something Eleanor did or said.'

'Used to?'

Lily nodded. 'I think it still does, but that's the thing about dementia. Mum's not the person she was a year ago, and it gets harder to know what she's feeling or thinking. She has moments of total clarity, when she's just like the person I've always known. Then she'll have a day when her memory is appalling and she's confused and can't carry out a basic task, like loading the washing machine. I went over to her flat the other week and found she'd put all the dirty mugs and glasses in the fridge. When I found them and tried to sort it out, she got furious and threw a glass against the wall. The hardest thing is that she's aware all this is happening to her, and I know it terrifies her. She doesn't want to lose herself – any more than I want to lose her.'

Jake put his arm around her shoulders and pulled her closer. 'I'm sorry,' he said. 'It's such a cruel condition. Are you both getting plenty of support?'

'We've had a diagnosis, but there's not much else they can offer us at the moment,' Lily said. 'That's why I agreed to make this trip. I was dreading it, to be honest, but I thought it was possibly the last chance we'd have to spend proper time together while she was still able to enjoy it. She's writing a book about her life – did I tell you that? Actually, I think she mentioned it, when you came to see her. I have no idea what's in there, but it's making her happy.'

The wine was finished, so Jake pulled a flask from the rucksack. 'Pudding,' he said, handing her a mug of steaming hot chocolate.

Lily laughed and wrapped her hands around it; she hadn't realised how cold she'd grown. 'This trip was so important to Mum. I know I have to take her home again, once she's better, but there are other places she wants to visit. Even though I know she's not up to doing that, it makes me feel guilty for bringing things to an end. I think I've let her down.'

'I doubt anyone else would see it that way. It seems to me, you're a very good daughter.'

'No, I'm really not. But I do love her very much, and I want to help her with this book. I'm sure it's doing her good.'

When the hot chocolate was gone, he packed everything back

into the rucksack and they walked slowly along the edge of the lake, his arm carelessly thrown across her shoulders, her arm tucked around his waist. It felt strange to be this close to a man. She had never wanted to let Dave get anywhere near, let alone put his arm around her, and even when they'd been together, she and Nick had never been a touchy-feely couple. But right now, she realised how much she had missed being physically close to another person; being one entity rather than two lonely individuals. Every now and then people walked past in the opposite direction: dog walkers, other couples, once a gaggle of squawking teenage girls. Lily smiled at them all, keen to share her happiness.

Just before 9pm, they walked up the hill towards the guest house. Lily pulled Jake back beneath the trees across the road from Glenmorrow. It was highly unlikely Eleanor or the Campbells would be looking out of windows at this time of night – anyway, they wouldn't be able to make out much in the darkness – but she didn't want anyone to see them. She stood up on her toes and kissed him, then drew away again. This was all so strange. She didn't know what to say, what to do. Could she ask to see him again? Would he want that, or had tonight just been a bit of fun for him, a way to pass an evening when there was nothing much on the TV and he was bored with sitting alone in his hotel room?

The possibility was slightly shocking, the last couple of hours had meant so much more to her. But maybe that was her own stupid fault? She was launching into something that had no future and would only end in tears.

'So!' she said.

'So!' he replied. 'Guess I'll say goodnight then.'

They stood for a couple of seconds, the silence stretching between them. Considering the fact they'd been rolling around naked in a hotel bed just a couple of nights ago, standing here like this so awkwardly felt all wrong, but Lily didn't know what to do about it.

She knew she was falling for this man. It wasn't just the way he looked – although staring up at his floppy fringe and his wide smile made her pulse race. It wasn't how he treated her either – although it was wonderful to be with someone who clearly respected her and was vaguely interested in hearing her talk about herself. But those things were just part of a bigger picture: there was so much else, like his voice – low and a little gravelly, hugely sexy – and the sound of his laugh, which started as a rumble and immediately turned into a huge, deep guffaw that was so infectious she couldn't help laughing along. There was the way he looked at her, and the way his arm felt so strong and muscular around her shoulders. Then there were all the things she'd started finding out about him as a human being: he was bright and interesting to talk to, he had great sense of humour – he'd had her doubled up earlier when he told her a story about a cycling trip he'd recently taken with his best friend from medical school. He was also incredibly self-aware – he'd been almost painfully open and honest when talking about his failed marriage and acknowledging the part he played in it.

So far, what little she'd seen, heard – and felt – of this man, he was the whole package. But Lily had no idea whether he felt the same way about her. Even if he did, they couldn't have any kind of future together.

'Well, thanks for a lovely evening,' she said, hearing the formality in her own voice, not sure where it was coming from.

He seemed to stiffen a little, or was that just her imagination?

'It's been a pleasure,' he said. 'Good to see you.'

'I'd better get back inside. Mum and Eleanor have probably been at each other's throats for hours.'

He smiled and nodded. 'Hope it's not too battle-scarred in there.'

'Well, goodnight then!' She turned and walked away, feeling his eyes boring into her back, desperate to stop and run back to him, to fling her arms around his waist and bury her head in the collar of his coat. But she made herself keep walking. As she went up the steps to the front door of Glenmorrow, she couldn't resist turning around. He was already walking away from her back down the road and, as she watched, he disappeared into the darkness.

CHAPTER TWENTY-FIVE

'HOW LONG DO you think we're going to be stuck here?' Eleanor crossed her arms in front of her chest. 'There's no way she can go home yet, but I'm supposed to be in London this weekend seeing a show with Paul, and next week I really need to go back into the office. Being stuck in this godforsaken place is far from ideal.'

'It's not godforsaken, it's beautiful,' said Lily.

'Whatever. The fact is, being here is really inconvenient.'

'No one asked you to come!'

'That's as maybe. But I'm here now, so I'm not going to leave you to deal with everything on your own. I'm just saying it's bloody irritating.'

Lily sighed. It was typical of Eleanor to give with one hand, then take away again with the other. She clearly felt she was being helpful, and it must have cost her a fortune to travel up from Brighton and stay in the rather exclusive Roxborough Hotel up the road. But, although it had been her decision to make the journey, it seemed as if she still couldn't resist making Lily feel bad about it.

They were sitting at a table in the Campbells' dining room,

waiting for lunch. Eleanor hadn't been keen on the idea, but it was pouring with rain and neither of them wanted to get soaked going out to buy a sandwich. The only alternative was balancing another of Joan's trays on the edge of an armchair in Moira's bedroom, and Lily didn't feel she could cope with that either.

'Ladies!' beamed Archie, flying through the swing door from the kitchen bearing two plates. 'A little something to put a smile on your faces on such a miserable day.'

He put down the plates in front of them, then stepped back and stretched out his arms, as if he was about to launch into song. 'Ta da!' he said. 'Quiche à la Campbell, with leafy greens and scalloped sweet baby tomatoes drizzled with a garlic and oil jus.'

'Gosh,' said Lily. 'Thank you.'

When he'd disappeared into the kitchen again, leaving the door swinging energetically in his wake, Lily looked up and her eyes met Eleanor's. They both snorted with laughter.

'Shh!' whispered Lily, feeling the disapproving glare from an elderly couple at a table by the window.

'What *is* he like?' Eleanor said, picking up her fork and prodding the food. 'How are these tomatoes "scalloped"? They've just been chopped in half. As for the jus – it looks like French dressing to me.'

'It's not exactly haute cuisine, is it? You'd be better off eating at the Roxborough.'

'That's fine,' said Eleanor, cutting into her quiche. 'I'd rather eat with you.'

Lily looked at her daughter in surprise; that had almost sounded friendly. She snuck quick glances at Eleanor as they ate. She had been a pretty little girl, who'd turned into a beautiful woman with defined cheekbones, large green eyes and an almost perfect nose. But, despite what Moira had said the other night, Lily couldn't see anything of herself in her daughter. There was so much of Nick in those features. It probably wouldn't hurt quite as much if Eleanor had less of her father's personality as well.

Out of nowhere, she suddenly remembered the two of them sitting across from each other at a similar hotel lunch table, many years previously. They'd all been in Sidmouth, on a week's break during the school holidays. Eleanor was eight and loved dressing up in her best clothes to eat in the restaurant. It had been a strangely peaceful week – endless sunshine and days spent on the beach, no arguments, hardly any childish tantrums from either Eleanor or her father. Lily remembered feeling more relaxed than she had in a long time. One day, Nick had booked a fishing trip and, while he was away, Lily and Eleanor had eaten lunch together in the restaurant. She had sat across the table from her daughter, listening to her chat about rock pools and stinky seaweed. She'd just found a starfish on the beach and was writing a story about it. Her eyes lit up as she went into detail about the plot and Lily had sat in silence, soaking up the animation and enthusiasm, bursting with love for the independent, bright little girl who had so much ahead of her. That had been the last family holiday they'd taken during which Lily had been unaware they weren't a proper family anymore; a few weeks after they got back to Brighton, Lily had learnt Nick was having an affair. It probably wasn't the first, and she already sensed it wasn't going to be the last.

Archie's quiche was actually rather good. After lunch they went back upstairs to Moira's room. She had hardly touched her food and her chest was sounding wheezy.

'I'm not sure the antibiotics are working,' Eleanor said. 'Do you think we ought to get that doctor back again?'

'No!' said Lily, immediately realising she'd sounded too abrupt. 'I mean, I doubt we could get someone here until tomorrow now, and it's probably too soon to tell whether the pills are having any effect. Let's leave it.'

'I'd quite like to see that lovely man again,' said Moira. 'He was extremely handsome.'

'Let's not bother him,' Lily said.

She and Jake had been exchanging texts since she got back from the lake last night – dozens of texts. Lily had started it, lying awake in bed on her own, wishing she was lying beside Jake in his hotel room. She was kicking herself for not being more forthcoming with him and being so formal when they said goodbye. So what if he might have knocked her back? She was forty-seven years old and was way past the hormonal posturing and emotional game-playing she might have indulged in twenty years earlier. Plus, she was hundreds of miles from home and due to be leaving Keswick soon and would never see this man again. So, what did she have to lose? After writing and deleting at least six versions of a text, she finally pressed send, then immediately wished she hadn't done it.

> Lovely to see you this evening, Dr Jake xx

Less than twenty seconds later, her heart lurched into her throat as a reply pinged in:

> You too, Ms Bennett. Thank you for joining me for wine and hot chocolate x

Oh my God, there was an x at the end! She squealed out loud in the darkness, then laughed at herself; what an idiot! She left it a couple of minutes before replying:

> You make excellent hot chocolate xx

It was another couple of minutes before his reply pinged in:

It's all about who you're sharing it with x

She read the message again and again and again. He must be keen. He sounded keen? He wouldn't be replying if he wasn't. Or maybe he was just bored.

'Lily Bennett, stop being so bloody paranoid!' she said to herself, her voice sounding very loud in the poky little bedroom at the back of Glenmorrow.

More texts followed; neither of them declared undying love – although she was sorely tempted – but the ongoing conversation was fun and familiar and made Lily feel happier than she had felt in a long time. They finally signed off shortly before 1am, and he had texted just after dawn to say good morning and tell her he was heading out on a run round the lake if she wanted to join him. She'd told him she didn't do running of any kind and then added a couple of heart and smiley face emojis. As soon as she'd pressed send, she wanted to drag the text back and replace it with something more sophisticated. But his reply – a row of *xoxox* – made her smile and she had run her finger across the screen, as if it would bring her closer to the man who'd sent the message.

Today she was feeling the after-effects of too little sleep and her head was stuffed full of an excess of Jake. Throughout the morning she kept remembering snippets of their conversation, the sound of his laugh, the way he subconsciously touched his forefinger to his right eyebrow when he was about to answer a question.

But now Eleanor was suggesting they call him back to see Moira, and although this wonderful man had taken up residence inside her head, she needed to keep him away from her mother and her daughter – the prospect of the four of them being in the same room again was enough to give her palpitations.

'Mum, what's the matter with you?' snapped Eleanor. 'It's not as if we have to pay for the doctor to visit.'

'That's not what I meant!'

'We should get him here again to check the antibiotics are doing their job. We need to be sure Granny will be well enough to travel. I'm going back to the Roxborough to do some work, so I'll call the surgery from there.'

'I just don't think there's any need...' Lily began. 'He must be very busy, with so many patients to see.' But Moira was coughing again on the bed in front of them.

'I can't believe you're being so selfish!' Eleanor said. 'I'm going to call to arrange it and that's the end of it.'

'I'm not bloody well going home!' Moira said. 'But I don't mind seeing that handsome doctor again. He did have lovely warm hands.'

After Eleanor left, Lily sat in the armchair. Her book lay open in her lap but she kept finding her eyes had skimmed across an entire page without taking in any of it. Moira was scribbling away in her notebook, chuckling to herself every now and then.

'He was good-looking, back then,' she said, suddenly.

'Who was?'

'Oliver! He had all that lovely hair and he was very muscly. Not like he is now – that belly is shocking.'

'I guess age catches up with us all.'

'Well, I haven't let myself go like that!'

Lily laughed. 'No, that's true.'

'You've got his height,' Moira said, staring at Lily across the room. 'Not the hair, yours is darker. But maybe the chin is similar as well.'

Lily's book fell off her lap onto the floor.

'I think I'm going to have a little doze now,' Moira said, carefully closing her notebook and putting it on the bedside table, She wriggled herself down in the bed, crossing her hands in front of her chest and closing her eyes. 'Just a quick nap.'

Lily's mouth had fallen open. She leant forward and picked up her book, straightening out the pages which had creased as it hit the carpet. Maybe she hadn't heard that properly? Or she might have totally got the wrong end of the stick; it was probably just Moira, wittering on in her usual way, and Lily had read more into what she was saying than she should have done.

But she knew she hadn't.

Her mother started to snore, the rasps loud in the silent bedroom. Lily got up from the chair and tiptoed across to the bathroom, clicking on the overhead light and shutting the door behind her. She stood with her hands on the basin, leaning forward so she was inches away from the mirror, close enough to examine every pore on her skin, every freckle, every tiny wrinkle. Her pulse was racing, blood pumping around her head making her temples thud.

She stared at this face she knew so well, the face she'd looked after so carefully: cleansing, toning, moisturising, adding subtle touches of eyeliner and mascara every morning. The face was starting to age, but it marked out who she was and where she came from. She had never thought she looked like either of her parents – though people had told her she was a lot like Moira when she was younger. But Lily couldn't remember anyone ever suggesting she looked like her father.

It could be that she needed to study this face with someone else in mind. Maybe she should be searching for traces of Oliver?

CHAPTER TWENTY-SIX

LILY HAD SPENT another fitful night in the back bedroom at the guest house. This time there were two men whose faces kept popping up in her head: Jake and Oliver. Imagined clinches with the former were definitely more enjoyable than worries about the latter. When she got out of bed, she was so exhausted everything ached and the beginning of a headache was playing around above her right eye.

But as she pulled back the curtains, daylight streamed into the room and she could see blue skies up above. She threw open the window, but quickly closed it again as she caught the stench of rubbish coming from the huge industrial wheelie bins below. Never mind, at least it wasn't raining, and since she was having to stay for longer than planned in Keswick, she really ought to make the most of it. The prospect of getting out of this claustrophobic guest house and being in the fresh air for a couple of hours was appealing. But realistically, that wasn't going to happen; she still didn't feel she could leave Moira, so the best she was going to manage was a quick walk up and down the road. Unless she asked Eleanor to stand in for a while? The two of them had got along quite well for most of yesterday – apart from a brief spat about whether or not to request another doctor's visit. But before that, Eleanor had been almost mellow over lunch, and later that afternoon the two of them had sat on either side of Moira's bed, showing her old photos on their phones, laughing at pictures taken of them all in fancy dress seven years ago, at Gordy's 50th birthday party.

Lily decided it was worth a try, but she also knew she couldn't give Eleanor any wriggle room. She typed out a quick text:

> Hello darling, hope you slept well. I need you to come and sit with Granny for a couple of hours this morning, I'm going out. See you about 10 xx

She felt quite proud of herself once she'd pressed send, and wasn't at all surprised when a furious reply pinged in a few seconds later; Eleanor was very busy and had some important work calls to make and the last place she could afford to be this morning was in Granny's stuffy room at the guest house. Usually, Lily would have backed off straight away, and apologised for even daring to ask for such an outlandish favour. But she was feeling a bit bolshy today, and for once she stuck to her guns.

> Sorry about that, El, but I'm going out and someone has to be here. Thank you! xx

She stood holding her mobile for a minute or so, waiting for a flashing grey bubble to indicate that Eleanor was typing out a rude response. But there was nothing. Ridiculously, Lily felt guilty, even though she knew that was silly – she had nothing to feel guilty about, she wasn't asking for much. She wandered into the en suite and picked up her toothbrush, wishing she had someone with whom she could share this momentous news. After all these years, it felt as if she had finally found a way to deal with her truculent daughter.

Two hours later she was stomping up a well-worn path to the Castlerigg Stone Circle, a couple of miles out of town. After so much rain, the ground was sodden and it was hard work, but the air was fresh and the views exhilarating. When she finally reached the top, she could see across the surrounding fells for miles. There were a handful of other walkers around, including an elderly couple who reached the circle just after she did and seemed barely out of breath, whereas Lily was panting so hard, she struggled to speak.

'Jelly Baby?' asked the woman, holding out an open packet. 'Looks like you need the sugar.'

'Thank you,' Lily said, dipping her fingers into the packet. 'Although I think I need a whole new pair of lungs.'

She sat up there for a while, wondering what Jake was doing. She'd texted him earlier, to ask if he was free to go on a walk. She'd guessed he would be working, but her spirits still fell when she read his reply:

At the surgery all day. But have fun x

In a way, this was good news. However desperate she was to see him, at least this meant it would be a different doctor who visited Moira this afternoon for the home visit booked by Eleanor.

Every now and then Oliver flashed into her mind, but she tried not to let him stay there. Before the conversation with Moira yesterday afternoon, she had felt nothing but pity when she pictured the overweight, lonely old man sitting in his stained clothes in his filthy house. But now the thought of him made her feel uneasy – almost anxious. Could that man really be her father?

She had plenty of photographs of herself as a young child with Moira and Ken. When she was back in Brighton again, she would get them all out and study them properly. Although she must have looked at those pictures dozens of times over the years, she'd never been looking for anything specific. She thought they were just normal family snapshots of a little girl and her parents – on the beach, at theme parks, gathered with groups of friends. She had never looked to see if she bore any resemblance to her father, because she never had the faintest idea she needed to.

Going back down to Keswick from Castlerigg took half as long as it had taken her to go up, although her knees were aching by the time she got into the town. As she walked along the main street, she found herself staring at every passing car and peering through every shop window. Somewhere in this place was Jake Jordan and she was so obsessed with the man that she kept expecting to see him around every corner. She wasn't just expecting it – she was yearning for it. It was ridiculous, he wasn't going to be out and about. Right now, he would be stuck inside the local GP's surgery, dealing with a long stream of bumps, bruises, bacteria and blood clots. But that didn't stop her hoping that he might walk out of a shop up ahead, or jump from a car as it pulled along beside her on the street.

When Lily got back to Glenmorrow, Eleanor was perched on the end of the bed, watching Moira, who was standing by the bay window in her nightie.

'It goes like this!' she was saying, sticking one leg out behind her and whirling both arms around to keep her balance.

'Mum! What on earth are you doing?'

Moira glanced over at her and tutted. 'Lily, do be quiet. I'm showing Eleanor how to do a Tree pose. I saw it on the television the other day.'

'I'm not sure that's a Tree,' Eleanor said. 'I think you need to stand upright for that, Granny. Are you sure it's not a Warrior?'

Moira put her foot back on the carpet again and stuck her hands on her hips. 'Don't be an idiot, Eleanor. What do I have to worry about? It's a fucking Tree.'

'You must be feeling a bit better at least, if you're out of bed doing yoga,' Lily said, taking off her coat and throwing it over the back of the chair by the desk. 'I'm not sure we really need to drag the doctor out again.'

Moira's shoulders visibly slumped and she started to cough.

'Mum, I know you're putting that on,' Lily said.

Her mother moved back towards the bed, coughing pathetically into her hand as she went. 'Oh dear. I think I've overdone it. I shouldn't have tried to show you that, Eleanor. This cough is bad again now, very bad. I really do need to see that lovely doctor man.'

'Granny, you're such a fraud!' Eleanor said. 'You've hardly coughed at all in the last hour!'

'It's getting worse,' said Moira, climbing back into bed and pulling the covers up towards her neck. 'I hope he comes soon. Such nice eyes he had, and lovely warm hands too.'

'He's not coming at all, Mum, he's not on duty. It will be someone else,' said Lily.

'How do you know that?'

Lily realised they were both staring at her, and knew she was blushing. 'I don't! I'm just guessing. I'm sure he won't be on duty today, if he was doing home visits on Thursday.'

Moira narrowed her eyes. 'Lily, that is bollocks.'

'Mum, don't be rude! I'm just saying I don't think it will be the same doctor.'

Moira sighed deeply and crossed her arms in front of her

chest. She turned to Eleanor and raised her eyes to the ceiling. 'Your mother is up to something,' she said. 'She's being very strange indeed.'

Eleanor nodded. 'She's right, Mum. You are being weird.'

CHAPTER TWENTY-SEVEN

HALF AN HOUR LATER, they'd nearly finished drinking their tea when there was a knock on the door.

'I'll get it.' Eleanor got up and went across to open it. 'Oh, hello, Dr Jordan! Nice to see you again, come in.'

Lily spluttered English Breakfast all over herself and the carpet.

'Lily!' Moira exclaimed. 'What a mess!'

As she wiped tea from her chin, Lily looked up and saw Jake grinning at her. She glared at him, aware her cheeks were bright red again. 'What are you doing here?' she said.

'How rude!' exclaimed Moira. 'You would tell me off if I was that rude. Ignore her, doctor. She's in an odd mood today. It's very good to see you, I must say. We weren't expecting you because my daughter thought a different doctor was coming?'

'I ended up doing the home visits again this afternoon,' Jake said, sitting down on the bed beside her. 'My colleague is off sick. You seem much better, Mrs Spencer.'

'Well, I'm still coughing,' said Moira, clearing her throat and harrumphing. 'I think you might have to listen to my chest again. Shall I take off this nightie?'

'No!' chorused Lily and Eleanor, again, at the same time.

'Well, I can already hear from your breathing that your chest has less of a rattle. But it would probably be a good idea to take a quick look at you.'

'Excellent!' said Moira. 'Are those hands all nice and warm?'

'Oh, God,' Eleanor groaned. 'Please tell me this isn't happening.'

Lily went into the bathroom, keeping her eyes averted from the bed as she went past. She stood in front of the basin and angrily swiped at her top with a hand towel, only managing to smear the tea and make the stain larger. What was he doing here? Her heart was pounding She was obviously delighted to see him, although humiliated at being placed on the back foot. How embarrassing she'd reacted like that! She'd been in pretty much constant contact with this man over the last couple of days, so he must have thought she was a right idiot when she spat tea all over herself at the sight of him. On the other hand, when he found out the rota had changed, he could have warned her? He knew Moira was on the home visit list, he also knew she would be here; he could have sent her a text so she wouldn't be quite so surprised when he walked through the door. He probably just hadn't thought about it. This whole situation was so peculiar. She had spent most of the morning thinking about this man, and he'd taken up permanent residence in her head – not just the image of him, but the things he'd said, the conversations they'd had, the regular flow of texts they'd been sending. But despite all that, it felt strange to suddenly have him here, just a few feet away, with his stethoscope on her mother's chest.

She finished trying to wipe her top. She could hear the hum of voices outside in the bedroom. Jake was talking, and then Moira was laughing at whatever he'd said. She ran her fingers through her hair to tidy it and took some deep breaths. She could cope with this, it was all fine. She would go back out into the bedroom and act normally, as if nothing was wrong and Jake was just the local GP who'd come to check up on her mother. She smiled at herself in the mirror and tilted her head to one side, nodding as if she was listening to their conversation. Apart from the brown tea stain splattered across her chest, she didn't look too bad.

'That's good to hear,' Eleanor was saying, as Lily opened the door. 'I'm sorry we called you out again, but yesterday there didn't seem to be any improvement. It's only today that Granny has started to seem better.'

'It's not a problem.' Jake stood up and began putting things back into his bag. 'That's what we're here for, and it's always better to be safe than sorry. It has been a pleasure to see you ladies again.' He turned to where Lily was standing in the bathroom door. 'I was just telling your mother, her chest is improving and she's making good progress.'

Lily stared at him; her heart was beating so hard and fast that she was sure Eleanor would be able to hear it from across the room. 'That's great,' she said.

'I know you're all keen to get back to Brighton, so I'd suggest that, if she takes it easy for another couple of days, Mrs Spencer should be fine to travel by Monday.' His eyes were boring into her as he spoke.

'Monday? Two more days?' Lily heard her voice catching in her throat.

'That's great news, isn't it?' said Eleanor. 'Only two more nights in this awful place, Granny, then we can get you back home.'

'I'm not bloody well going home!' said Moira.

'I'm afraid you are,' said Eleanor. 'This road trip of yours is well and truly over. Now we know you're on the mend, we can make plans to get you back to Brighton.'

'You can't tell me what to do!'

'I can and I will. Anyway, it's not just me. Mum agrees that she needs to take you home.'

Lily was aware of them sniping at each other in the background, but couldn't take her eyes off Jake. He was still staring at her too, and she wished she could read his mind, find out what was going on in his head. He looked tired today, the bags beneath his eyes were more pronounced than when she'd last seen him; although maybe it was because they were indoors, under artificial light. The last time she'd stared into these eyes, two nights ago, they'd just walked up the hill from the lake and had stood lurking in the darkness on the other side of the road. She wanted to reach out and touch him, run her fingers down his cheek, put her hand around the back of his neck and drag him towards her. But with Moira and Eleanor right beside them, she couldn't make a move.

'Two days?' she said again. She was near enough to smell his aftershave – that damn smell was addictive. She would have to find out what it was, so she could go and buy a bottle and surround herself with it, once he was no longer around. The very thought of him not being around, the prospect of having to slam a door on something the two of them had only just started to explore, made her want to cry.

He nodded. 'Yes, that should be plenty of time, the course of antibiotics will be finished by then. After that, there's no reason why you and your mother shouldn't make the journey home.'

She nodded. She tried to smile, but her mouth felt wobbly, so she pursed her lips together and dropped her eyes to the carpet. He stood in front of her for another second or two, then she saw his feet moving away and only looked up again as he opened the door; he went through it without turning back.

As the door clicked shut behind him, Moira and Eleanor were still arguing.

'You can't force me to do anything I don't want to do!' Moira was saying.

'No one is forcing you to do anything, Granny. You just need to be sensible.'

'You're forcing me. You always force me.'

Lily walked across to the bay window and looked down into the parking area. Below her the front door slammed, and she watched as Jake came out and down the steps and began to walk away from the guest house.

There were so many reasons why she should make the journey home, and they all involved Lily being a selfless, dutiful daughter – as usual – and putting her mother first. There were also many reasons why she shouldn't make the journey home – and they all involved Jake, and would mean Lily making a stand and putting herself first for a change. She just wasn't sure she was ready to do that yet.

CHAPTER TWENTY-EIGHT

> Meet me for a drink? Xx

HAVING SENT THE TEXT, Lily sat holding her phone, watching for the little grey dots to appear, which would confirm he'd seen it and was writing a reply. Just as she was on the point of giving up, there it was.

> Right now? x

> Yes, right this minute. Well, 10 minutes. In the bar at the Hamilton xx

Lily couldn't believe what she'd done, but was as excited – and nervous – as a teenager who'd told her parents she was staying over at her best mate's but was actually smuggling a bottle of cheap vodka out of the house to take to her first proper party. She dragged a brush through her hair and whizzed some eyeliner quickly along the top of her eyelids.

She was suddenly desperate for a gin and tonic, some Dutch courage before she saw him, but the facilities at the Glenmorrow didn't stretch to minibars in the bedrooms. If she wanted a drink of anything other than tap water, she'd need to go into the residents' lounge downstairs and ring the bell to summon Archie or Joan. There was no way she could risk that – she'd almost certainly get drawn into a long conversation with them, and after she'd left, she could just imagine them raising those Scottish eyebrows in tandem and discussing the fact that, because she was a middle-aged woman drinking alone in a guest house, she must surely be a functioning alcoholic. She didn't really care what the Campbells thought of her, but could do without the hassle.

She pulled on her coat and went out of her bedroom, tiptoeing along the corridor and poking her head through Moira's door. Her mother was asleep, a soft snoring coming from under the duvet. Perfect. She was highly unlikely to wake up, and anyway Lily wasn't going to be out all night this time; this was going to be just one drink, she told herself as she ran down the main stairs. She just needed to see him for an hour.

By the time she walked through the front door of the Hamilton Hotel, her hair was dishevelled again and the skin on her cheeks was numb. The temperature had dropped today and a strong breeze had picked up around the lake. Keswick felt grim and exceptionally wintry.

A group of people were standing by the bar and several of the tables were taken – it was busier tonight than it had been earlier in the week. Jake was sitting in the far corner – in the same chair he'd been in when he'd glanced up and caught her eye as she came through this door five nights ago. Her pulse quickened at the sight of him and she walked across. He stood up too quickly and his chair toppled backwards, hitting the wooden floor with a crash.

'Drunk already, Dr Jordan!' yelled a man who was sat on one of the bar stools.

Jake grimaced at him and turned to pick up the chair. Lily

suddenly realised he would know people here tonight. Of course he would. Not only was he one of the town's GPs, but he had been staying in this hotel for weeks – he'd be a well-known face. Was this going to be awkward for him, being seen with her? Oh hell, why hadn't she thought to suggest somewhere else. He gestured to the empty chair beside his; he did look a little uncomfortable.

'I'm so sorry, this wasn't the right place to meet, was it?' she said. 'Do you want to go somewhere else?'

'No, it's fine! Sit down.' He picked up the bottle of wine on the table. 'We can't go anywhere until we've had this. Although, at the rate you drink, Lily Bennett, we'll be out of here in fifteen minutes.' He was smiling again now, the skin on either side of his beautiful brown eyes crinkling as he looked at her. Those eyes! She smiled back at him, shrugging off her coat and hanging it on the back of the chair. He leant forward and poured wine into a second glass and pushed it across to her.

'Cheers, Ms Bennett. This was a nice surprise.'

'Was it?' she said before she could stop herself. 'I know it was a bit sudden. Sorry. I was just sitting up there, in that awful bedroom in the guest house and I really wanted to see you.'

'I'm glad you did,' he said, as they clinked their glasses together. 'Very glad.'

They took a sip of the wine, not taking their eyes off each other. Even in this crowded bar which smelt of woodsmoke and spilt beer, she could smell his aftershave.

'How's your mother?'

'Oh, she seems much better. She got up after you left this afternoon and had an early supper with me downstairs in the dining room, so she's getting her strength back. She also told the Campbells that her piece of steak looked and tasted like a dead rat, so she's definitely feeling more like herself.'

He laughed and put down his glass, reaching his hand

across the table. His fingers found hers and rested on top of them before sliding further forward. She looked down at them as they turned her own hand over and he began to run his thumb across her palm. As she looked up again, he was moving towards her and she closed her eyes as their lips met.

'I'm glad you sent me that text,' he whispered.

'I'm glad I sent it as well.' She couldn't stop herself smiling.

They drew apart again and picked up their wine glasses.

'Is this okay, us being here?' she asked. 'I mean, people obviously know you, and I don't want to embarrass you.'

He nodded. 'Don't worry. I may be a pillar of the local community,' he grinned at her, 'but I'm also a grown-up and I can decide who I spend my time with – and what I do with them.'

'But, what with your wife living here too, and everything.'

'Ex-wife,' he said. 'We're divorced.'

'I know, but it still might be awkward – this is a small community and all that. Everyone knows everyone else's business.'

'That's true enough. But I refer you to my first answer – I'm a grown-up.'

'Is she...' Lily paused. This was really none of her business. 'I mean, I know you told me things were amicable between you, but do your paths still cross? You must have friends in common and you probably bump into each other – Keswick is a small place.'

He nodded and looked down at the table as he twisted the stem of his wine glass between his thumb and forefinger. 'Yup, it happens. But it's all relatively easy because it's just the two of us and there aren't any children involved. I think she's seeing someone else, although she hasn't told me specifically, but a mutual friend hinted at it.'

'How does that make you feel?' asked Lily, not really wanting to hear the answer.

'A bit odd,' he admitted. 'But not in a sad sack, stalking ex-husband sort of way. I'd be lying if I said I didn't still love her, because we shared a lot together, but I'm not in love with her anymore and she's not in love with me. I've already told you that and it's true. Anyway, I can't criticise her for moving on, because I'm sitting here with you, also moving on.'

Lily liked the sound of that. A lot. Although she was cross with herself for letting his words make her feel so happy. What was the point? She was leaving in a couple of days and taking Moira on the 360-mile journey back to Brighton. After which, she would never again see this handsome, gentle, funny man. So, they weren't really moving on, in the traditional sense of the word – because there was nowhere for them to move on to. But that shouldn't stop her enjoying this last, precious little bit of time with him.

She lifted up her glass. 'Cheers,' she said. 'I'm very much enjoying being here with you, Dr Jordan. I just wish we weren't in such a public place so that, to quote my mother, you could put those soft, warm hands all over me.'

She could hardly believe those words had come out of her own mouth – what on earth was happening to her? She had never been this forward with a man in her life. But sod it, life really was too short.

Jake snorted into his wine glass. 'The feeling,' he said, leaning forward to kiss her again. 'Is mutual.'

CHAPTER TWENTY-NINE

'MUM, Eleanor and I have been talking, and we've decided that – now you've got the all-clear – we'll definitely head home on Monday, like Ja... like the doctor suggested.'

Moira crossed her arms and glared at Lily.

'Don't look at me like that. I know you don't want to end this trip early, but you've not been well and we think it's the sensible option.'

Her mother huffed and tipped back her head, staring up at the bedroom ceiling. 'La-la-la. Not bloody listening to you two fuckety fuckwits!'

'Granny, you do need to be reasonable,' Eleanor said. 'We're only thinking of what's best for you – and for Mum as well. This whole business has been pretty stressful for her, you know. She's been very worried about you.'

Lily turned to stare at Eleanor, her eyes wide with surprise; this was all very strange, she wasn't used to them being on the same team about anything. Although, interestingly, her daughter had seemed much calmer and more rational than usual over the last day or so. Maybe it was because there was finally an end in sight to her stay in the Lakes.

'It's a long drive,' continued Eleanor. 'But if we get you on the road first thing on Monday morning, you'll have time to make as many stops as you need to along the way.'

Moira uncrossed her arms, stuck her fingers in her ears and sang more loudly. 'La-la-la, tra-la-dee-dum!'

'Mum! Stop it!'

'La-la-laaaaaa. Not listening!'

Lily walked across to her mother and took hold of her hands, gently moving them away from her head. 'I know you don't want to listen, but you have to. We aren't going to be able to finish this trip now, but we will do it in the spring, I promise.' Moira was staring at her, and Lily saw tears glistening at the edges of her eyes. 'When the weather's better, we will come back here and we'll pick up where we left off. We'll work it all out in advance and we'll go to Durham and to Yorkshire and to all the other places you had on your list.'

She hoped her words sounded believable to her mother; they didn't to her. She was absolutely convinced they wouldn't be able to undertake another trip like this one, however much they planned and prepared. Spring was half a year away, and by that time who knew what sort of state Moira would be in? She was still struggling with her memory, and her temper and unpredictability seemed to be getting worse by the day. The Good Mum/Bad Mum behaviour was never going to go away and Lily doubted that the mother she knew now, would be the same as the one she'd be dealing with in six months' time. It wasn't a prospect she wanted to have to think about, but it was always there in the back of her mind and, while she could keep up a pretence with Moira, she wasn't going to kid herself that whatever lay ahead of them would be easy.

'But what about finishing my book?'

'You will be able to finish it! Spring is just around the corner, it's not long to wait. In the meantime, when we get back home you can spend some time going over all the notes you've made on this trip and then you can write them up in detail, so you're ready to start again.'

'Bamburgh Castle,' whispered Moira. 'Your father and I took you there when you were a year old. We went to Holy Island too. I remember trying to get your pram across the causeway and it was too rocky. In the end your dad went over on his own, and you and I sat on the beach and waited for him.'

'We'll go there, definitely,' Lily said.

'And the Norfolk Broads, do you remember I told you about that?'

'Yes, Mum, but that was just a holiday, nothing exciting happened.'

'Ken fell overboard, that was exciting.'

Lily smiled. 'Yes, I remember you saying.'

'Well, he only fell in up to his knees, so I suppose it wasn't earth-shattering. But I'd still like to go there. It's all for my book.'

'No problem, I promise we will go to the Norfolk Broads.'

Moira sat back in the armchair, nodding. 'That's good then. That's all fine. In that case, we'll do what you want.'

Lily and Eleanor exchanged a quick glance. They hadn't thought it would be this easy, but, the singing outburst aside, Moira was noticeably less strident than she had been yesterday afternoon. After Jake left, her argument with Eleanor seemed to have exhausted her, and she'd looked pale and shrunken, like a woman who had little fight left in her. Now, she wiped her eyes with her fingers and blew her nose noisily on a paper tissue. 'That's good then,' she repeated.

Lily hated seeing her mother upset, and hated even more that she was the cause of it. But there was no other option, they couldn't continue with this journey. The relief was overwhelming because taking Moira home against her will would have been awkward and upsetting. At least now, they could all start to plan their return journey properly.

'There's just one thing...' Moira said.

'What's that?'

'There's somewhere I want to visit, before we leave Keswick.'

'Where's that?'

'The Pencil Museum.'

Eleanor snorted with laughter. 'The *Pencil* Museum? What on earth is that?'

'Don't be thick, Eleanor,' said Moira. 'It's a museum all about pencils.'

'Okay, well that's logical. But, Granny, why do you want to go there?'

'Because I like pencils.'

'Who on earth likes pencils?'

'I do. I like them very much. I have been using pencils to write in my notebook and I like them a great deal more than pens. So, while we're here, I want to go to the Pencil Museum – which is actually world famous. There's a leaflet about it over there on the desk, along with something about bird watching – but I don't want to go and watch any birds.'

Eleanor was standing by the window, arms crossed, shaking her head. 'I've heard it all now. Pencils.' She looked at Lily. 'Please don't tell me we're really going to do this?'

'Fine,' Lily said. 'If that's what you want, Mum?'

'I do.' Moira nodded so vigorously her whole body shook in the armchair. 'And I want you both to come with me. I think pencils will be just what the three of us need.'

CHAPTER THIRTY

'THEN, in 1950, the factory closed and relocated to Yorkshire...'

Lily had tuned out. She knew nothing about graphite, but that lack of knowledge hadn't held her back in any way over the last forty-seven years and she wasn't worried if she didn't do anything to improve on it now. There was a display board on the far wall behind the guide's head. She was too far away to see properly, but the photograph seemed to show a huge sculpture in a city square; presumably it had earnt its place on the wall because the sculpture was made entirely from pencils.

'...by which time, the company had built up a healthy customer base in the Far East and China.' The guide's voice was slow, measured and on the quiet side, which did nothing to liven up his subject matter.

Moira elbowed Lily in the ribs and held the Pencil Museum leaflet up in front of her face. 'See? I told you this would be interesting. This guide person with the big ears has got his photograph on the back here. His ears look even bigger in real life.'

'Shhh! Mum, put that thing down.'

Lily was already going over tomorrow's route in her head. It wouldn't be a complicated drive – mostly motorway – but the campervan wasn't built for speed so it would take at least seven hours, and that was without factoring in stops for fuel, food and Moira's weak bladder. If they left at nine the following morning, they'd be lucky to get home by early evening.

'Of course, the improvement in the quality of the colour was something appreciated from the start by the artistic community...'

Lily could see Eleanor's attention had also drifted; she had her phone out and her head was bent over the screen. It couldn't be work on a Sunday; she was probably texting Paul. She'd reminded Lily earlier that they'd had to cancel their London plans because she was still in Keswick. Lily had apologised – again – but couldn't help feeling irritated, she really didn't think any of this was her fault – she hadn't asked Eleanor to come and stay. Why did her daughter always need to cast blame? Nick had been the same; if something went wrong, it was invariably someone else's fault – usually Lily's, even if she hadn't been directly involved.

She watched her daughter push a stray lock of hair behind her ear, and saw her smile down at the phone screen as her finger flew across it, typing out a reply. It was interesting to be able to watch Eleanor without her knowing she was being observed, and it was good to see her looking relaxed – happy even. However much they bickered and bitched and irritated the hell out of each other, she did love this girl of hers, so very much.

Over the last day or so she'd realised that, despite the fact that they'd been thrown together in Keswick, she was pleased Eleanor had stuck around. The two of them hadn't spent this much time in each other's company for years. Because Eleanor and Paul also lived near Brighton, they'd never needed to stay overnight at Lily's; even when there was a family birthday or other cause for celebration, they rarely hung around for longer than a couple of hours. Last Christmas, they had arrived at Lily's little terraced house just before midday and were gone again by the time the credits were rolling on the King's speech.

It hadn't occurred to Lily until now, but the diluted amount of time they all spent in each other's company, meant they knew little about each other's lives. She obviously knew Eleanor worked for one of the largest legal firms in Brighton, and that she specialised in employment law. But she didn't actually understand what her daughter did on a daily basis, other than yell at people down the phone and hammer away so furiously on her laptop keyboard that she looked as if she was about to break it. But Eleanor was clearly good at what she did; a couple of months ago Paul had mentioned she'd had unexpected success representing a client at a tribunal about unfair dismissal. 'She's a firebrand when she's standing up there, defending someone!' he'd said, proudly. Lily had congratulated Eleanor, who'd brushed it off with a dismissive wave of her hand, and the conversation had ended. But now Lily wished she'd pushed harder and tried to find out more. Over the years she had learnt to back off when she got nothing in return from her daughter, possibly as a form of self-preservation. Eleanor clearly didn't need her, so why bother trying to get closer to her? But, if she was being honest with herself, the lack of communication between them wasn't just Eleanor's fault. It was hard discussing Eleanor's work because Lily had always got the impression that her daughter thought her dim mother wasn't really capable of understanding what she did. But that could just as easily be Lily projecting her own insecurities onto the situation? She suddenly realised that she hadn't once asked Eleanor about work since she'd arrived at the guest house, four days ago. That hadn't been intentional, she just hadn't thought about it. But what if Eleanor actually found that upsetting and misread her mother's reticence as a lack of interest in what she did? Come to think of it, Lily hadn't asked her daughter about the rest of her life either – she hadn't thought to ask what she and Paul had been planning to do during their time in London. She hadn't even asked any general questions, such as whether they'd booked any weekends away or whether Paul was enjoying the new job he'd started a couple of months ago.

It wasn't that she didn't care – she was fond of her daughter's boyfriend and had always admired the patience and tolerance with which he dealt with Eleanor and her tantrums. But even when the two of them had been sitting together, eating quiche à la Campbell, their small talk had been very small indeed. It was as if they'd both become so used to squabbling and picking holes in whatever the other one did or said, they'd forgotten how to have normal conversations. They'd forgotten how to care for each other, like mothers and daughters were supposed to do. It meant that the distance between them – created by years of existing as a dysfunctional family unit – had grown larger recently, and they hadn't even noticed.

The guide was now leading them into another room. 'This is the biggest pencil in the world!' he was saying, pointing towards an outsize model, suspended from the ceiling. 'Can anyone guess how long it is?'

'Three miles long!' yelled a small child, and everyone laughed. Lily met his mother's eye and smiled at her.

She must do something to improve her relationship with Eleanor. Maybe the best thing to do was start talking to her daughter about her own work? She never bothered doing that because she'd got the impression years ago that Eleanor thought the job at the garden centre was lowly and beneath her. But she loved being at Beautiful Blooms and was proud of the part she'd played there. Maybe she should talk about it a bit more and explain how happy it made her? She might even mention

Gordy's relationship woes to Eleanor. She was pretty sure that, when she started talking about Hilary walking out, her daughter would give an exasperated eye-roll and suggest Gordy needed to get a grip on himself. But she didn't actually know that for a fact; Eleanor might just be sympathetic?

The guide had announced the actual length of the gigantic pencil – Lily wasn't concentrating and had missed it – and was now taking questions from the group. Eleanor had moved forward to stand beside her grandmother and, as Lily watched, they both laughed at something Moira was saying, then looked apologetic when the guide frowned in their direction.

After the tour, they came out of the museum through the gift shop. Lily felt sorry for the bored girl sitting behind the till, so bought a pack of sketching pencils which she knew she'd never use.

'Are you ready, Mum?' she called.

Moira was leaning forward peering at a wall display, where hundreds of pencils were arranged by colour. 'It's like a rainbow!' she beamed. 'Who would have thought there were so many different types of blue! Take a photo of me, Lily, by all these pencils. Lily pulled out her phone as Moira puffed out her chest and grinned inanely at her. 'Camembert!' she yelled.

'I'll need copies of all these photographs,' she said, as she turned back to the wall display. 'To go into my book.'

'We'll wait for you outside,' Lily said, and pushed open the door to the courtyard. Eleanor was already out there, sitting on a low wall, her head tilted up towards the sun.

'I was thinking,' Lily said, perching down beside her. 'Why don't you come back with us, in the van?' She was surprised at herself, she hadn't been thinking about that at all, but it suddenly seemed like a good idea.

'I've already got my train ticket,' said Eleanor.

'Can't you get the money back? I just thought it might be a

nice idea, for us all to travel back together. It seems crazy for you to pay for a train, when we're heading the same way anyway.'

'It will be quicker by train.'

'Not necessarily. You've got to change twice, and then you have to get across London with all your luggage.'

'I suppose so, although that's not a big deal,' said Eleanor. 'Anyway, it's not exactly comfortable in that van. It's noisy and the suspension is crap. How would I get on with any work?'

'You could sit at the table in the back and you'd have lots of space,' said Lily. 'It's no different to sitting on a train, except it would be more fun, because you'll have our scintillating company for the journey!'

Eleanor was looking at her, frowning, her head on one side. Lily realised she was probably as taken aback by receiving the invitation, as Lily was by having given it.

'Well, I suppose I could see if I can get the ticket refunded? I'll check on the app.'

'Good! Yes, do that. Excellent. I'm thinking we'll head off after an early breakfast, say about 9am?'

'Okay.' Eleanor seemed bemused by the whole conversation. 'Thank you.'

The shop door swung open and Moira came out, carrying a bulging carrier bag. 'Ah, there you are,' she said. 'I've bought a few pencils.'

'You look like you've bought more than a few,' Lily said, getting up and peering into the top of the bag. 'There are hundreds in there!'

'Oh, don't exaggerate, Lily.' Moira tutted. 'At least these should keep me going over the winter. I've got a lot of writing to do.' As she turned to walk away, the toe of her shoe caught on the edge of a paving slab and although she managed to stop herself falling, she dropped the plastic bag and pencils scattered across the ground.

'My pencils!' she screeched.

'Don't worry, Granny.' Eleanor went down on her hands and knees and began to gather them up.

'They'll all be broken though,' wailed Moira, as Lily held her arm tightly to steady her.

'They're fine!' said Eleanor, putting the final few back into the bag and standing up again. 'Here, good as new. Shall I carry it for you?'

As she took Moira's other arm and helped guide her towards the car park, she looked across and caught Lily's eye.

'*Well done!*' mouthed Lily.

Eleanor grinned back at her.

'If any of those leads are broken, I'm going to come straight back and complain to that guide with the big ears,' Moira was saying. 'Did you see the size of them? He was a proper Mr Spock.'

CHAPTER THIRTY-ONE

SHE HADN'T EXPECTED to hear from Jake all day, but still hoped for it. Every time her phone pinged, she grabbed it and swiped to wake up the screen, desperate to see his name appear, only to slump with disappointment when the message was from someone else. Once it was Gordy, another time her friend Rowena. There was even an automated message from Southern Water saying her next direct debit payment was due. But nothing from the one person in the world she wanted to hear from.

It was ridiculous to be on tenterhooks like this – she knew he wasn't free because, over wine in the Hamilton last night, he'd told her he was going to see his ex-wife to clear up a few final issues; there were documents to be handed over, one last outstanding joint bank account to be closed, a couple of boxes from the house move which had ended up going to her new flat but which belonged to him.

Lily had never met Claire, but she disliked her with an irrational passion. There was absolutely no logic to how she was feeling. Claire and Jake both had copies of their decree absolute, and were starting out on their separate, newly single lives. Jake had told Lily he wasn't in love with his ex-wife and was glad they'd made the break. But he'd also told her he still loved Claire. That wasn't surprising – in many ways it was a good thing, because if they cared about each other, it meant the whole business would be less antagonistic and unpleasant. But Lily was surprised at how much it had hurt to hear that. She wouldn't know Claire if they passed within inches of each other in the street, but the woman's very existence was like a little dark cloud, sitting over her shoulder, overshadowing whatever it was that had been going on with Jake. Which was madness! Claire and Jake had eleven years of shared history; Lily had known him for precisely six days, which was no time at all. Despite the fact that they'd fallen into bed together on the night they met, they still hardly knew each other; she had no rights over this man. But she didn't want Jake to love Claire – even as a friend. Over the course of the last six days, she hadn't been able to stop herself starting to feel very strongly about him. It had been wonderful to snatch an hour and a half in his company last night. He had walked her back up the hill to the Glenmorrow again, once the bottle of wine was finished – she'd been remarkably self-restrained and resisted his attempts to buy them another one – and they stood and hugged beneath the darkness of the trees across the road from the guest house. One long, lingering kiss turning into several more. And ever since she'd woken up this morning, she had been thinking about him and resenting the fact that he couldn't be with her. She wanted this man she hardly knew to love and adore her – and her alone. It was crazy and baseless and stupidly insecure, but she didn't want Jake to be spending Sunday with his ex-wife. Especially when she had spent a good proportion of the same Sunday at the bloody Pencil Museum.

'What now?' asked Moira, as Lily started the van and they drove back into town.

'Now, we go back to the Campbells and you rest.'

'I don't need to rest, I'm fine.'

'You start packing then. We're leaving early tomorrow morning, straight after breakfast. We all need to be ready to get on the road.'

'I'm coming with you,' Eleanor announced, from the back. 'I've cancelled that train ticket.'

'Oh good!' Lily smiled at her in the rear-view mirror. 'I'm so pleased. It will make the journey much nicer for us, won't it, Mum?'

'I suppose so,' Moira said. 'But I have to sit in the front. I get very car sick if I sit in the back of vehicles.'

Lily laughed. 'Mum, I've never known you to get car sick in your life.'

'You don't know everything about me, Lily. You think you do, but I've got complex needs.'

Lily looked in the rear-view mirror and saw Eleanor grinning back at her and rolling her eyes.

'Also,' Moira continued, 'I'm now fairly old, so my comfort has to be your priority.'

'Right,' said Lily. 'Got it.'

'And another thing, Eleanor, you can't keep shouting into that phone of yours. I know what you're like when you're working. You yell at people and cause all sorts of commotion.'

'Granny, that's ridiculous,' said Eleanor. 'I do *not* yell at anyone. I just have to deal with people who sometimes don't know their arse from their elbow, and in certain situations I need to sort them out.'

'Fucking glad I don't have to work for you,' said Moira. 'You're far too bossy.'

'My role is very wide ranging and I have a team behind me, so it involves a certain element of management,' said Eleanor. 'I need to *manage* people.'

'Well, just don't *manage* them too loudly,' Moira said. 'If you need to run the entire bloody world while we're driving down the motorway, please do it quietly.'

Eleanor muttered something else behind them, but Lily couldn't hear what it was.

They were waiting at a set of traffic lights and her phone pinged. She let out a small cry of delight as the screen lit up with his name.

'What's the matter with you?' asked Moira.

'Nothing. I'm fine.' She couldn't read the whole message, but the first line was enough:

Meet me later? I have...

The relief of hearing from him was so immense, she could feel her face flushing and her heart rate increasing as blood pounded faster through her veins. How insane to get this excited by one text! But she felt as if someone had just called to tell her she'd won the entire prize fund of this week's EuroMillions draw. All of a sudden, the sky didn't look so overcast and the streets of Keswick didn't look so grey.

'Lily! People are tooting!' Moira said.

The lights had turned green. She started to drive forward, but her foot slipped off the clutch and the van stalled; she had to turn the key in the ignition three times before the engine roared back into life. 'Sorry, sorry!' she muttered, as horns blared out behind her. They lurched across the junction, just as the lights turned red again.

'Please don't drive this badly on the way home,' said Eleanor. 'I'm beginning to wish I hadn't cancelled that train ticket.'

'I'm beginning to wish I'd bought the train ticket from you,' said Moira.

'Do shut up, both of you.' But Lily couldn't stop smiling. Those five little words on the phone screen were enough to brighten her day, lighten her mood and help her cope with any amount of bad temper and ridicule from her mother and daughter.

CHAPTER THIRTY-TWO

THE FULL TEXT had asked her to meet him down by the lake again at 4pm, further along than before, beside a blue and white boathouse. He had signed off with *xoxox* and there was a ps:

bring armbands!

She was out of breath when she got there, and stood staring around, wondering if she'd got the right place. She was in front of a blue and white boathouse, but there was no sign of Jake. An elderly man was walking past her with a terrier, yapping and straining so hard on the lead it threatened to pull him over, while a group of lads had thrown their bikes on the ground and were lounging on a nearby bench. She could smell their cigarette smoke and hear the tinny sound of music playing through a portable speaker.

Where was he? She pulled out her phone to see if there was another message.

'Lily!'

She turned around, then back again. Then towards the gang of boys.

'Lily, over here!'

And there he was; that handsome man with his floppy fringe and huge smile and still slightly tanned face. He was down by the edge of the lake, standing in a rowing boat.

'What's going on?'

'What does it look like?'

'It looks horribly like you're expecting me to get into that thing with you.'

'Yup. That just about covers it.' He grinned. 'I did tell you to bring your armbands.'

'I know, but I didn't understand. I thought you were just messing about.'

'Come on,' he held out his hand, 'hop on board, Ms Bennett.'

'I don't think this is a sensible idea. I'm not good on water.'

'Me neither.'

'Why do you own a boat then?'

'I don't.' Jake was bending over to pick up an oar and the little wooden boat began to rock from side to side. He put out his arms and windmilled them to get his balance. 'Shit! Hang on a minute. Okay, that's better. Right, grab my hand and leap across. Don't worry, it's fine – I've got you.'

He hadn't. As Lily launched herself off the grass and into the boat, her foot slipped on the wet wooden slats at the bottom and she plummeted forward into him. Her chin hit his chest, his arm caught her on the ear and there were a couple of terrifying seconds when they were both flailing in the air with the boat tipping from side to side, before Jake fell backwards with a thump against the wooden bench seat, while Lily landed on top of him.

'Shit!'

'Ouch! I'm sorry! Are you okay?' She tried to get up, but her legs were tangled with his and one arm was trapped under his waist. As she struggled to free herself, she pushed him further down into the bottom of the boat. He twisted to the side and his knee caught her sharply on the thigh. She could hear howls of laughter coming from the boys on the shore.

Suddenly, both his hands were around her waist and he was dragging her up towards him. She felt the hard buckle of his belt scuff against her jumper and the rasp of his stubble against her cheek. Then their faces were next to each other and they were kissing.

'Oh, Lily,' he breathed, as he pulled away. 'I've missed you.'

'I've missed you too,' she said, and closed her eyes as she leant in to kiss him again.

The laughter from the shore had now turned to catcalls.

'Give her one from me, mate!' yelled one of the lads.

'Let's get out of here,' said Jake. They eventually managed to pull themselves upright, disentangling limbs and straightening clothing. The little rowing boat was still rocking precariously, and Lily sat down on one of the bench seats, stretching out her hands and clinging to both sides. Now she was upright again, she could feel a sharp pain in her right shin and Jake was rubbing his shoulder.

'I really don't like boats,' she said. 'Just to warn you.'

'I don't like them either,' he said. 'This belongs to a friend and I asked him if I could borrow it because I thought it would be fun to go out in it. Something a bit different.'

'Can you row?'

'Of course!' He picked up the oars and shuffled himself carefully into the middle of the seat facing her. 'Well, sort of. Hang on to your hat. Off we go.'

It took a couple of minutes for him to get the hang of using both oars at the same time, then another five minutes to get far enough away from the shore that they could no longer hear the lads calling out to them. Jake wasn't bad at rowing, but it wasn't his finest hour either, and even out here in the increasing darkness of the lake, she could see sweat glistening on his forehead.

'Right, I've had enough of that,' he said, pulling the oars out of the water and stowing them in the bottom of the boat. 'We can drift for a bit. Look in that bag under your seat.'

Lily bent over and found a carrier bag stuffed beneath the bench seat. She pulled it out and found several cans of pre-mixed gin and tonic, together with a large packet of crisps. 'You really do think of everything, don't you?' She smiled at him, wallowing in the warmth of his smile, loving being this close to him again, despite the fact that she was in a rowing boat that was pitching from side to side and the shore looked frighteningly far away. There was an inch of water sloshing around in the bottom of the boat and her trainers were already soaked. 'Is that water meant to be there?' she asked, looking down.

'No idea, but let's hope so.' He cracked open one of the cans and clinked it against hers.

'I'm going to miss you so much.' It hadn't been what she'd intended to say. But it was the only thing going through her mind.

'I'm going to miss you too,' he said. 'Are you still leaving tomorrow?'

She nodded. 'There didn't seem any point in delaying it. Mum is so much better – thanks to you – and once Eleanor and I had persuaded her to give up the road trip, it was just a case of when, rather than if, we set off.'

'Is she okay about heading back home?'

'Not really, but I think she accepts it has to happen. I've promised her we'll do the trip again in the spring, but to be honest I don't know if she'll be up to it then. It's been tricky enough now, and if she gets more forgetful and her behaviour gets worse, I don't think I'll be able to cope with taking her away. But there's no point worrying about that now. We'll just have to play it by ear.'

They ripped open the packet of crisps and took it in turns to pull out handfuls.

'How did your afternoon go, with Claire?' Lily hated herself for asking; she didn't want to know. But she also very much *did* want to know.

'It was fine. I wasn't there for long, she was going to see her parents, so we just did what needed to be done, then I came away again.'

'Is it strange, seeing her now?'

He shook his head. 'Not really. She's in her own flat, it's nothing to do with me. We haven't been properly together for a long time.'

'When Nick moved out, I remember feeling very odd when he came to collect Eleanor. I'd dread seeing him, but also be quite glad to see him – God knows why. It was just that, after all those years, he was so familiar. He'd been a part of my life for such a long time. It wasn't that I was expecting us to get back together, I just didn't know how to be on my own. The future felt scary.'

Jake nodded. 'It was more complicated for you, because you had a child. Claire and I were always very focused on our careers, which is probably why we grew apart in recent years. We both had other things that were important in our lives, and they came to matter more to us than each other.'

'But you still love her.' Lily wanted to bite the words back in again. She stared down at the can in her hands. Why was she ruining this moment?

'I do,' he said. 'But...'

She looked back up at him, as the pause grew longer.

'But?'

'But I'm not in love with her anymore. Whereas, I think I may be a little bit in love with you, Lily.'

She breathed in and tried to swallow at the same time, and ended up choking on her gin. He reached out and clumsily patted her on the back, while she spluttered and started laughing at the horrified expression on his face.

'Don't die on me,' he said. 'I haven't said that to anyone in a long time. Maybe I ought to take it back?'

'Please don't,' she said, clearing her throat one final time. 'Can you just say it again, and I'll try not to overreact this time?'

He grinned at her and reached forward to push a strand of her hair away from her face.

'I think I may be a little bit in love with you, Lily Bennett.'

She wanted to kiss him and hug him and throw her arms around him. She wanted to stand up in the boat and do a little dance in the inch of water slopping around in the bottom. She wanted to sing and cheer and yell the news to the group of lads, now far away on the shore.

'I think I may be a little bit in love with you too,' she said. 'And I'd almost forgotten what that felt like.'

They leant closer and shared a long, gentle kiss. When Jake put his hand up and stroked her cheek, she could feel her heart pounding so loudly, she was sure he must be able to hear it. Eventually, after what seemed like no time at all, they sat back, just inches apart, smiling at each other.

Jake reached down into the plastic bag and popped open two more cans of gin and tonic. 'Cheers,' he said. 'Here's to crazy road trips.'

'Cheers,' Lily echoed. 'And to crazy mothers. If mine hadn't insisted on a crazy road trip, I wouldn't be sitting here now.'

The rowing boat drifted slowly and they watched the sun setting on the far side of the lake. Jake pulled a camping lantern out from the bottom of the boat, turned it on and balanced it on the bench seat beside Lily. She found herself getting light-headed much more quickly than she would have expected. 'Getting drunk on the water is more fun than getting drunk on dry land,' she said, tipping back the can. 'I don't mind that wobbly feeling anymore.'

'We need to start getting back,' said Jake. 'It's going to get dark quickly and it will probably take me ages to row to the shore. I definitely need to practise my oar technique.'

'Just before we do,' Lily said. 'Kiss me one more time.'

She leant forward and put her arms around his neck, feeling his hands move around her waist, one of them working its way up inside her top across her back, his palm warm and soft against her bare skin.

'It's been such a lovely evening,' she said, her voice muffled against the collar of his coat. 'Being with you has made me really happy, thank you. I'll never forget it.'

'You sound like you're saying a proper goodbye?' he said, putting his hand under her chin and turning her face up towards his.

She wasn't sure how to answer him. 'How can this work? I've got to take Mum back home to Brighton in a couple of days and you've got your practice here.'

'I'm not tied to Keswick,' he said, gently. 'Claire is here, my old life is here. But it's beginning to feel like quite a big deal to me that you aren't here.'

'What are you saying, Jake?' Lily pulled away slightly, her hands still on the sleeves of his coat.

'I don't really know. But I don't want to this to be a proper goodbye.'

'But the whole thing is insane! We've only just met.'

'I know.' He leant forward and kissed her again. 'Listen, I was thinking I might take some time off, at the end of the month, maybe get on a train and come down to see you?'

She pulled away from him, surprised.

'Sorry, is that not what you want?' he said. 'I could come for a weekend, or even overnight, we could go out for dinner. But if that's not going to work for you, just say.'

'I...' Her mouth couldn't keep up with her brain, which was whirring into action. Already she was imagining showing him around her little terraced house, walking along the beach arm in arm in the evening, wandering through the Lanes and stopping for a drink in her favourite bar.

'It's a bad idea,' he said. 'I shouldn't have mentioned it. Forget I said anything.'

'No!' Her voice sounded squeaky. 'Don't forget it! Sorry, I was just surprised, I wasn't expecting it. But yes please, let's do that. I'd like it very much.'

He grinned at her and raised his can up to clink it against hers. 'Deal then. Maybe in a couple of weeks' time.'

'Deal,' she said. 'But I wish I didn't live so far away. I wish I'd had more time here. Oh God, I just wish everything was different. It's so unfair.' She pictured the campervan waiting in the Campbells' car park, remembered the journey tomorrow which would take so many hours.

'I know.' He nodded. 'It's really unfair.'

Just seconds ago, she had felt ridiculously happy, but suddenly everything was ruined again as reality wormed its way into her mind, forcing aside the daydreams; she was almost choked by the anger that was overwhelming her. She wasn't angry with Jake, or even with Moira, she was furious with the universe. She wanted to stand up and scream at the lake, yell at the surrounding fells. She wanted to punch the side of the boat and bring her fists down on the little wooden bench seats. It was all so horribly wrong. This man sitting beside her was special; the most wonderful person she had met in many years. Possibly in forever. Spending time with him felt like she was being offered a chance at happiness.

But she couldn't take it. In the morning, she would have to pack all their belongings into the campervan, strap Moira into the front seat and get Eleanor and her laptop set up in the back. She would then have to drive away from Keswick without looking back. Life was so unfair. What she wanted to do and what she needed to do, were two completely separate things. She couldn't think about Jake, she couldn't think about what might have been. She must walk away from all this and be a responsible daughter and a responsible mother, and concentrate on getting everyone back home safely.

CHAPTER THIRTY-THREE

'LET me know when you want a hand with the cases!' trilled Archie at breakfast. He then disappeared until an hour later, by which time Lily had lugged both her and Moira's suitcases downstairs and they were standing by the reception desk, settling the bill.

'It's been such a pleasure having you lovely ladies stay at our humble abode,' he said, as he popped Moira's credit card into the machine. 'I hope you'll be back next year, when you continue the trip?'

'We absolutely will,' Moira said. 'But you'll need to improve your cooking. Those scrambled eggs I had this morning were bloody awful.'

'Mum!' Lily turned and glared at Moira. 'I'm so sorry, Mr Campbell. That's not true at all. Breakfast was delicious.'

'Bollocks,' said Moira. 'Lily, you said yourself that you've never known someone to make such a fuck-up of a fry-up.'

'Anyway!' Lily turned and picked up the cases. 'I'll just get these out and into the van. Mrs Campbell, thank you so much for your hospitality and for all your help when my mother was ill. We really appreciate it.'

Joan was standing by the front door wearing an apron with a picture on it of a French maid's uniform. 'We have loved having you to stay,' she said, watching as Lily puffed past with the heavy cases. 'What a pity Toby isn't here. He'd be able to help you with those.'

Eleanor's things were already stowed in the campervan, and she had set up a temporary office on the table in the back. Her mobile was on charge, she had two water bottles and a notebook within easy reach, her laptop was open and she was tapping away furiously. 'I'm hot-spotting at the moment, but we'll need to stop to get proper wifi at some stage,' she said, not taking her eyes off the screen as Lily heaved the cases in through the open side door. 'I've got a meeting at 11.30 so I've worked out all the timings and we'll need to have got to the Charnock Richard services by then. It's near Chorley, about ninety miles away. But we should be fine provided we don't get held up in too much traffic.'

'Right,' said Lily, stopping to catch her breath. 'Fine. We've got Granny's weak bladder to factor into the journey too, don't forget. She may well need us to stop before then.'

Eleanor looked horrified. 'Well, she won't be able to! We've got a schedule to stick to.'

'I'm not sure seventy-nine-year-old bladders are very good at sticking to schedules,' said Lily as she slid shut the side door.

Moira was making her way down the front steps, with Joan Campbell holding on to her elbow. 'I can manage!' she snapped, trying to pull herself away. 'You people are so clingy!'

Lily held open the passenger door and thanked Joan effusively, trying to make up for her mother's bad temper.

'Ladies!' called Archie, coming down the steps with something in his hands. 'I have a wee gift for you. It's a little token of our esteem. We give it to all our favourite customers.'

'Food poisoning?' asked Moira.

'Mum, shut up. Thank you so much, Mr Campbell,' said Lily. 'How very kind of you.' She held out her hands and accepted the package, which was a plastic bag wrapped around something and sealed with Sellotape.

'Bon voyage!' called Joan, running her hands up and down the front of her apron. Lily had to turn away, it looked suspiciously as if she was a French maid caressing herself.

'Safe travels!' said Archie.

As the van engine roared into life, Lily let off the handbrake and began the first part of a seven-point turn to get out of the ridiculously narrow car parking space.

'Bye!' called Joan.

'Ciao!' called Archie.

'Wave at them, Mum!' said Lily, through gritted teeth as she hauled the steering wheel back and forth. 'Keep waving until we're out of sight.'

'Goodbye!' yelled Moira, through the closed passenger window, before starting to sing. 'So long, farewell!'

'For God's sake,' muttered Eleanor.

'It's from the *Sound of Music*!' Moira said, turning round. 'Do you remember this one, Eleanor?'

'Granny, please stop singing.'

'Adieu, goodbye, to all of you!' Moira belted out, as Lily changed gear and the campervan crawled back up the hill.

'Jesus Christ, please don't tell me we'll have this all the way to Brighton,' muttered Eleanor.

'Oh, do be quiet, both of you,' said Lily. She was pushing the accelerator to the floor and willing the old van to keep on grinding up the hill to the main road, where she would join the A66 and start following signs towards the motorway. As she stared through the windscreen, she wondered where this shower had come from? She had checked the weather forecast last night and no rain was forecast. She flicked on the windscreen wipers but they scraped back and forwards across the glass, making no difference at all.

When they reached the junction at the top of the hill and she slowed to wait for a gap to join the faster moving traffic, she realised it wasn't raining. The blurriness ahead of her was due to her own tears; they were welling up in her eyes so fast, she couldn't have wiped them all away again even if she hadn't had both hands firmly fixed on the steering wheel.

'So long again and goodbye to you!' Moira belted out, at the top of her voice.

'Granny, stop singing!' yelled Eleanor.

Lily tried to take a breath, but let out a sob instead. Above the roar of the engine and the sound of Moira's singing, neither her mother nor her daughter noticed. She accelerated onto the A66 and sat back in her seat as a sign ahead told her there were eighteen miles to the M6.

Her head was full of him. She could picture his broad back, his shoulders, his taut stomach, his forearms as they wrapped themselves around her. She could see his beautiful brown eyes, his smile, the slant of his cheekbone as he'd turned sideways in the rowing boat last night, laughing at something stupid she'd said. She could smell him, that aftershave, as well as the salty sweat of him when she'd woken up in his arms in the Hamilton Hotel. Had that really been less than a week ago? In some ways it seemed like no time at all, but it also felt like a lifetime. Just a week previously, this amazing man hadn't been in her life, but now she could hardly remember what it had been like not to know him. But he wasn't even in her life! That was the whole point – that's what was making her feel so damn sad.

She had slept badly last night, when she got back from the lake. Maybe it had been a mistake to agree to meet him one last time? It would have been easier to set off this morning if he wasn't still so fresh in her mind. Or possibly not easier, just slightly less raw. The pain she felt at leaving him behind was all-encompassing, but she had to be realistic and sensible and accept that this was probably going to be the end of Jake and whatever else might have happened between them. Her mood had instantly lifted, last night, when he'd talked about coming down to Brighton to visit her, but she was pretty sure that, in the cold light of day, he would think better of the idea. It was too far to go for a quick visit; the Lake District to the East Sussex coast just wasn't practical. It was sad and depressing – and bloody unfair – but sometimes life just didn't work out the way you wanted it to.

'I leave and say goodbye!' Moira sang. 'Goodbye to all of you!'

Lily took more deep breaths. It will be fine, she told herself, I can do this. But even as she chanted the words inside her head, she didn't believe them. It felt as if there was a hole in the pit of her stomach, and the more miles she put between herself and Keswick, the more empty she felt. There was nothing left inside her, because she'd given her heart to a doctor who'd taken her out last night in a little wooden rowing boat on Derwentwater.

CHAPTER THIRTY-FOUR

'THIS WAS A STUPID IDEA!' Eleanor slammed her laptop shut and sighed loudly enough to be heard above the thunderous engine of the VW van. 'There's no way I can work properly in these conditions. God, I wish I'd got the train.'

'So do we,' said Moira.

There was surprisingly little traffic on the road, which was a relief because Lily was so exhausted, it was an effort to just cling on to the vibrating steering wheel as the van roared down the motorway. They'd only been going for thirty minutes, and Eleanor had spent twenty of those on her mobile, yelling at someone in her office who hadn't done the earth-shatteringly important task she'd assigned to him. Lily hated being forced to listen to these conversations, her daughter came across as hard and insensitive. She must be awful to work for and it made Lily sad that she seemed so hard-nosed, with little affection for any of those around her. Lily felt responsible, she'd played a major part in breeding this firebrand.

Her phone pinged in its holder on the dashboard and she saw Jake's name, followed by the first few words of the text:

> How far have you…

A few seconds later it pinged again, then again. Each time she could frustratingly only see the start of each message:

> I can't stop thinking…

> Can't get anything done…

'Who on earth keeps texting you?' Eleanor asked.

'Just Gordy,' Lily replied, immediately feeling guilty because Gordy was the one person she ought to be texting, but hadn't. Her phone pinged again. Every time Jake's name appeared on the screen of her mobile, her heart did that now-familiar little flip. Would she ever get over the excitement of hearing from him? She hoped not. But while she loved it, there was no point letting herself think too much about it, nothing would come of this, there was no point building it up into something it could never be. She had only just met this man and there was no way she could ask him to give up his whole life for her. Admittedly, they hadn't got to that stage, but that hadn't stopped her thinking about it.

'Drink a little drink, drink, drink!' Moira started to warble, now waving her arms in the air, conducting herself in song.

In the mirror, Lily saw Eleanor drop her head on to her arms on the table.

'That's from the thing about "Lily the Pink",' Moira said. 'Not you, Lily. A different one. But I don't know where the pink bit comes in.'

The further away she got from Jake, the more Lily wished she'd had the nerve to push things a little harder, despite the fact that they lived hundreds of miles apart and had separate lives that would be almost impossible to knit together. But being pushy wasn't in her nature, she had always been the one to compromise, put other people first and let them make the decisions. Years ago, when Nick got a new job in Portsmouth, he hadn't even told Lily he'd applied for it, let alone asked her how she felt about what it would involve. He had come home late one evening, staggeringly drunk having accepted the position and spent the evening in the pub celebrating his good news. He presumed Lily would be happy to hand in her notice at her own part-time job, rent out their house in Brighton, take three-year-old Eleanor away from the nursery she loved and move to a new city. She wasn't happy, but he'd presented her with a fait accompli, so she did it anyway. A few months later, when Nick's contract wasn't renewed after his probationary period, she was made to feel it was somehow all her fault. The night he got the news had been horrible. He sat slumped at the kitchen table, working his way through the best part of two bottles of wine, increasingly morose as he justified his own failings and blamed everyone else. His employer hadn't recognised his potential, his colleagues were useless and self-serving – even the job description hadn't been put together properly. But it was Lily who got the whip end of his tongue; she hadn't been supportive enough; she hadn't believed in him; she hadn't wanted the move to work.

'You're glad, aren't you?' he'd slurred. 'You're glad it hasn't worked out, because that means you get to go back to your small little life in Brighton and you can drag me back with you.'

Lily had hated him for that. But she'd hated herself almost as much, for taking the path of least resistance – which meant letting him get away with blaming her for the whole mess.

'And then he invented something!' Moira was singing.

'Granny!' Eleanor lifted her head from her arms. 'You're giving me a headache!'

'When we go back to Keswick next year, I don't want to stay

in that place again,' Moira said, turning to Lily. 'The food was awful and the bed wasn't comfortable.'

'You never mentioned that about the bed, before?'

'I didn't get the chance. You put me in that room and forced me to stay there – against my will.'

'You were sick, Mum. You needed to rest so you'd get better. It worked, didn't it? You're doing well again now. But last week you had a bad cough and we were worried. Anyway, I seem to remember that the day we arrived at Glenmorrow, you sat down on that bed and told me how comfortable it was!'

'Oh, pah!' Moira said, swatting away imaginary flies with her hand. 'I'm sure I didn't do that. You're making things up again. Why would I have said that about a hard, lumpy bed?'

Lily sighed. 'Whatever. Have it your own way, Mum.'

'And now you're patronising me.'

'I'm not! But there's no point arguing with you sometimes.'

'I can't stand it when you all treat me like a child.' Moira crossed her arms in front of her chest.

'Oh please, let's not start again. I'm too tired for all this.'

'We only treat you like a child because you behave like one,' put in Eleanor, from the back.

'That is *not* helpful!' snapped Lily, looking at her daughter in the rear-view mirror.

'It's true! We couldn't trust her not to do a runner. That's why we had to keep you in that room, Granny. I didn't want to be holed up in that awful place, either, but I had to be there in order to keep an eye on you.'

'I don't know what you mean?' Moira said, indignantly. 'I don't do *runners*. You're exaggerating, as usual.'

'Granny, you went for a barefoot walk around Keswick at dawn without telling anyone where you were going. That's why we had to keep an eye on you.'

'I did no such thing!' Moira turned round in her seat and

glared at Eleanor. 'Why do you all tell these terrible lies about me? You and your mother, you're as bad as each other.'

'It's like the swimming pool thing last summer.'

'Stop going on about the swimming pool, Eleanor, it was fine!'

'It wasn't fine, Granny. It was yet another example of you going off on your own, doing something crazy and irresponsible...'

'Shut up, both of you!' Lily shrieked, banging her hands on the steering wheel. 'For God's sake, just shut up!'

There was a shocked silence and, although Lily didn't take her eyes off the road, she could sense both of them had turned to stare at her, open-mouthed. 'I have had enough of your pathetic bloody bickering,' she yelled. 'Just stop it! I can't believe you're both so selfish. Mum, I wasn't happy about making this trip, but I put everything in my own life on hold, took time off work and went along with this because I thought it would be good for you. I've driven hundreds of miles and we've followed your memories all around the bloody country, which has been exhausting and not always a bundle of laughs, but that was fine, because it was what you wanted to do. Even though, in the meantime, I've not been able to support Gordy in his hour of need. But I didn't mention that to you because I didn't want to worry you. Then, Eleanor, you rocked up like Wonder Woman, thinking you were coming to save the day – which I didn't ask you to do – but once you were here, I thought fair enough, maybe it would be good for you to share this experience with us. But I stupidly hoped you'd help me out with Mum, whereas what you actually did was insult her at every turn and constantly tell me off for doing such a useless job. We hardly ever get to spend time together, all three of us, so these few days could have been great. We could have talked properly and found out what was going on in each other's lives. But actually, all we've done is fight! And all the two of you have done, is wind me up. And – now we're on the subject – what about me? Have either of you stopped to think about me in all of this? How I've been feeling? Has anyone thought to ask how I'm coping with the driving? Was I all right stuck in that poky back bedroom at the guest house? Is there anything else I would have liked to do on this stupid bloody road trip, other than be at your beck and call and try to keep the peace between the two of you and fit in with everyone else's plans?'

A sports car sped past the campervan and cut into the lane in front with no warning and leaving very little space.

'Signal, you dick!' yelled Lily, pressing the heel of her hand repeatedly on the horn. 'Use your sodding indicators!'

'So,' she said, breathing heavily now and no longer shrieking. 'That's all I want to say to the pair of you. I've just about had enough and I have nothing left to give. You've both pushed me to my limit. Now, I'd be grateful if you would please be quiet and let me get on with trying to drive us back home.'

Even over the roar of the campervan's engine and the rattle of every single cupboard door in the back, the silence that stretched between them seemed very loud. Moira still had her arms crossed and was glowering through the windscreen; Eleanor was staring out of the side window. Lily sighed; should she apologise for yelling? No, bugger it. Just for a change, why shouldn't she say it like it was? She kept her mouth shut and let the silence simmer on. She imagined being able to stand Moira and Eleanor side by side and bang their silly heads together.

A huge blue sign flashed past on the side of the motorway, announcing they were 248 miles from London. This was going to be one hell of a long day.

CHAPTER THIRTY-FIVE

NO ONE HAD SAID a word for the last twenty minutes. Lily had been half hoping her mother or daughter might apologise, but neither did so and she was now feeling bad about her outburst. She was relieved when signs showed they'd reached Charnock Richard services.

'We all need coffee and some time to calm down,' she said in the car park, as she helped Moira down from the passenger seat. 'Eleanor, you go ahead. We'll see you in there.'

'Please don't sit anywhere near me!' her daughter said, as she hauled the side door of the van shut. 'I've got a Zoom in ten minutes and I need to concentrate. So, make sure you're over the other side of the café.' She began to walk across the car park to the entrance, yelling over her shoulder. 'And *don't* let Granny sing!'

'Rude,' Moira said, as they watched her march away.

It took another quarter of an hour for Lily to guide Moira to the toilets, help her choose a new magazine in the shop, then get her seated in Starbucks and order coffee and some food. Eleanor was at a table by the window, with her laptop open and headset on. Every now and then she leant forward and tapped frantically at the keyboard or scribbled notes in the pad on the table beside her.

'Oh, to be that important.' Moira tutted.

'At least she's being important out of earshot,' Lily said. 'How are you feeling, Mum? You seem much brighter today.'

'Never better,' Moira said, sawing away at a cheese and ham toastie. 'Glad we've got something decent to eat though. I must have lost about a stone when we were staying at that place. Fucking awful eggs.'

Lily sipped at her cappuccino and watched her mother make short work of her food. She seemed to have totally forgotten about the scene in the campervan earlier. Maybe it was just as well. At the table behind them a family of four were ignoring each other as well as the drinks they'd ordered, while they individually swiped and tapped at the mobile phones in their hands. Further along, an elderly couple were sitting on either side of a table, staring over each other's shoulder, seemingly with nothing to say. It made Lily sad and reminded her of Gordy's depressing view of their future, that they were two middle-aged, lonely people who'd left it too late to find love again. Except that she *had* found love – or almost had. She just hadn't managed to hold on to it.

'He loved a cheese and ham toastie,' Moira said, running her fork around the edge of the empty plate to scrape up the last blobs of melted cheese. 'We had one of those funny machines where you put everything in between two hot plates, then close them together, and the cheese always used to run out at the sides and burn.'

'A toasted sandwich maker?'

'That's it! Clever you. Anyway, we used to have quite a lot of those sandwiches, and he really loved ham and cheese.'

'Who did?'

'Your father, of course!'

Lily's stomach contracted, as if someone had punched her. Your father.

'In those days I used to count calories, so I didn't eat nearly as many toasties as he did. I did like a bit of Marmite with mine though. We used to experiment with lots of different fillings – I didn't like tuna, that was disgusting.'

Lily had been trying not to think about the conversation she'd had with Moira in the guest house on Saturday morning. But trying not think about it hadn't worked. Every time she looked in a mirror, she examined herself yet again for signs of who she was. When she turned her face to one side, she could almost imagine herself having Ken's nose, and her chin was definitely his. But her eyes weren't like either of her parents; they were green, like Oliver's, as Moira had pointed out. Lily was also so much taller than either of her parents. By the time she was fourteen she had already towered over them, and the three of them used to laugh about the fact that she must have taken after distant relatives who had height on their side. Now it didn't seem at all funny. Lily couldn't remember ever meeting any of those mysterious tall relatives, or even seeing any photos. She *had*, however, met Oliver, and he was very tall.

'Mum,' she said, stirring the dregs of her coffee with a teaspoon. 'There's something I need to ask you.' Her heart was pounding, her cheeks flushed. She really shouldn't bring this up now; it wasn't the time or the place. But there was a voice inside her that wouldn't be stilled.

'That was delicious!' Moira said, pushing her clean plate away from her.

'Mum, why was Oliver so special to you?'

'Oliver?'

Lily studied her mother's face for any sign that she knew what was coming, but there was nothing. 'Yes, what did he mean to you?'

Moira sat back in her chair, frowning. 'Well, we were all good friends. There was a big group of us, and we spent most of our weekends together. Me and Ken, and this couple called Jan and Derek. Oliver was always there too, with one of his pretty girlfriends.'

'But you were especially close to Oliver.'

'Too right I was! He was such a handsome man. All the ladies wanted to spend time with Oliver. He was so funny and smart. I loved him very much.'

'Did Dad get on with him?'

Moira looked puzzled. 'Yes, of course he did. What a silly question. I told you, there was a big group of us and we all got on.'

'Mum, is Oliver my father?'

Once the words were out there, they sounded so stark. Lily wanted to suck them back in. But at the same time, she was desperate to know the answer – one way or the other. She stared across the table at her mother, watching for her expression to change, looking for clues.

For a moment, Moira didn't move, then her brow furrowed. 'Why would you ask me that?'

'Because I think it might be true.' Lily could hear the wobble in her own voice.

Moira sat back in her chair and clasped her hands together on the table in front of her. 'Lily,' she whispered. 'Oh, my dear Lily.'

'Please just be honest with me, Mum. It won't make any of this easier if you don't tell me what really happened. I need to know. After you said all those things the other day, I haven't been able to stop thinking about it. You told me I had his green eyes and his height, and you keep saying how special he was and how much he meant to you. I don't know if you've been subconsciously trying to tell me this, or if you're not even aware you've been doing it. But it feels like you've been drip-feeding me clues that I'm supposed to be picking up and linking together.'

Moira's expression had changed; she now looked appalled. She reached both her hands across the table, putting them on top of Lily's. 'Oh, my darling,' she said. 'I'm so sorry.'

'You don't have to be sorry,' said Lily. 'I'll understand if this is something that happened a long time ago. And I guess it's not a subject you'll have talked about to anyone else. If you had an affair of course you wouldn't want to tell anyone about it. But please, you do now have to tell me.'

'There's nothing to tell!' said Moira, leaning forward. 'Nothing! Oliver is not your father.'

Lily breathed in sharply, hearing what her mother was saying, but not quite taking it in.

'He was a very good friend, and he was charming and funny to me, but it wasn't just me – he was like that with everyone! I wasn't special – there were so many of us, and Oliver always had his girls. There was never anything more to it than that. Ken was your father and he loved you very much.'

'Okay,' Lily said. She knew there were other things she ought to say, but she was so drained, she couldn't kickstart her brain into action.

Moira was now shaking her head from side to side. 'Why would you even ask me that question?'

They were still clutching hands across the table, and Lily now squeezed Moira's, running her own fingers across her mother's, staring down at the pale wrinkled skin. On the third finger of Moira's left hand were her wedding ring, which she never took off, and her engagement ring with its tiny twinkling diamond, which she slid off each night and kept next to her on the bedside table. Over the years they had both become a little tarnished and were now slightly loose on the finger which had grown thinner and more bony than when the rings had been bought. Lily ran her own forefinger across them.

'It just seemed to fit together. All the things you said about him, the fact that you clearly loved him so much – I thought you must have meant more to each other. Why else would you want us to go and visit him on this trip?'

'Not because he was your father!' Moira said. 'I can't deny I was probably a little bit in love with him. More than a little bit. We all were – he was that sort of man. Everyone fell in love with Oliver. But nothing happened between us.'

'Okay,' said Lily, again. 'That's all right then.' Her head was thumping now and her eyes were suddenly prickly with tears, which was stupid – she didn't need to cry, this was good news, it was what she'd wanted to hear. It was as if a huge weight had been lifted from her chest and she could finally breathe freely again. But a part of her also felt inexplicably sad for Moira. Looking at the confusion on her mother's face, she wished she hadn't brought this up; if only there had been a way to find out the answer to her question, without them having to have this conversation.

'I'm sorry, Mum,' she said, swiping at the tears on her cheeks. 'I shouldn't have asked you. It just seemed to make sense. You'd been saying some strange things, but I obviously misread it all.'

'This is my fault,' Moira said, softly. 'I'm a silly old woman and I don't always say what I want to say. I know that, but I can't seem to help it. Sometimes I get so confused. But I never meant to hurt you, Lily.'

'You haven't!' Lily tried to laugh now, as she pulled a tissue from her bag and blew her nose. 'I've just been stupid.'

'Oh dear,' Moira sniffed. 'What a to-do. The last thing I would ever want to do is upset you. You're my world and you mean everything to me.'

Lily got up from her seat and went to the other side of the table, squeezing in on the bench beside her mother and putting her arm around her shoulders. 'I know,' she said. 'I'm sorry to have brought this up, Mum. Let's just forget about it.'

A shadow fell across the table.

'What's going on?' Eleanor asked. 'Why are you both crying? For God's sake, I leave the two of you alone for half an hour and you fall to pieces.'

CHAPTER THIRTY-SIX

> Where are you now? xx

LILY PULLED her phone onto her lap as she replied, making sure the others couldn't see who she was texting:

> Just leaving services near Bolton. 270 miles to Brighton xx

She slotted the phone back into its holder on the dashboard and started the engine. There was more traffic around now, and they had to queue to get out of the car park and back onto the slip road leading to the motorway. Another text pinged in, this one displayed in full as the screen hadn't had time to lock itself again.

> I hate this. You're getting further and further away from me xx

She jabbed at the screen, trying to swipe away the message. His words were so beautiful they made her heart swell, but she almost couldn't bear to read them because he was right; every mile nearer to Brighton was another mile she was putting between herself and the only person in the world she wanted to be with right now.

As she accelerated onto the motorway, Moira leant back against the seat. 'I think I'm going to have a little sleep,' she said. 'It's been a very tiring day so far.'

Lily caught Eleanor's eye in the rear-view mirror. 'Are you all right, sweetheart?' she asked. 'Did your meeting go okay?'

Her daughter nodded. 'It was fine. There are some issues I'll need to sort out when I get back into the office tomorrow. But nothing too awful.'

'Good,' said Lily.

'Mum.' Eleanor was looking down at her hands and Lily couldn't see her face in the rear-view mirror. 'I'm sorry about earlier.'

'Earlier?'

'You know, those things you said about us. The way we've been behaving. I'm sorry you think we haven't been supportive and haven't thought about you during all of this.'

Lily was so surprised, she was temporarily speechless. Eleanor didn't usually do apologies – in fact Lily couldn't remember her ever apologising for anything, because she was invariably convinced that whatever she said or did, was gospel.

'Well!' Lily said. 'Um... okay.'

'It was very unfair of us to do that to you,' Eleanor continued. 'You're right, Granny and I have both been a bit selfish.'

'Oh, never mind,' Lily said. 'It's just one of those things.' It wasn't. As the words came out of her mouth, she realised she was doing what she normally did – and had been doing for years – downplaying the hurt. 'But thank you for apologising.'

'We've been taking you for granted,' Eleanor said. 'I didn't think about it like that before, because you're always just there, doing stuff for us – Granny in particular – and you always have done. So, I guess it never occurred to me that you weren't happy in that role.'

'I am happy!' Lily glanced in the mirror again, catching Eleanor's eye. 'I love looking after Granny, and I feel awful that I told her I resented bringing her on this trip, because that's not the case. But some days I feel like I'm a bit-part player in everyone else's life. I keep things on track and ticking over and every now and then a bit of resentment about it builds up inside me.'

'That's not surprising.'

'Also, if I'm being honest, I'm feeling a bit down today, and I think that's why I lost my rag. I'm sorry for yelling like that. But in another way, I'm not sorry at all, because it helped us to start this conversation, which I think is well overdue.'

Eleanor nodded. 'It's good you told us how you feel. You had every right to shout at us.' She looked up and their eyes met in the mirror. Lily grinned and her daughter smiled back her. It was so good to feel that they were on the same side. Lily still felt guilty about her outburst, but for once her words had hit home and had clearly made Eleanor stop and think. In her daughter's reaction, there had been a touch of humility instead of sarcasm. Lily was relieved, and also extremely surprised. Maybe she should have stopped trying to keep everyone happy for all these years, and tried asserting herself instead. A little bit of yelling seemed to have gone a very long way. She was seeing a new, softer, side to this feisty daughter of hers.

'I'm so glad you came back in the van with us, El,' Lily said. 'I know it's not comfortable for you, and you can't work properly. But I appreciate your company.'

Eleanor looked surprised. 'Really? I didn't think you wanted my company at all on this trip!' She laughed, but it was a slightly brittle laugh.

'That's not true,' Lily said. 'Well, maybe it was a bit true at the start. But only because I resented you flying in like the cavalry, thinking you needed to sort out the mess I'd made of everything in Keswick.'

'You had made a bit of a mess of things, Mum. Be honest.'

'I hadn't! We were fine.'

'You'd lost Granny!'

'Well, okay. I *had* lost her, but I would have found her again.' She laughed. 'But despite all that, it has been good to have you around. I don't see much of you or Paul nowadays. This is probably the longest amount of time we've spent with each other since you left home.'

Eleanor nodded. 'I suppose you're right. At least you'll get to spend time with both of us again in a couple of weeks.'

'What do you mean?' Lily frowned.

'At the wedding!'

'Wedding?'

'Dad's wedding! Don't tell me you've forgotten.'

'No!' Lily had temporarily forgotten. 'Of course I hadn't. But I won't be going.'

'What do you mean?'

'I'm not going to your father's wedding.'

Eleanor looked shocked. 'But you must! You have to be there!'

'I certainly don't.' Lily signalled and pulled out into the middle lane to overtake a lorry. 'I was at his last wedding, to horrible Sophie, and it was awful. He made those cruel comments about my dress looking like I'd dredged it up from a charity shop – and there were all the nasty digs in the best man's speech about his marriage to me.'

'Were there?' Eleanor looked confused. 'I don't remember.'

'Well, it was really upsetting and I was embarrassed.'

'Best man's speeches are always a bit unpleasant.'

'That one was particularly vile about me. Then Sophie's

maid of honour made a so-called joke in her speech about Nick's "baggage" and everyone sitting nearby turned to stare at me.'

'I don't remember any of that,' said Eleanor, shaking her head. 'I guess I wasn't old enough to be aware of all the nuances. I just enjoyed poncing around in my bridesmaid's dress and being the centre of attention!'

'That's fair enough,' Lily said. 'You were at a difficult age. I was more worried about how you'd cope with it all.'

'Sophie was a cow,' Eleanor said. 'Anyway, she had no reason to be smug, she didn't last long. They were divorced by the time I started in sixth form, and he was soon on to the next one. You were with him for much longer than any of those other women.'

This wasn't really relevant, but Lily thought it was meant as a back-handed compliment and was strangely touched by it. 'I know, El. But I can't go through all that again, and I don't want to. It's weird he even invited me to this wedding, to be honest. We never see each other nowadays and I don't know his fiancée – what's her name? Helen. I can't understand why he'd want his first ex-wife at his third wedding.'

Lily hadn't actually sent back the RSVP slip. It had arrived weeks ago and she'd put it on the stack of paperwork she kept at the end of the kitchen worktop, where it had got lost amongst unpaid bills, insurance renewal reminders, bank statements and flyers that had been pushed through the door advertising dog walking, babysitting and aromatherapy. Every now and then she had come across it, while looking for something else entirely, and had then shoved it back into the pile. It was one of those things she always intended to deal with another time. But the wedding was now so near, it was rude of her not to have replied; she must send back the reply slip first thing tomorrow.

'Mum, please!'

Lily looked into the mirror in surprise; Eleanor looked distraught.

'You have to come! I really need you to be there with me.'

'Why?'

'As moral support! It's not that he's getting married again – God, I really don't care about that, I'm used to his stream of bloody girlfriends. But Helen is so young, it's humiliating! She's younger than me and the whole thing is going to be awful. Dad doesn't understand what people think about him, he can't see when they're laughing at him. Even people he's known for years, like John and Tony, they say awful things about him. He had a party a few weeks ago and they all got really pissed, and when he was out of the room, they were joking about him being a cradle snatcher and how they ought to shop him for sleeping with young girls.'

Lily couldn't hide her surprise. Not at the news that Nick's friends bitched about him behind his back, but at the fact that her hard-nosed, self-confident daughter was suddenly displaying such vulnerability.

'I just really need you to be there,' Eleanor said. She wasn't looking at Lily in the mirror anymore, she was staring out of the side window of the van, biting at the skin around her thumbnail. 'The whole thing will be hideous, but Dad is so madly in love with this girl that he won't see any of it. He'll just get really drunk and make a dick of himself and be fawning all over her at the reception. Then, within six months I bet you anything they'll have fallen out and he'll be back on his own again and everyone will be laughing about it.'

There was a string of red taillights in front of her, and Lily dragged her mind back to the road, braking as the traffic bunched up ahead. She was amazed at what she'd just heard. She couldn't remember hearing Eleanor criticise her father like this. Ever since he'd left them, fifteen years ago, she had only ever got one version of events from their daughter: Dad is so amazing; Dad is such fun to be with; Dad is so laid-back about life now he's not living with you anymore. When Eleanor was younger and still so bitter about the divorce, Lily knew the comments were primarily intended to hurt her. But more recently, they had just seemed like a factual report about Nick's life: Dad is so happy now he's met a new girlfriend; Dad and his new girlfriend seem so good together; Dad this, Dad that. Dad, Dad, Dad. Eleanor had always been the loyal little girl who took her father's side against Lily and the rest of the world. But particularly against Lily.

'I can understand how hard the wedding will be for you,' Lily said. 'And if there was something I could do to make it easier for you, I would. But the one thing I won't do is put myself through the stress of being there. It's too much. I'm sorry if that sounds selfish, but I just can't bear to do it. Even for you.'

Eleanor looked up at her again. 'I get it, and I don't blame you. I just don't want him to marry this bloody girl, she only left university a couple of years ago. It's all too awful.'

'Do you have to go, if you feel that strongly about it?'

Eleanor took a deep breath and nodded. 'I've been thinking about it a lot, but I know I have to be there. He needs me. He hasn't really got anyone else.'

Lily nodded. 'I guess that's true. You're a good daughter, El. He's lucky to have you.'

CHAPTER THIRTY-SEVEN

'BUT YOU CAN'T NEED to go again?'

Moira huffed and starting fiddling with her seat belt. 'I can and I do. It's been a very long drive.'

'But we only stopped an hour ago? Mum, don't unbuckle that now! Please let me get off the motorway first.' Lily glanced in the rear-view mirror and signalled to move into the inside lane. 'There's another services coming up in a couple of miles. Just sit tight and we'll go in there.'

They had already made four stops since leaving Keswick – twice for food and fuel and then twice more for Moira to use the loo. Lily wasn't convinced this fifth visit was necessary – she hadn't seen her mother drink anything since the small cup of coffee in Starbucks, hours ago.

'It's all very well for you, but I have a weak bladder,' Moira was saying. 'When you get to my age, things aren't as good as they used to be, down in that particular department.'

'It's fine,' Lily said, gritting her teeth. It really wasn't. They weren't far from Brighton now and she was exhausted after a full day's driving, desperate for it all to be over. She looked up and met Eleanor's glance in the mirror. Her daughter rolled her eyes again and they grinned at each other. It was good Eleanor had been with her on this journey, it would have dragged by and felt so much longer if Lily had been on her own listening to Moira work her way through a medley of every song she'd heard since the fifties.

They pulled into a parking space at the services and Lily picked up her bag from the floor. 'Want anything?' she asked Eleanor.

'Nope. Make it quick please, Granny. Paul was going to have supper ready for me by eight, at this rate it will end up being breakfast.'

'That was rude again,' Moira muttered, as Lily led her across the car park. 'Bloody rude, that daughter of yours.'

It was dark now and, when they went through the entrance doors, the overhead lighting in the cavernous space felt harsh and unwelcoming.

'Shall we have something from there?' Moira asked, as they went past Greggs.

'We ate at the last stop. You really can't be hungry again?'

'I fancy one of those veganism things – sausage rolls. The ones with pretend meat in them? I had one a few months ago and it was very tasty.'

Lily pushed open the door to the Ladies and held it for Moira. 'I'll wait out here,' she said, pulling her phone from her pocket. There were three more texts from Jake; she couldn't fault this man's enthusiasm. They weren't about anything in particular, he was just checking in. She read them all, then read them again before sending one of her own:

> At another bloody service station – Mum has a
> bladder the size of a pea xx

What would he be doing right now? It was nearly 7pm on a fairly miserable Monday night in October. He must have finished work, but would he have anywhere to go after that? Despite the hours they'd spent in each other's company, she still knew so little about this man. He'd suggested his divorce hadn't gone down well amongst the mutual friends he and Claire had made in Keswick, but he must have mates of his own there too – male friends he could have a beer with or drag along to see a film? Otherwise, he'd end up staying in his hotel room, or maybe going down to the restaurant, eating dinner alone, as he had done on the night they met. Lily pictured him there, sitting at the round table in the corner with his book open in front of him. What if there was another single woman sitting nearby tonight; a woman just like her who wasn't looking for anything other than an evening meal, but might end up meeting a man who would alter the entire course of her life?

What was the matter with her? Of course Jake wouldn't go and talk to anyone else. Why would he? But then again, why wouldn't he? He'd approached her, so there was nothing to stop him making a similar play for someone else. The thought made her so unhappy, it was like she'd been punched in the gut. She shoved her phone back in her pocket. *Stop it, Lily!* She was tired and emotional and was letting her imagination run riot. She just needed to get home. Where the hell was Moira?

She pushed open the door to the Ladies and went in. 'Mum? Are you finished yet?' There was no reply. She walked along past the cubicles – only one door was closed and behind it she could hear a mother chatting to a small child.

'Mum – are you in here?'

Her pulse racing a little faster, she went back towards the entrance, this time pushing open all the unlocked toilet doors so they slammed against the cubicle walls.

'Hey! Stop that,' the woman called, as a door thudded against the cubicle she was in.

'Sorry!' called Lily. 'I'm looking for my mother.'

She went back out into the corridor and glanced in both directions. No one. She started walking back to the main area, stopping to peer in through the doorway of a room full of slot machines and video game consoles.

'Excuse me, have you seen a little old lady?' The cleaner looked at her blankly, still mopping the floor. 'She's about five foot tall, with white hair and she's wearing a pink cardigan?' The man shook his head and moved away.

'Shit!' Lily muttered to herself. 'Shit, shit, shit!'

There were more people out in the foyer area, milling around outside WHSmith and queuing to buy food at the concessions. She ran past Leon, then Starbucks, scanning the tables. The queues were longest in front of McDonald's, but there were no little old ladies, no pink cardigans. She pulled out her phone – she would call Eleanor and ask her to come in to help, the two of them could cover more places. But what if Moira was no longer in the building? She could have wandered outside and right at this minute she might be walking around the car park, looking for the van. She probably would have no idea where they'd parked – these places were confusing, even in daylight. Maybe she'd gone the wrong way, towards the petrol station, or even towards the road that led back towards the M25?

Lily felt bile rising in her throat. This was all her fault. Why hadn't she just gone into the toilets with her mother? She hadn't been concentrating on what was happening – all she'd been thinking about was checking her phone for messages from Jake. How could she have been so irresponsible? She'd already lost Moira once on this trip, now she'd somehow managed to do it again.

'Hey, you! Stop that!'

There was some commotion up ahead; a woman was yelling and people were turning to stare.

'Get away from the counter!'

Suddenly, Lily caught a glimpse of something pink. She ran forward, pushing past people standing in her way. As she got to the front, she found herself beside a large woman wearing a Greggs uniform towering over a little old lady in a pink cardigan, who was grinning up at her and hanging tightly on to her arm.

'Come on then, twirl with me?'

The Greggs woman was looking confused and not a little exasperated. 'Madam, please let go of me and calm down.'

'Mum! There you are!' Lily reached out her hand, but Moira ignored it. She was stepping from side to side, humming to herself, beating out a rhythm as if she was holding a conductor's baton in her hand.

'Mum! Why didn't you wait for me?'

'And back, two, three, four – and twirl around!'

She pulled the woman from Greggs towards her as she sidestepped, then bumped her hips against hers as she moved back the other way. People were starting to laugh and Lily had an awful sense of déjà vu, remembering that Sunday afternoon, just over a week ago, in the aisles at Asda.

'And now you spin me, like this, as the music goes ta-ra-da-dummmmm!'

The woman was trying to pry Moira's fingers off her arm while being dragged backwards and forwards as she danced. She was heavy on her feet and looked as if she was about to fall over. 'Get off me!'

'There you are, Lily!' Moira's face lit up as she saw her. 'I was waiting for you, but I didn't know where you were, so I started dancing by myself.' She suddenly dropped the woman's arm and began to shrug off her coat, flinging her arms from side to side as they slid out of the heavy material. As it landed on the floor, she kicked her legs out in front of her and whirled around in front of the Greggs counter.

'La-dee-la!' she sang. 'Tra-la-la, dum dum!'

Eight days ago, Lily had felt her face redden as she looked around at the people laughing at her mother. She'd been humiliated and couldn't wait to get her out of the store. Now, standing watching her mother cavort across the shiny tiled floor, all she could think about was how much she loved her.

'Doo-dah-dah!' warbled Moira, still spinning. She went too close to the edge of the Greggs fridge section and her outstretched arm sent several packets of sandwiches flying onto the floor. 'La-la-laaaaaah!'

Lily noticed a teenager had pulled a mobile from her pocket and was holding it out in front of her, filming Moira. She stepped forward and swiped at the phone. 'Hey! Stop that!' she shouted, above the sound of her mother's singing. 'How dare you? Show some respect!'

The girl looked shocked and took a step back. Lily realised she was now attracting almost as much attention as her mother, but suddenly she didn't care. 'Fuck off, all of you!' she yelled, turning in a circle to glare at the onlookers. 'Haven't you got anything better to do? Bugger off and get back to stuffing your faces with burgers, you nosy-bloody-parkers!'

She turned to Moira and held out her arms, catching both her hands and joining in with the strange dance.

'Oooh, you're very good!' Her mother laughed. 'Lovely footwork! La-dee-dum!'

'La-la-la!' sang Lily, as loudly as she could. 'Doo-dee-dum.' She had no idea what she was singing, but it didn't matter. Her foot trod on something squelchy and, as her shoe slid sideways, she looked down to see that one of the sandwich packets had split open when it fell off the shelf. Bits of lettuce were on the floor, and Lily was treading a bright green trail across the tiles.

Keeping hold of one of Moira's hands, she reached down and picked up her crumpled coat from the floor.

'Do the hips thing, Lily!' called Moira. 'Push them in and out.'

Lily found she was laughing. 'Like this?' she asked, gyrating her hips backwards and forwards.

'Perfect!' Moira was laughing as well.

The crowd of onlookers was bigger than ever now, and as Lily whirled her mother around, feeling sweat gathering on her forehead, she caught sight of people shaking their heads and looking appalled, amused, angry and alien. Then, out of the corner of her eye, she saw a very familiar face.

'Well, this looks like fun,' said Eleanor, grabbing Moira's other hand. 'Hello, Granny, look at you on the dance floor!'

'Yes, look at me!' Moira laughed. 'This is the rhumba, Eleanor. Your grandfather and I used to do the rhumba on a Thursday night, after I'd had a couple of Campari and sodas.'

'Fantastic!' Eleanor said. 'Shall we do it along here, away from all these people.' She looked at Lily and signalled towards the entrance with her head.

'Good riddance!' the Greggs woman yelled after them. 'She needs locking up!'

'Sod off!' said Lily. 'Come on, Mum, show me that hip thing again, off we go.'

As they made their way towards the doors to the car park, Lily realised she didn't give a damn about the dozens of people standing staring at them, she didn't care about the snorts of laughter or the cat calls. 'Goodbye, everyone!' she yelled. 'Happy Monday!' A woman in a Welcome Break shirt had come out of the shop and was gaping at them. Lily waved at her as they went past. 'Thank you for having us!' she called. 'Really sorry about the mess on the floor!'

They sang as they made their way across the car park and

Eleanor held open the passenger door of the campervan, while Lily helped Moira back up into the seat, then wiped the remains of the salad from the bottom of her shoe before climbing into the driver's side. Slamming the door shut, she leant back in her seat, breathing hard, her heart still racing.

Moira was staring ahead through the windscreen, still humming softly to herself and nodding her head from side to side.

'Thanks, El,' said Lily. 'I don't think I could have got her away from there without your help.'

'I was wondering what had happened to you,' Eleanor said. 'You'd been gone for ages, so I came looking for you.'

'Mum, what was that all about?' Lily reached out and pushed a stray wisp of white hair away from her mother's forehead. 'Why didn't you wait for me when you came out of the toilets?'

'Why was I there?' Moira asked suddenly. She turned to face Lily. 'What was I doing there?'

'I think you might have wanted a vegan roll,' Lily said, gently. 'You talked about it when we were walking in, and I guess you came out of the toilets and decided you'd go and get yourself one?'

Moira shook her head slowly. 'I don't remember that,' she said.

'Never mind,' said Lily. 'You must have forgotten I was waiting for you.'

Moira's shoulders were shaking. 'I don't want to be like this,' she said. 'I don't want to forget things and get everything wrong. I hate what's happening to me.'

Eleanor leant over from the back and put her arms around Moira's shoulders. 'Granny, I'm so sorry. This must be horrible for you.'

'I don't want to cause you all these problems.' Moira was

crying properly now, gulping back sobs as she tried to get her words out. 'I didn't understand why all those people were shouting at me! I just wanted them to go away. I'm a mad old woman and I'm losing the plot, I know I am.'

'Mum, don't cry. It's all going to be fine.'

'This is only going to get worse, isn't it, Lily? This thing that's happening to me, it's never going to go away?'

'No,' Lily said gently, surprised by how calm she felt. 'It's never going to go away, but we're going to help you deal with it. We're both here for you, me and Eleanor. Between us, we'll cope with whatever happens.'

'I'm sorry for everything I'm going to put you through over the next few years,' sobbed Moira. 'I know it will be so hard for you. I wish I could stop it all and just be me again. I wish I could be the me I used to be, before my silly brain started going all wonky on me.'

Eleanor rested her own head against her grandmother's. 'It will be okay,' she whispered. 'It really will.'

Lily passed Moira a tissue, and she blew her nose loudly. 'Look at me,' she muttered, scrunching the tissue in her fingers. 'What a mess. What a terrible mess. I'm a silly old fool.'

'You're not,' said Lily. 'This is all very hard.'

'A silly old fool who doesn't even know what she's doing.' Moira dabbed at her eyes.

'It really doesn't matter,' said Eleanor. 'We'll look after you.'

'This is why my book is so important,' Moira said, resting her head against Eleanor's arm. 'It's my gift to you, my darling girls. When you can't get any more sense out of me, you'll be able to read all the things that I won't be able to carry on telling you.'

'It will be lovely for us to have it,' said Lily.

'Everything will be in there, but there will be no dark secrets, I promise.'

'That's good.' Lily smiled.

'I can't understand it. Why don't I know what I did in that place, just now?'

'I have no idea either, but don't worry. It's over now.'

Moira shook her head. 'I just remember that woman with the big boobies, standing shouting at me.'

Lily reached across to grab her mother's hand. 'She wasn't very nice,' she said. 'She didn't need to shout at you like that.'

'No,' Moira said. 'And she did have enormous, big boobies, didn't she?'

Lily laughed. 'They were huge.'

CHAPTER THIRTY-EIGHT

AS THEY DROVE down through the centre of Brighton, the streets were full of people and lights shone from the windows of bars and restaurants. Lily was so happy to be home; this little seaside city was truly one of the best places on earth. She reversed into a parking space a few doors up from Moira's block of flats.

'Oh, it's wonderful to be back!' her mother said, clapping her hands together in delight. 'I can't tell you how much I've missed being here. That was quite a long trip, wasn't it? I don't know why you suggested we go for such a long time, Lily. I really don't like being away from home for more than a day or so.'

Lily got out of the campervan and mimed a silent scream up to the sky, before walking around the other side, plastering a smile on her face and helping Moira onto the pavement. She was so tired, every muscle in her body was throbbing, and all she could think about was getting back to her own house, running a hot bath and collapsing into it, preferably with a large glass of wine.

Eleanor was pulling Moira's case out through the sliding side door. 'Go ahead, Granny. I'll bring this up for you.'

'I wonder if I've had a lot of post?' Moira was saying. 'It's always rather fun, isn't it, opening the post that comes when you've been away on holiday. It makes you feel very popular, getting all those letters.'

The flat was chilly and smelt musty. Lily turned up the heating thermostat and unpacked a bag of groceries she'd picked up at the Marks & Spencer store in one of the first services they'd visited.

'I've got you a chilli con carne ready meal, which you can just pop into the microwave for tonight,' she said. 'Plus, I've put some milk in the fridge and there's a loaf of bread and some butter for toast tomorrow. I'll come back in the morning and take you out to the supermarket, so you can do a proper shop, but you should be fine until then.'

Moira was standing in the hallway, peering through all the doors in turn. 'I'm glad I made the bed before we left, I hate coming back to a messy flat. Oh, look at that plant – I must have forgotten to water it before we left, the leaves have gone all droopy.'

Lily took the packaging off the ready meal and put it into the microwave. 'I've set it to the right time, you just have to shut the door and press the start button. Do you think you'll remember that? Maybe I should write it down for you.'

'Lily, I'm not stupid!' Moira tutted. 'I know how to work a microwave.'

'I'm sure you do, but I might just put it on a piece of paper and leave it on the worktop, in case you get distracted. Right, here you go – I've written down how many minutes it needs to cook for and what to press.'

Eleanor had brought the suitcase in through the front door. Moira turned to her and shook her head. 'Your mother thinks

I'm completely doolally,' she said. 'Can you put that in my bedroom? I need to get my slippers out. I'm so glad we visited that pencil museum – Eleanor, have you got the plastic bag with all my pencils in? I want to have a look through them all again.'

'Your pencils are here. Also, I found this in the back of the van,' said Eleanor, holding out the badly wrapped parcel Archie had given Lily when they left Keswick.

'God, I'd forgotten about that,' Lily said, holding out her hand. 'I wonder what it is?' Moira and Eleanor watched as she ripped long ribbons of Sellotape from the plastic bag. 'It looks as if he's used an entire roll,' she said. When the plastic bag was finally off, she was left holding a slightly less large item, covered in bubble wrap. Lily pulled it away until she had a piece of bubble wrap nearly a metre long. Finally, she unwound the last section.

'Oh dear,' she said.

Eleanor snorted with laughter. 'That's hysterical!'

'What is it? Let me see,' said Moira.

Lily showed her what she was holding, a framed colour photograph of Archie and Joan Campbell standing on the front steps of the guest house. Joan was wearing her French maid's apron and Archie had one hand on his hip, the other pointing upwards to the Glenmorrow sign above the door.

'Why would they think we'd want that?' Moira exclaimed.

'What's really funny,' Lily said. 'Is that they've signed it. Look down here at the bottom, there's Archie's signature on the left and Joan's next to it.'

'Unbelievable,' said Eleanor. 'What kind of ego do you have to have to send guests away with signed photographs of yourself?'

'He probably thought it would be nice for us to have something to remember them by,' said Lily, trying to be kind.

'I'll never forget those bloody awful eggs, as long as I live,' Moira said.

Lily sat down on the sofa and watched her mother bustle around her little flat. It didn't seem possible that, just over an hour ago, this same woman had been weeping uncontrollably in the front seat of the campervan, devastated at the way she'd behaved in the services – but even more so at the fact that she couldn't remember what she'd done or why she'd done it. This was the aspect of her mother's encroaching dementia which she felt least able to cope with, the loss of memory was worrying, but the dramatic changes in mood always brought Lily up short. It was the familiar Good Mum/Bad Mum scenario and, although Lily was still never sure which version of her mother she would be dealing with, until now it had always felt like Moira was in control of what she was doing. She recognised she was behaving badly, but didn't give a damn. The scene in the services had suggested something different, her mind was wiping itself clean after an awkward episode, leaving Moira with no idea why she had acted in a certain way, let alone any memory of doing so.

'That was such a lovely trip, Lily. Thank you for taking me. I'm glad we managed to fit it all in. Chepstow, Cirencester, the Lake District. And where does Oliver live again? All of it was lovely. And the Broads, of course, that was special.'

Eleanor looked puzzled. 'You didn't go to the Norfolk Broads, Granny?'

For a moment, Moira's expression froze, then her face relaxed and she beamed at her granddaughter. 'Of course we didn't! I know that. I was just teasing you.'

Eleanor went back into Moira's bedroom and Lily heard her lifting the suitcase up onto the bed and undoing the clasps. 'I'll put all your dirty washing into the laundry basket in the bathroom, shall I, Granny?'

'If you like, dear.' Moira was sitting in the armchair with the plastic bag of pencils on her lap. 'Oh, these are spectacular. What beautiful colours! Have you seen these ones, Lily? They're called Lightfast, and the woman in the museum shop told me they won't fade for a hundred years!'

Lily nodded, smiling at her mother but not really listening. She was in the middle of composing a text to send to Gordy – at long last. She felt awful about neglecting him, but now she was back in Brighton, she was going to start making amends for being such a useless friend over the last few days. She wasn't due back at work, because she'd taken two weeks off, but tomorrow she would pop in to see him at Beautiful Blooms. Once they'd debriefed about the whole Hilary thing – and she knew it would be an extensive debrief, which would probably need to take place over an entire evening, with the help of a couple of bottles of wine – she was going to make it her mission to get that man back out in the world again. He needed to realise that finding himself on his own after so many years, wasn't the end of everything. Somewhere out there was Gordy's next love interest, and Lily would stop at nothing to help him track down that special person. She pressed send and watched as the text message turned blue and told her it had been delivered.

'Are you sure you're going to be all right tonight, Mum?' Lily asked, putting down her phone. 'Maybe I could pop back later, to check on you. I'll just go home and get myself sorted out, then...'

'There is no need for that!' Moira said. 'I will be perfectly fine. I'm back in my own home. What on earth could go wrong?'

Lily had a flashback to the evening she'd popped in on Moira to discuss the trip, less than two weeks ago, and had found her trying to boil wash tea towels in the slow cooker.

'Nothing will go wrong, of course it won't,' she said. 'Just don't worry about doing anything tonight, other than having something to eat and watching a bit of telly. You're tired and you need to get a decent night's sleep. In the morning, I'll help you do your washing.'

Her phone pinged with a reply from Gordy:

I've missed you! I'm so glad you're back x

'Where are my slippers?' Moira asked. 'I'm sure they're usually by the front door.'

'They're here, Granny,' said Eleanor. 'I just got them out of your case.'

'Oh yes, that's good. Right, off you go, you two. I'm going to be absolutely fine on my own so you don't need to hang around here. I'll heat up that meal and look at all my beautiful pencils. Are you going to be talking to that handsome doctor, tonight, Lily? He'll be waiting for a phone call, I'm sure.'

Lily's mouth dropped open and she felt her face heat up as Eleanor turned to stare at her. 'Well, I may... I guess I might... How do you...?'

'Oh, stop being so coy,' Moira said. 'A blind monkey couldn't have missed all the signs that something was going on between the two of you.'

CHAPTER THIRTY-NINE

'WELL, I guess that makes me a blind monkey,' Eleanor said, as they came back out onto the pavement. 'Does she mean that Dr Jordan? The one who came to see her in the guest house?'

'Yup,' said Lily, fumbling in her bag for the keys.

'That good-looking one, with the brown eyes?'

'How did you know he had brown eyes?'

'Mum, let's revisit Granny's blind monkey analogy. Anyone would have noticed that man's eyes, they were incredible. Actually, the rest of him was pretty incredible as well, to be honest – for an older man. But I don't understand – does Granny mean that you and he...?'

'Yup.' Lily unlocked the van and walked around to the driver's door.

'Stop walking away from me! So, you and that doctor were actually getting it together, while we were up in Keswick?'

'Oh, Eleanor! Don't make such a big thing of it. Yes, in answer to all your questions. Jake and I were seeing each other. Well, sort of seeing each other. It's a bit complicated to explain. But we did, as you put it, "get it together" briefly, while we were up in Keswick.'

'Bloody hell.' Eleanor sat back in the passenger seat. 'That's extraordinary.'

'Why is it so extraordinary? I'm not exactly a withered old hag with no sexual desires.'

'I didn't mean that! I mean, how did you keep it quiet? I can't believe I didn't know about it, or even pick up on any signs that something was going on.'

'More incredible, is that Granny *did* pick up on it.' Lily started the engine and adjusted her rear-view mirror. After all these hours, it was strange to have her daughter sitting beside her now, instead of perched behind the table in the back of the van.

'True.' Eleanor nodded. 'She's a wily old thing. What amazes me is that she knew what was going on, but managed not to say anything about it. If I'd had the faintest clue about it, I would have said something way before now.'

'Maybe she kept forgetting?' Lily said, and they turned to each other and grinned. 'Sorry, that's unkind of me. But I wouldn't be surprised if that was the case.'

'Well, she knows now,' Eleanor said. 'And more to the point, so do I. What's your plan then? Are you going to stay in touch? Keswick is a bit of a distance – as we know after today. Did you finish things or will you go back up there?'

'Oh, I don't know, El. I can't go back up there, can I? To be honest I think I may just have to put it down as a holiday romance.' Lily sighed. 'Not even that really, it wasn't like I was on an exotic foreign holiday and he was a handsome waiter in a taverna somewhere.'

'Wow, Mum, it's so great that you met him, I'm pleased for you!'

Lily turned to look at her, half expecting sarcasm, but her daughter really did seem happy to hear about all this.

'Thanks,' she said. 'It was fun. He was lovely – more than

lovely. He was funny and kind, and I just really enjoyed spending time with him.' It felt strange to be saying those words out loud; sharing them with Eleanor made what had been going on seem very real. 'But it's not such a good thing really, because he's up there and I'm down here and we've both got our own lives. I had a wonderful time, but I can't let myself get carried away. He *is* lovely though, El – I think you'd like him. Meeting him made me very happy.'

Eleanor reached out and put her hand on Lily's arm. 'It's wonderful. It's about time you had someone in your life. Are you sure you can't work something out?'

Lily smiled at her. 'No idea. He talked about coming down to visit in a couple of weeks' time. But he's busy, so we'll have to see what happens.'

'I have to say, speaking as someone who knows what it's like to have to sit back over many years and watch her father shack up with jailbait,' added Eleanor. 'It's a huge relief that he's a middle-aged man and not some fit toy boy who's hardly out of his teens.'

'Do you know, I have no idea how old he is?' Lily said. 'I never thought to ask him. He looks about my age, and he sounds about my age. But he might be a bit younger? In which case, I *have* been carrying on with a toy boy.'

'What does it matter,' Eleanor said. 'He's mature in the best possible way, and gorgeous with it. I have to admit, I'm a bit jealous.'

Lily laughed as she turned the key in the ignition. 'Right,' she said. 'Enough of all this. Let's get you back home, to your lovely Paul. Your supper will be incinerated by now.'

'Hang on a minute.' Eleanor pulled something out of the side compartment in the passenger door. 'Granny has left something in here. It's her notebook!'

'Oh hell,' said Lily, turning off the engine again. 'We'd

better take it up to her. She'll get herself into a real state if she can't find it.'

Eleanor had opened the book and was flicking through the pages.

'El, don't do that!' Lily said. 'It's private. Why are you reading it?'

Her daughter was shaking her head. 'I don't get it.'

'What? Listen, please put it down, Granny would hate it if she knew we'd been looking at her book before it was finished. She keeps going on about how she's going to work on it and carry on writing, so we can have her whole life story when it's done.'

Eleanor looked up at her, frowning.

'What's the matter?' Lily asked. She suddenly realised her heart was thumping loudly and her mouth was dry. What had Eleanor just read? Her mind flashed back to the conversation she'd had with Moira earlier today, in the first services. Had her mother been lying to her about Oliver, after all? She might just have been saying what she knew Lily wanted to hear, reassuring her that there was nothing for her to worry about, that she was Ken's daughter. But in this book – the one she kept insisting would tell them all about her life – she may have decided to be truthful. And if the truth was that Oliver was Lily's father, what kind of a mess was that going to cause?

'Eleanor, please don't read it. For one thing, it's private! Whatever she's saying in there, you mustn't pay any attention to it. Seriously, put the notebook down. It's just Granny, getting carried away and imagining things. Don't believe any of it.'

Eleanor was now looking back down at the book, flicking through the pages. Lily itched to reach out and grab it out of her hands.

'None of what she's saying in there, makes any difference,' Lily said. She knew she was gabbling, could hardly hear herself speak above the pounding of the blood flooding across her temples. She wanted to reach over and grab the book from her daughter's hands, but was frozen in her seat. 'None of what you're reading in there, changes who I am or who you are.'

Eleanor turned the notebook so that they could both see the pages and flicked back to the beginning. Then she slowly began to turn the pages, each one moving across with a snap that sounded like a knife on metal.

'Oh my God,' whispered Lily. She reached out both hands and took the book, flicking through the pages more quickly, almost in desperation. She looked up at Eleanor, then back down at the book. There were no words. On some pages there were scribbles, on others little drawings and doodles. Twirly decorations covered the edges of most of the pages. In some places there was patterned shading, in others curling or symmetrical designs that were repeated dozens of times across a page.

'She hasn't written anything,' Lily said. 'Not one word.'

'What does it mean?' Eleanor asked. 'I don't understand? She hasn't stopped talking about her book and the fact that she's writing her life story for us. This book has been the focus of your entire trip! But all this time, she hasn't been doing anything with it. She hasn't even been writing any proper words in here.'

Lily closed the notebook and sat with it on her lap, her hands shaking as they rested on top of it. She felt shattered, drained of every ounce of energy as if she'd just run a marathon or cycled up a mountain.

'Mum, what are you thinking?' asked Eleanor.

Lily really wasn't sure what she was thinking, or how she was feeling. Part of her was relieved; she'd had no idea what she was expecting Moira to write about, but there had definitely been an expectation of dark secrets. Even if none were going to be revealed – as her mother had reassured her – Lily had still been nervous about what she might discover. Or what other people might discover about her.

But now none of that was going to happen. Nothing at all would be revealed. To her own surprise, she realised what she was mostly feeling, was incredibly sad. This book had played such a big part in their trip, precisely because it had seemed so important to Moira. Writing it had kept her mother going, it had helped her carry on through her illness and deal with the disappointments she'd encountered along their journey – the scruffy house in Chepstow, the long-forgotten dance hall, Oliver's inadequate welcome.

'What do we do?' Eleanor asked.

'I don't think we do anything.' Lily sat staring out of the windscreen at the back of the car in front, its rear window so filthy that someone had used their finger to draw a row of smiley faces on the glass. 'I think we just pretend to Granny that we haven't looked inside her book, and we don't know what she's been doing.'

Eleanor nodded. 'Okay.'

'She doesn't need to know, it would just upset her. We have to let her carry on with it and she can keep pretending to write in it, setting down her life story. It really doesn't matter. None of this is about us, El, it's about her.'

'Maybe you're right.'

'I'll take it back to her when I go along in the morning, and pretend I've only just found it. We both have to forget about it.'

Eleanor nodded again. 'Yes, that's the best thing.'

As Lily put the key in the ignition and started the van engine again, her phone pinged. She glanced at it and couldn't help smiling when she saw it was from Jake. 'Just a sec,' she said. 'I need to check this.' She pulled the phone from its holder on the dashboard and swiped to unlock the screen. The text opened; just the latest in a long trail of messages that had been sent backwards and forwards between the two of them over the last few days. But this one was the best of the lot:

> Just booked a train ticket to Brighton, for Friday. Block your diary out for the weekend, I'm coming for you, Lily Bennett xoxox

THE END

ALSO BY SARAH EDGHILL

A Thousand Tiny Disappointments

~ A gripping novel about grief and friendship

His Other Woman

~ A compelling and suspenseful women's fiction novel

The Bad Wife

~ A totally absorbing psychological suspense

ACKNOWLEDGMENTS

Memory Road started life years ago, but back then it was a very different book: much darker and more intense. Jake wasn't in it – even Moira only played a supporting role. My friends from Faber may remember something about that original version in 2015, and I'm grateful for all the feedback they gave me at the time.

I tucked that version away in a drawer and forgot about it, while I wrote something else. Then, in 2020, I dug it out again and, with the help of editor Alison May, had a rethink and made some major changes, and Lily and Moira's story began to emerge. However, life got in the way and back into the drawer it went, only to get pulled out again in 2022, when I was looking for a new project. I'm so grateful to Hannah Todd, whose support and editing skills helped knock the most recent version of this book into shape, and also to Betsy, Tara and Shirley at Bloodhound.

This is my fourth novel, and it's very different in tone to the three that came before. But I've loved writing it, and I hope you enjoy reading it, and that Lily and Moira will stay with you. Dementia isn't an easy subject to write about, and it's certainly not one to be treated lightly. But it's also true that even life's toughest times feel a little easier, if we can deal with them with a smile on our faces.

If you'd like to find out more about me and my writing, please visit www.sarahedghill.com or follow my Amazon Author page by clicking on any of my novels.

A NOTE FROM THE PUBLISHER

Thank you for reading this book. If you enjoyed it please do consider leaving a review on Amazon to help others find it too.

We hate typos. All of our books have been rigorously edited and proofread, but sometimes mistakes do slip through. If you have spotted a typo, please do let us know and we can get it amended within hours.

info@bloodhoundbooks.com

Printed in Great Britain
by Amazon